INTRODUCTION TO THE
MUSIC INDUSTRY

SECOND EDITION
Midwest Edition

ROBERT WILLEY

Kendall Hunt
publishing company

Diagrams throughout text created by Robert Willey
Cover © Shutterstock.com

Kendall Hunt
publishing company

www.kendallhunt.com
Send all inquiries to:
4050 Westmark Drive
Dubuque, IA 52004-1840

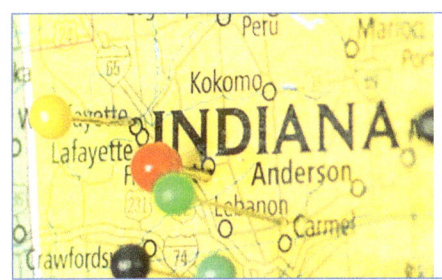

Contents

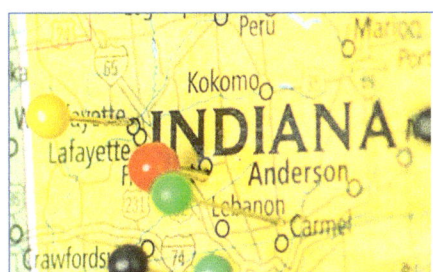

What You Will Learn

This book is an introduction to the music industry, and can be considered a *primer* for two reasons.

1. It covers the **primary, most important information** about the present state of the music and entertainment industry and how we got here. You will also learn how music is recorded, marketed, licensed, and performed.

2. It is meant to help **prime the pump** and contribute to the development of the music and entertainment industry in the Midwest, by identifying and reporting on special opportunities in the region.

The foundation in music industry practices and pointers toward new opportunities are designed to help you understand the business and where you might fit in. The suggestions for practical activities will help you begin.

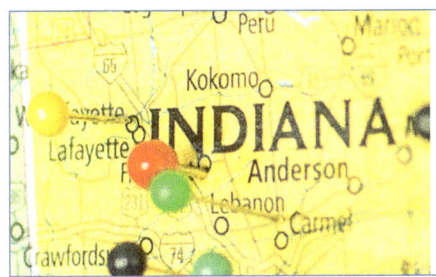

Acknowledgments

Thanks to all the friends, colleagues, contacts, and students who contributed directly or indirectly to this book. Here is a short list of those who were most directly involved:

John Snyder—Chair, Film & Music Industry Studies, Loyola University. One of my first mentors, and the man behind Artists House Music.

Dan Porter—Music Media Production and Industry, Ball State University. A great colleague who shares my passion in preparing students for the real world.

Jeff McDonald—Vice President for Human Resources, Sweetwater Sound, Inc. A strong supporter of the MMP program at Ball State, he appreciates what we are doing to help our students develop grit, self-control, and communication skills.

Eric Harvey—Marketing Instructor, Miller College of Business. He and his students help with the social media content and analytics in MMP 100, his son's band is launching a career out of Colorado.

Travis Harvey—Owner, Village Green Records. Super-knowledgeable about music and contemporary culture, on a mission to widen students' musical horizons.

Whitney Stump— Owner, Be Here Now. Operates an oasis for bands playing original music.

George Litterst—President, TimeWarp Technologies Inc. A great collaborator on the Joplin and other technology projects. Having one person who gets what I'm doing makes all the difference.

Ball State students in Survey of Music class (MMP 100). You know who you are!

Julius Bucsis—guitarist, composer, helps with the administration of the MMP 100 class. Good conversations about the role of music in a post-industrial age.

Michael Pounds—Professor of Composition, Ball State University. Co-director of the MMP program and my faculty mentor.

Bobby Owsinski—Author. We used his textbook *Music 4.1* for many years, knows lots about the recording industry and social media marketing, leads by example.

Wilbur Davis—Innovation Connector. Moral support, helped untangle intellectual property issues on campus.

Ryan Hourigan—Director, School of Music, Ball State University. The champion of the MMP program, helps me focus.

Michael O'Hara—Assistant Dean, College of Fine Arts, Ball State University. Supportive of Middletown Music and our efforts to be remarkable.

Brian Wampler—Owner, Wampler Pedals. Inspiring example of ingenuity and customer service.

David Concepcion—Chairperson of the Department of Philosophy and Religious Studies, Ball State University. Another mentor, and supervised my Diversity Associates study of hip-hop and the laws around sampling.

Robert Thompson—Professor, Composition and Music Technology, Georgia State University. So helpful with perspective on academia and the music industry.

Chris Dobrian—Professor of Integrated Composition, Improvisation, and Technology, University of California, Irvine. A wise and funny friend.

Garth Alper—Coordinator of Jazz Studies, University of Louisiana at Lafayette. A good musician and leader. Helped me build a foundation in Cajun/Zydeco country.

Jennifer Blackmer—Associate Provost for Entrepreneurial Learning, Ball State University. Creativity meets energy, showing how to get things done on campus.

Suzanne Plesha—Director of Faculty Support and Assessment for Entrepreneurial Learning, Ball State University. Supportive of the entrepreneurial focus of the MMP program.

Roy Tamanaha—Drummer. My best friend and partner at Rebel Rd. Productions.

Maria Oneide, Samuel, and Barbara Willey—My World-Go-Round Makers.

Ryan O'Shaughnessy—Acquisitions, Kendall Hunt Publishing. Got me excited about working with Kendall Hunt, hooked me up with music business people in St. Louis.

Rachel Guhin—Project Coordinator, Kendall Hunt Publishing. Patient and organized.

Interviews (on companion website):

Ariel Hyatt—Entrepreneur, Cyber PR. There's always something to learn from her books and newsletter. *Music Success in 9 Weeks* lays it out in a compact form.

Randy Chertkow—The book he wrote with Jason Feehan called *The Indie Band Survival Guide* is well-organized and overflowing with useful information. Their new one, *Making Money with Music*, is an essential read for aspiring indie musicians.

Katie Carlson: Super fan makes (real) good, now WALK THE MOON's day-to-day Manager at Mick Management.

Tim Hays: Thanks for your perspective on Chicago and reflections on how touring has changed.

T.J. Müller: It's great to see someone take up the torch and preserve the culture in a such a lively way.

Brandon Meeks: Good information on putting together a career combining jazz, hip-hop through social media and other online tools.

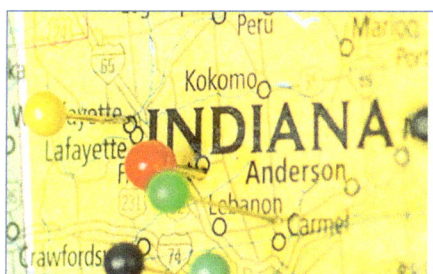

Credits

Chapter 9:

"Moore's Law" By Wgsimon (Own work) [CC BY-SA 3.0 (http://creativecommons.org/licenses/by-sa/3.0) or GFDL (http://www.gnu.org/copyleft/fdl.html)], via Wikimedia Commons.

"Full History Disk Areal Density Trend" courtesy of Barry Whyte [CC BY 4.0 (http://creativecommons.org/licenses/by/4.0)], via Wikimedia Commons

"Will Pay to Work" drawn by Barbara Willey.

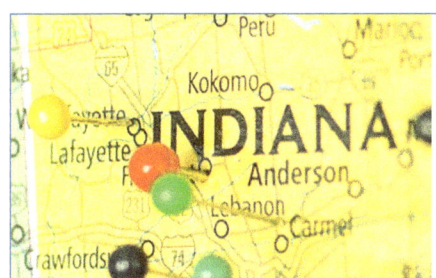

Introduction

Music makes the world go round.

There are many books about the music industry. The challenge for each author is to remain relevant, since this business is changing at an ever-increasing rate. By the time a book has been written, edited, printed, advertised, distributed, purchased, and read, much of the information is out of date and new trends are left out. The reason that I chose to work with Kendall Hunt is due to their rapid development cycle, and the ability to put out electronic versions and a new edition whenever one is needed. I decided to integrate a companion website into the project in order to be able to quickly respond to the most important developments.

This textbook was written for the 125 students in the Survey of Music Industry (MMP 100) that I teach each semester at Ball State University, located in Muncie, Indiana. Ninety-five percent of the students in the class take it to fulfill a general education requirement, the rest are preparing for careers in music production and telecommunications. I have used a number of textbooks in this and other classes over the years here and at other institutions. Donald Passman's *All You Need to Know About the Music Business* is a classic treatment of the traditional music business revolving around record contracts. David and Tim Baskerville's *Music Business Handbook and Career Guide* brings the business forward in time, and in 2009 I created the ancillary material for its companion website. Richard Weissman's book, *Understanding the Music Business* provides a good overview at a price that students appreciate. I switched to Bobby Owsinski's *Music 4.1* because of the good job he does dividing the business's developments into stages along with the tips on how to use social media, which he covers in greater detail in his separate book, *Social Media Promotion for Musicians*. I've supplemented the textbooks with additional material from Daniel Pink's *To Sell Is Human*, Ariel Hyatt's *Music Success in 9 Weeks*, Clara Dweck's *Mindset*, Angela Duckworth's *Grit*, Jeff Goins's *The Art of Work*, Seth Godin's *Purple Cow*, Randy Chertkow and Jason Feehan's *The Indie Band Survival Guide*, Martin Atkins *Tour Smart*, and Gabrielle Oettingen's *Rethinking Positive Thinking*. These and other titles are listed in the Bibliography at the end of this volume.

I finally decided to write this book for my students and anyone else interested in having a condensed survey of the music industry, combined with information on the Midwest that other books don't cover. The music business is a network of interdependent industries including songwriting, performance, engineering, design, marketing, promotion, and merchandising. It has multiple layers, beginning with an artist at home, going out to explore the local scene on their own, working with an indie label to tour regionally, and ultimately signing with a major label to emerge on the national and international scene.

I came to Indiana after teaching at the University of Louisiana at Lafayette for 11 years. It was easy to figure out there what we could be the world's best at, since we were located in the heart of Cajun and zydeco country. I co-wrote a book on Creole Fiddle, co-produced a DVD of zydeco music, and was involved with my students in recording groups representing Southwest Louisiana's unique musical culture. It took longer to discover our unfair advantage in Central Indiana. The manufacturing of glass jars and canning products by the Ball family had already moved to Colorado. Being the inspiration for the bad big-city opponents of the underdog heroes in the movie *Hoosiers* wasn't something most people wanted to build on. The TV series *Parks and Recreation* has many connections with our town, but not all Hoosiers seem comfortable enough to chuckle at themselves, and production of that show had wrapped.

What continued to interest me was the legacy of being the site of sociological studies beginning in the 1920s in which Muncie's identity was concealed by referring to it in reports as "Middletown". Muncie was chosen by the researchers because it was identified as being representative of an average or typical American small city, and offered an opportunity to study "the interplay of a relatively constant . . . American stock and its changing environment." While at first glance being statistically average might not be the best choice for a unique selling proposition, I've decided that Muncie's niche in the music industry could be its "Hometown U.S.A." heritage with its fingers lightly tapping the pulse of the nation. Our new motto has become "If we like you here, they'll like you everywhere!" and we are ready to serve as your next test bed or focus group. Muncie is home to a good, well-equipped university that is centrally-located, one with the time, energy, and vision to champion the development of Midwest music, something that no one else is presently doing.

The second purpose for writing this book was to include information on the Midwest music scene and its special opportunities, and to provide a tool that can help contribute to its development. This text is designed to provide the theoretical foundation for students to become involved and participate in Middletown Music's initiatives.

Each chapter concludes with suggestions for further investigation, DIY activities, and vocabulary definitions.

The interviews conducted with industry professionals are available on the book's companion website located at http://willshare.com/mmb. There you will find updates and links to the resources discussed in the book along with supplemental material.

I hope this book can help you understand how the record industry affects your taste in music, and opens avenues of exploration if you want to broaden your musical horizons. If you are interested in pursuing a career in music and entertainment, especially in the Midwest, it should make you more aware of your options and ways to get involved.

+Robert Willey
July, 2017
Muncie, Indiana

Legal disclaimer: The information presented in this book is not intended as legal advice. Consult an attorney who specializes in entertainment law when making legal decisions like, but not limited to, liability, copyright, and contracts.

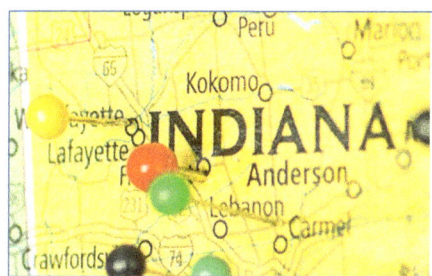

CHAPTER 1

A Short History of the Music Business

Topics

Classical Music
Player Pianos
Sheet Music
Radio
Vinyl Records
Portable Players
Compact Disks
Music Television (MTV)
Consolidation of Radio Stations
Consolidation of Record Labels
Other Factors Causing a Drop in Diversity
Digitization
Napster
Apple to the Rescue
Review and Preview
For Investigation
Do It Yourself
Vocabulary Review

Main Ideas

- At the beginning of the 20th century, many families were playing sheet music and piano rolls at home.
- Radio began to take over the home entertainment market in the 1920s.
- By the 1950s, teenagers had their own playback systems, records, and style of music.
- MTV launched in 1981 and put more emphasis on how artists look.
- The introduction of the CD format in 1982 resulted in huge profits for record companies.
- The passing of the Telecommunications Act in 1996 led to a consolidation of radio stations and an increased use of playlists.
- The consolidation of record labels increased pressure for safe investments and instant hits.
- Digitization and the MP3 file format made electronic distribution easy.
- File sharing and piracy are (unfairly?) blamed for the collapse of CD sales.

See the book's companion website for supplemental information, updates, and links: http://willshare.com/mmb

Classical Music

Every culture that we know of has had some type of music. There seems to be something that music expresses that can't be communicated any other way, and people sing and play instruments for rituals, personal satisfaction, and to entertain their friends and families. In the Middle Ages, it became possible for musicians to make

Ludwig van Beethoven:
Professional Composer.

a living from their art, primarily as part of their duties as monks in the Catholic church. By the time of the Baroque period, composers found work composing music for church choirs and to entertain royalty, like Johann Sebastian Bach (1685–1750), who was known for his skill playing pipe organ. In the Classical era that followed, composers like Wolfgang Amadeus Mozart (1756–1791) sought patronage from royal courts. Like Mozart, Ludwig van Beethoven (1770–1827) was a skilled pianist and improviser, and one of the first to earn a livelihood from income from his published music and subscription concerts. From then on, musicians sought to earn a little money from many people in the middle class rather than large sums from a few wealthy individuals.

Player Pianos

Up until the Classical music era, music had almost exclusively been something that had to be played in the moment. Today, when life is accompanied by a continuous soundtrack supplied by recordings played through loudspeakers and earphones, it may be hard to imagine how much more special music was when you or someone else had to perform it and was something that might require effort to seek out. The only way that people had of storing music and playing it back at a later time was through mechanical devices such as music boxes, which became popular in the 1800s.

Music boxes store compositions as bumps on
disks or cylinders.

In the late 19th and early 20th centuries, mass production of pianos resulted in a lowering of the cost of instruments for the home, and the same punched card technology that had been developed to control the weaving of looms was soon added on to create player pianos. These could be played normally like any piano, or played automatically by reading punched holes on paper rolls, which could hold longer compositions and were cheaper to produce than the metal disks used with music boxes.

When a punched hole in the piano roll passes over the tracker bar, the corresponding key on the piano is played.

See the companion website for videos of music boxes and player pianos in operation.

There were eventually hundreds of companies around the world producing rolls for the player piano market. The Copyright Act of 1909 established the first compulsory mechanical license, which allowed anyone to make a copy of a piano roll if they paid a fee set by Congress. This compulsory license system continues to be used today, not to pay royalties for piano roll copies, but by musicians who want to record and distribute cover versions of songs written by other songwriters.

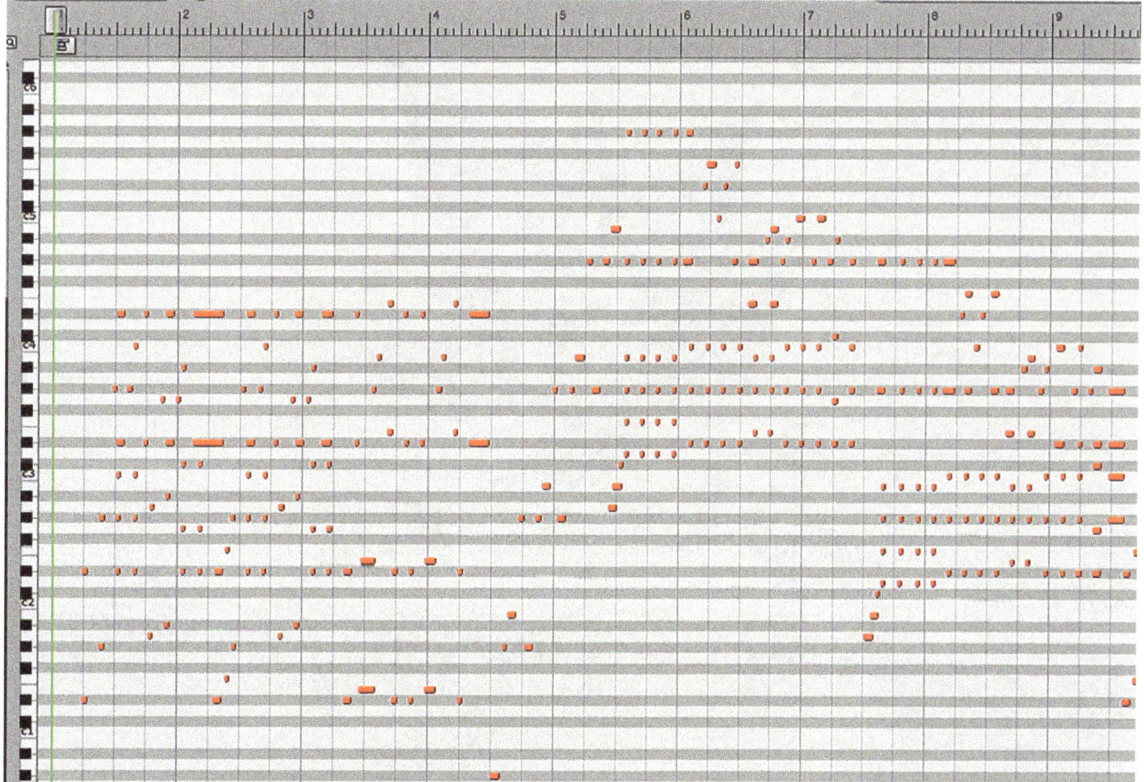

Scott Joplin's "Maple Leaf Rag" displayed graphically in a MIDI sequencer program. Time is represented on the horizontal axis and pitch on the vertical axis. Each little blob represents a single note, like the bumps on the cylinders of music boxes.

The sales of player pianos peaked in 1924 as phonographs, loudspeakers, and later radios began to offer customers new options for entertainment. There was also a similar decline in the publishing of player piano rolls, and the Stock Market crash of 1929 virtually ended their production. Today computers have replaced paper rolls as the control system in player pianos like Yamaha's Disklavier, which offers new capabilities such as connecting to the Internet and playback synchronized with video. The player piano's model of registering the timing and pitch of notes as time passed on a paper roll became the basis for the Musical Instrument Digital Interface (MIDI) protocol developed in the 1980s, which replaced punches on paper with bytes of binary data in a digital stream. This information can be displayed and edited easily using a computer and sequencing software.

Sheet Music

The printing of music, which had begun in the 1500s, dominated the music industry by the 19th century. Sheet music arrangements of single songs were a popular form of home entertainment for those who wished to play the songs themselves rather than listening to piano roll arrangements of them on player pianos. Scott Joplin, the King of Ragtime Writers, was one of the first of his generation following slavery to learn to read and write music. His biggest hit was "Maple Leaf Rag" and became the first ragtime song to sell over a million copies. Joplin had fortunately negotiated a royalty with his St. Louis publisher, John Stark, and the on-going income stream allowed him to dedicate his time to composing. Later in his life, Joplin moved to New York City in search of other publishing opportunities, such as those found in the area called Tin Pan Alley, known for its collection of songwriters and publishers of sheet music.

The cover from the sheet music for "Maple Leaf Rag."
Courtesy of TimeWarp Technologies

Radio

Changes in player piano technology were just one of the many breakthroughs that have affected the evolution of music and the entertainment industry. While we live in an age that focuses on developments in electronics and communications, all the instruments musicians use today show signs of the evolution in materials and manufacturing techniques. For example, pianos became louder after cast iron was invented and allowed for frames to withstand more tension. Cast iron was also used in the construction of wider balconies in larger auditoriums, requiring louder pianos to fill them up with sound. Radio became a popular form of home entertainment in the 1920s after more homes started to be supplied with electricity. Gradually more and more families gathered around the radio in the living room to enjoy a variety of programming that eventually combined music, drama, news, and sports coverage.

Radio became the primary avenue for listeners to discover new songs. It is a sit-back experience that you can enjoy while you are doing something else, like (carefully) driving a car. In the early days, disc jockeys had the freedom to pick the songs they wanted to play. The voices of radio personalities provided a sense of connection and companionship, and a sense of place. Many DJs served as knowledgeable curators and created a mix of familiar and new songs to entertain and educate their audiences. Regionally-owned stations can be engaged in the community and cover local news.

© Everett Historical/Shutterstock.com

1930s family listening to the radio together.

Vinyl Records

After radio, the next major shift in the music and entertainment business began in the 1950s. The main system for music delivery was 45 and LP vinyl records sold in stores. In some ways, we've come full circle. Music lovers bought 45 singles in the 1950s, moved to LP albums in the 1960s to 1990s, and then back to downloading singles after 2000. The growth of the record industry set the stage for the music business as we know it today.

© Swill Klitch/Shutterstock.com

LP records offered greater fidelity
and playing time than 45 disks.

The phonograph had been invented in 1877 by Thomas Edison with a system using cylinders wrapped in tin foil, and Alexander Graham Bell made improvements by switching to wax. Emile Berliner followed with a different type device that played flat discs. The waveform of the audio signal is stored on a record in its spiraling groove, which is travelled by the needle tip of a stylus. Both the groove and the stylus are gradually worn down after repeated playing. Disc recording became the dominant format for most of the 20th century.

© Gustavo Escribano Delgado/Shutterstock.com

A stylus reading the grooves in an LP.

There was limited interaction during these years between artists and the public, who learned of new releases from listening to the radio. Artists worked with record companies to make recordings, which were distributed to stores and then sold to listeners.

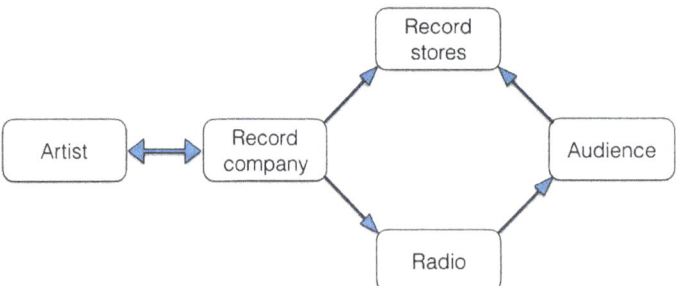

Companies promoted their records to radio stations, which generated interest in the audience to purchase copies at record stores.

At first, record labels stocked the stores with new records and promoted them to new radio stations to get air play, but after radio personality Alan Freed was convicted in the payola scandals of the 1950s, labels began to insulate themselves from direct contact with stations by hiring independent radio promoters, whose job is to get their records into heavy rotation on the air.

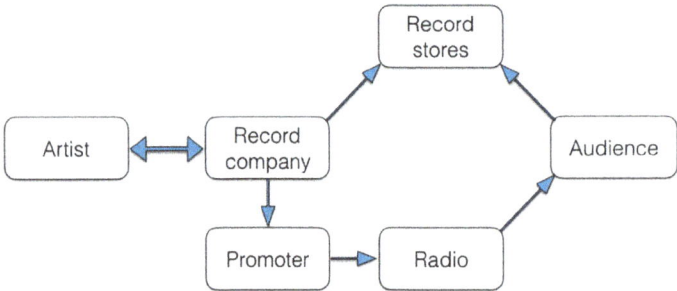

In order to insulate themselves from promotion, record companies began to hire independent promoters to work with radio stations.

During this time, record companies were owned primarily by music lovers, who gave producers like John Hammond time to nurture new artists and discover how their talent could best connect with an audience over the course of a series of albums. For example, he discovered 18-year-old gospel singer Aretha Franklin, and after trying several different styles she developed into the Queen of Soul.

Portable Players

In 1954, another breakthrough product appeared—the transistor radio—and provided the first portable individual listening experience. Steve Wozniak, the co-creator of the Apple computer loved what it could do said that "It opened my world up."

The transistor radio provided the first portable listening experience.

Personal radios, inexpensive record players, and the increase of teenagers' spending power led to the development of a youth music market, which continues to be the driving force in the industry today. Suddenly young people could go off anywhere and enjoy their own music—rock and roll, a style that most parents did not keep up with and could not relate to. Purchases supported the growth of large record chains like Tower Records, which grew between 1960 and 2006 to have stores across the United States and in many other countries around

A portable cassette tape system.

the world. Cassette tape was the recordable format that developed in parallel with vinyl records. Listeners could buy prerecorded tapes, or blanks to use to make copies of records. Many enjoyed making "mix tapes" combining their favorite songs from different albums. In 1979, the Sony Walkman was introduced—a portable system for playing cassettes, and over three hundred million of them were sold.

While most large record stores have disappeared since 2006, and all that is left are small displays to Walmart and Best Buy, there has been a resurgence in the last few years in vinyl sales to younger fans for their listening and collecting enjoyment. Small stores are hanging on, and celebrating the movement each year on Record Store Day.

Compacts Disks

In 1982, the CD format was introduced, and two years later the Sony Discman became the first portable device to be able to play them. Advantages over vinyl records included greater capacity, fidelity, and durability. If handled carefully, the surface of a CD never wears out as it is read by a laser beam instead of a record player stylus.

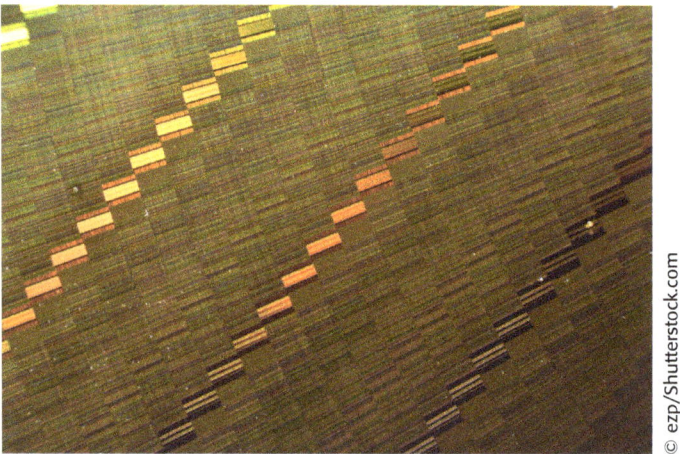

A close-up of the surface of a CD.

Record companies understood that once the music was in a digital form it could be easily copied and shared, and were concerned when Apple's slogan for the marketing campaign for their computers in 2006 became "Rip. Mix. Burn." A levy was instituted, as had been previously done with blank cassettes. It was a royalty of 2% on the price of the recording devices and 3% on blank media such as CD-ROM discs, despite the fact that the majority of them are actually used in the computing industry for data storage, not music. This money created a revenue stream for the music industry and reduced some of the complaints from record companies.

The real benefit, however, to the recording industry from the popularity of the compact disc format was that consumers went out and repurchased many of the recordings they already owned on vinyl in order to get a version with greater dynamic range and less noise. The labels charged $15–$18 for a CD, making the excuse that they were a higher form of technology, when in actuality it costs less to manufacture and transport than an LP. Better yet, the labels had no new development costs, as they already owned the master recordings. This created a cash cow for record labels and lulled executives into a feeling of complacency so that they were not alert to, nor prepared for, the coming revolution brought on by the Internet.

Music Television (MTV)

Viacom launched MTV on cable and satellite networks in 1981, becoming the first 24-hour station devoted to music videos. Having videos of performers helped shift music from an auditory to a visual experience, which changed the priority for artists from sounding good to looking good, and in some cases, dancing well. In recent years, MTV's programming has shifted to reality, comedy, and drama in order to try to hold on to its teenage audience.

Consolidation of Radio Stations

The Telecommunications Act of 1996 allowed for media cross-ownership, and a single company to own as many as eight stations in the same market. This helped continue the decline in the number of corporations that control newspapers, magazines, TV, and radio.

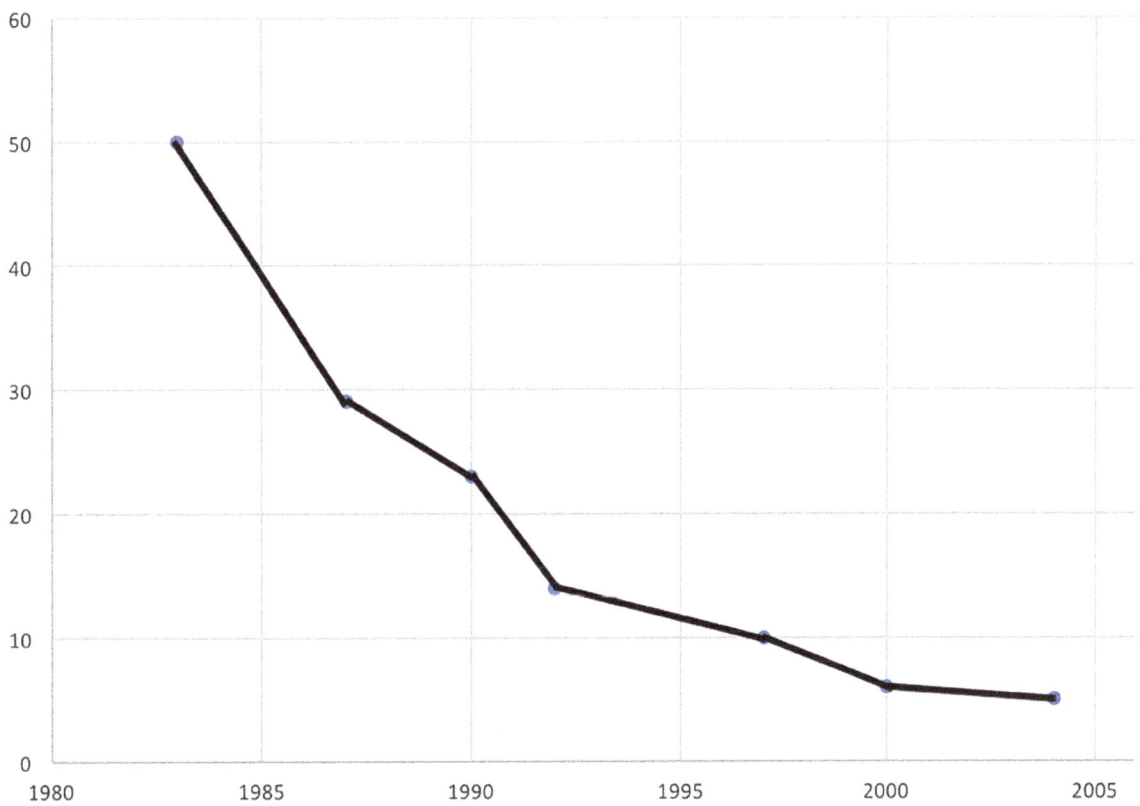

The number of corporations owning major media outlets.

Over time, Clear Channel Communications, Inc. spent $30 billion to become the largest operator of radio stations in the United States and transformed into iHeart Communications. By the year 2000, it had bought nearly 1,200 stations nationwide. Voice-tracking software allows for smaller market stations to be partially or completely operated by people who may never have visited the town from which they are broadcasting. In order to make the program seem more natural, companies audition and hire actors to call in and pose as listeners. iHeart's subsidiary, Premiere Radio syndicates radio programming to 245 million listeners a month, including 90% of the #1 stations.

The formalization of planned rotation reached its most limited form of expression in playlists based on the results of research with focus groups. The only place now to hear much variety in music on the radio is through SiriusXM satellite and college stations. In 2018, iHeart filed for bankruptcy, so some of the stations may be sold off which may lead to an increase in the variety of programming.

Consolidation of Record Labels

The consolidation of record labels that began in the 1990s ended in 2012 with "The Big Three"—Universal Music Group (French), Sony Music (Japanese), and Warner Music Group (American) that control over 90% of the world market. Record labels are no longer owned by music-lovers. Instead, music is viewed as a commodity, and large, publically-owned companies have to show quarterly profits to investors. There are no more John Hammonds nurturing talent through a series of records to develop a career. Instead, if a group doesn't have a hit record right out of the gate it is dropped and another one brought in.

We will return to look at the recording process and record labels operations in Chapter 6.

Factors Causing a Drop in Live Music

I remember being taken aside early on in my career as a musician by a bar manager. He explained that as far as he was concerned it didn't matter how well a band played. It all came down to the total number of drinks sold on the bar receipt that was printed out on paper at the end of the night. He had a number that he needed to make every night to meet his payroll and expenses, and if the number went above that line he would consider having the band return for another engagement. I was advised to announce drink specials over the P.A. and to encourage patrons to consume more. This new reality was later formalized in Willey's Law of Music & Entertainment, which shows the direct relationship between alcohol sales, music, and money:

music + alcohol = money

Willey's Law of Music & Entertainment.

In 1984, the federal government passed a law that tied funding for highways to the drinking age, and by 1990 nearly every state had fallen in line and set the minimum age to 21. This cut into the revenue stream for bars and clubs, and in turn, reduced the pay rates and number of performance opportunities for bands—both local and those on the road. Musicians need to perform regularly in order to hone their musical and communication skills in front of an audience. Musicians also learn from watching each others' performances, and the establishment and development of new musical styles depend on a critical mass. For example, Cajun and zydeco music developed in south western Louisiana due to the fact that there were many opportunities for musicians to learn from each other and to grow in front of an audience. The same happened in the 1890s with ragtime in St. Louis, and with country music in Nashville and jazz in Chicago in the 1920s. Many trace the growth of the Beatles' act to grueling weeks playing long days and nights in Hamburg in the 1960s.

A second factor in the drop in live music is the competition with other forms of entertainment. Consumers in the 21st century have a multitude of options for leisure time, and one of the main challenges for musicians today is to get anyone's attention. YouTube, video games, Instagram, and email are among some of the electronic diversions that are consciously designed to hook and hold users.

Digitization

Digitization (or "sampling") in music is the process of converting a song to binary form. Once an audio or video recording has been digitized, it is easy to copy or transmit it over a network. Audio tracks are digitized and stored on CDs in WAVE format, which uses about 10 MB of space for each minute of a stereo recording.

A number of compression algorithms were developed in order to reduce the size of files and the amount of time it takes to send them over networks, the most popular being MP3. Depending on the amount of compression, an MP3 file sounds almost as good as the full-resolution WAVE file, especially when listening with cheap earphones, small speakers, or in a noisy environment. The software to do the encoding was released to the public in 1994, and MP3 audio files soon began to spread on the Internet, first on the Internet Underground Music Archive and mp3.com, and later in large numbers on Napster.

We will go into the ramifications for the music business and hip-hop culture in Chapter 5.

Napster

Napster was developed in 1999 by Shawn Fanning, a college student at Northeastern University. His software helped users locate MP3 files stored on the computers of other users anywhere on the Internet. The MP3 files that could then be copied from these "peers" became available on their own computers for any other user.

A perfect storm of factors combined to cause it to quickly catch on—the ubiquity of the MP3 file format, plunging prices for hard disk file storage, proliferation of high-speed Internet connections (especially in dormitories on college campuses), a growing disregard for law, and resentment over the high prices charged for CDs. Many people who would not steal a CD from a store felt comfortable illegally downloading songs using the service. Napster attracted huge numbers of users and at times accounted for as much as 61% of network traffic from campus dormitories. Napster's server that ran the search software and closed down in 2001 following a lawsuit filed by the Recording Industry Association of America (RIAA). The RIAA prosecute users for violating copyright, and referred to file sharing as "piracy," and claimed that illegal downloading was responsible for the drop in CD sales in 1999, the year that Napster started to take off:

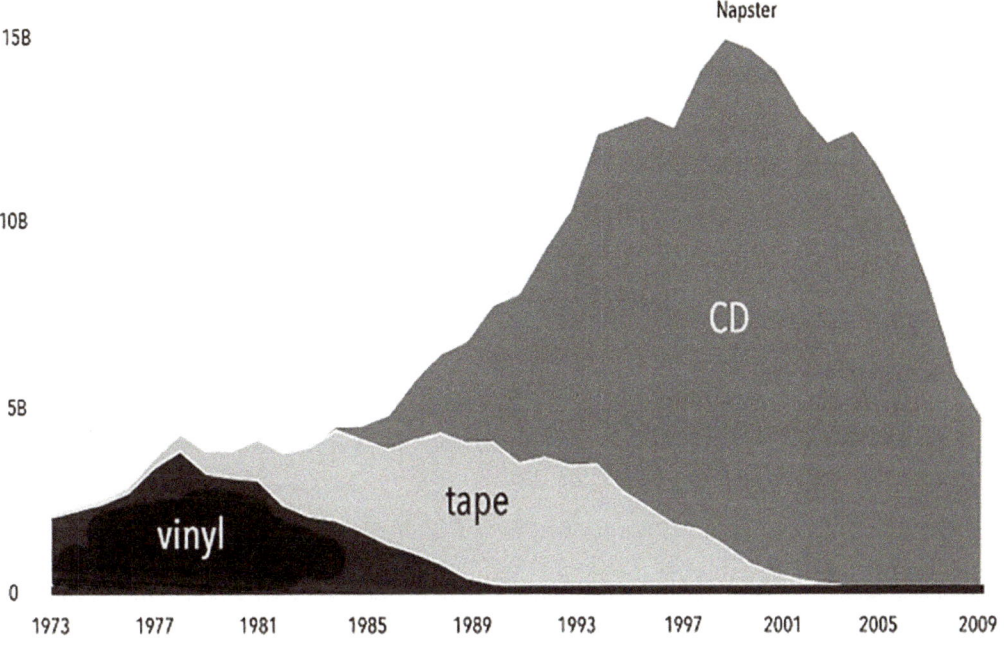

Sales of CDs began to drop in 1999.

There are other opinions, however, as to what turned the tide as just another product in the market. The "Product Life Cycle" expresses what typically happens to sales of any product over time:

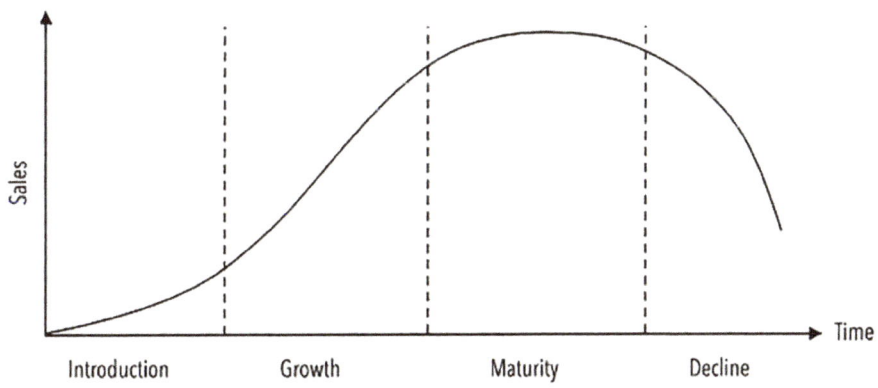

The four stages of the Product Life Cycle.

During the first phase, demand starts to build up. Products are introduced to the market and come to the attention of early adopters, who like to be the first to try something or who are looking for an edge over the competition. This is followed by the growth stage, in which revenue increases rapidly as retailers and customers take notice and new markets open. The third phase is the most profitable, even though growth slows down and competitors introduce similar products in hopes that customers will switch. During the last phase, sales begins to decline as the market has become saturated and customers start to look for the next thing.

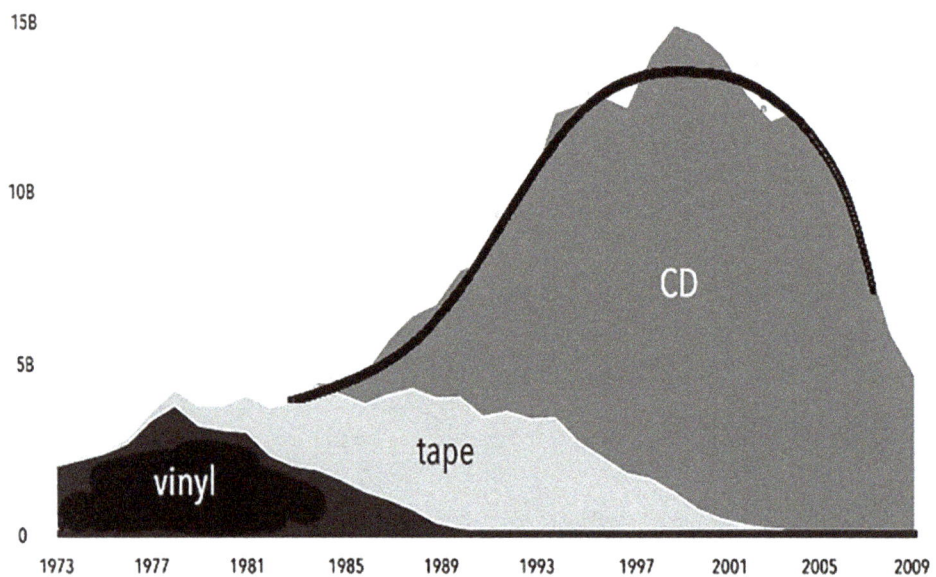

The Product Life Cycle superimposed over CD sales.

If we superimpose the Product Life Cycle over the graph of CD sales starting in 1982 (the year CDs were introduced), we can see that sales followed the natural progression predicted by the Product Life Cycle, suggesting that CD sales would have dropped off, with or without piracy and file sharing.

Apple to the Rescue

Steve Jobs loved music. His favorites included Bob Dylan's "Highway 61 Revisited", Cat Stevens "Tea for the Tillerman", The Grateful Dead's "American Beauty", Glenn Gould's "Goldberg Variations", and Miles Davis's "Kind of Blue." He and Apple wanted to make products that they would like to enjoy music with themselves.

Apple's iTunes store was introduced at the right time for the music industry. CD sales were declining and there was not a legal alternative to peer-to-peer file sharing networks, so Jobs was able to strike a deal with the five major record labels of the time to offer make their songs available in the iTunes store. When he launched the store in 2001, he said that it solved several problems for consumers—it was the quickest way to get high-quality music, was more reliable, and didn't create the bad karma that peer-to-peer file sharing did, which was stealing.

Later in 2001, Jobs announced the iPod. Apple's style is to not be the first to market, but to wait and see what is out there, and then to make the most elegant version of it. The first portable MP3 file player was developed by a South Korean company in 1997. One of the first for the U.S. market was the Rio, whose success caught the attention of the RIAA, who claimed that the device encouraged illegal copying of music. They filed a suit against its manufacturer but lost. Jobs believed that an important motivator for a consumer would be the chance to have a device that could hold a lot of songs. The iPod had a tiny internal hard drive that held 1,000 songs and fit in a pocket. Songs were accessed with a scrolling wheel, and the user's library synced with songs purchased through the iTunes store with a fast firewire connection. The sale of the 25 different iPod models was a big success and the profits from them funded the development of the iPhone.

Apple iPod.

Jobs announced the iPhone at the Macworld convention in 2007, telling the audience that it was actually three products in one—a revolutionary mobile phone, a widescreen iPod with touchscreen controls, and an Internet communications device. The last of the three features got the least reaction from those in attendance, but turned out to be the most important. Few foresaw how quickly people would come to rely on a pocket-sized, networked-connected device, or the popularity of apps that would be developed for it.

In 2008, Apple passed Walmart as the number one music retailer in the United States, with over 50 million customers, the largest music catalog with over six million songs, and four billion songs sold. Jobs believed that people wanted to own their own music and would continue paying for downloads. The one thing that he didn't see coming was how streaming would become the preferred method of music listening.

Review and Preview

We have arrived at the end of our short history leading up to the dawning of the 21st century, ending with technological changes that would drive the music industry for the next 25 years—the blossoming of the Internet, the services offered on the World Wide Web, and Internet-enabled media-playing smartphones.

We will return to the social media layer that was built on top of this new technology in Chapter 4, and review other changes such as globalization and a move toward streaming as the primary distribution method for media in Chapter 10.

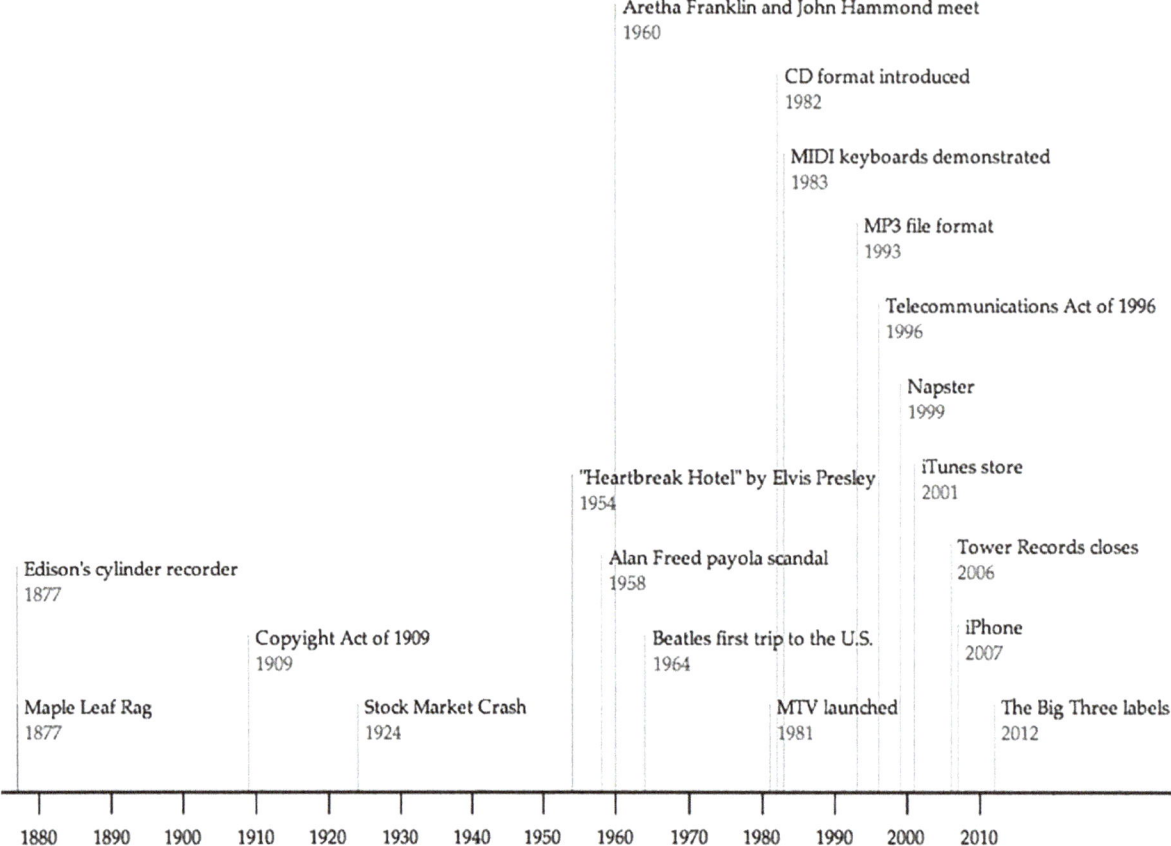

Timeline of milestones in music industry history, from the invention of the record player through the formation of The Big Three record labels.

For Investigation

1. Study a classical music composer who lived before 1850. How did they support themselves? Whom did they serve? Try to estimate many hours of music they wrote during their lifetime. How does this compare with songwriters today?

2. Visit http://scottjoplinarchive.org and listen to a recording of a composition by Scott Joplin as performed by a classically-trained pianists such as Joshua Rifkin. How do Joplin's compositions, and their approach to performing it, compare with "flashier" honky-tonk entertainers such as Jo Ann Castle?

3. Find a piece of sheet music. List every type of information that it includes. Find an experienced pianist that can play it by sight. Ask their opinion of how hard they think the arrangement is to play. Have them play it for you. How does it sound compared with the original recording or other songs you've heard in the same style?

4. Listen to 20 minutes of a commercial radio station. Write down the sequence of things that you hear by category, such as announcements, commercials, news, and music, along with the time that each started. Estimate how many minutes were devoted to each category. Next, do the same thing with a college radio station. Finally, do the same with a public radio station. How do the proportions compare? What was your reaction listening to each one?

5. Compare the listening experience of playing MP3 files on a portable player with the same music in WAVE format (i.e., CD quality) on a good pair of speakers. How do the two compare? What effect does it make depending on where you are sitting in the room relative to the speakers?

6. Make a list of radio stations in your area. Find out who owns them.

7. Go watch a band play live. Take notes on the quality of compositions, the performance, the engagement of the audience, number in attendance, which songs the audience responded to the most, the quality of the sound system, atmosphere, etc. What are they doing best? What would you suggest they try differently?

8. Encode a track from a CD with different MP3 bitrates, from 192 kbps to 320 kbps. Can you tell the difference when you listen back?

9. Visit a record store and talk to someone who works there about their collection. Who makes the decision on which records to stock? How interested do they seem to be in music? Did you find anything there you were interested in or didn't know about? What attracts you about the way products are packaged?

10. Compare the difference in presentation of album art and liner notes on LPs compared with CDs and single downloads.

11. If you have a record or CD collection, what are some of your favorite recordings, which artists perform them, and what label are they on? How many are from "The Big Three" companies?

12. If you've never listened to a whole album before, find a way to do so. How does the experience compare with listening to an assortment of songs by different artists as you might hear on the radio or on Spotify?

13. Trace the changes in laws enacted by Congress and rulings by the Supreme Court covering the copying of piano rolls. Links to the relevant court cases can be found in the book's companion website.

14. Watch Steve Jobs product announcements for the iTunes Store, the iPod, and iPhone. What was his style of presentation? What percentage of the projections on the screen were words, graphs, and pictures? What do you think was it in his manner that captivated people? What changes did the music and entertainment industry go through as a result of these products?

15. How do you feel about downloading songs for free without paying royalties to the composers and performers? Are you, or anyone you know, interested in earning their livelihood from their creative works? Should music be free?

16. Watch the documentary *Before the Music Dies*. Much of the first half covers changes in business and technology in the late 20th century, and how it has negatively impacted musicianship along with radio station and record label management. Take notes and pay attention for the main themes, including:

    • MTV
    • The consolidation of radio stations following deregulation
    • The use of focus groups and playlists
    • The consolidation of record labels and change in ownership from music lovers to executives who have to report to stock owners and show quarterly earnings
    • Studio tricks like autotuning
    • The drop in work ethic today
    • Doyle Bramhall II's experience with the "failure" of his records
    • Opportunities for musicians who go do it themselves
    • Whatever Erykah Badu says

    What were some of the opportunities that were described in the second half for do-it-yourself musicians? What others have come along since the movie was made?

Do It Yourself

1. Visit a radio station. See if you can talk to the Music Director and get some feedback on one of your songs.

2. Get your song played on a college radio station.

3. Try your hand and ears at being a disc jockey and video jockey. Make a Spotify playlist, and a YouTube channel and playlist(s) and share them with your friends and social media.

4. Make a lead sheet of one of your songs using Noteflight. Link to your online score from your website and share it on social media.

5. Make a single copy of a CD of your songs or those of a friend using the kunaki.com service. Link to the product page the service sets up for you from your website and post it on your social media.

Vocabulary Review

Alan Freed—an internationally-known radio disc jockey famous for promoting a mix of country, blues, and R&B credited with coming up with the term "rock and roll". His career was destroyed after his conviction in 1960 for accepting a payola payment of $2,500.

CD (Compact Disc)—the first commercial digital audio format, launched in 1982 by Philips and Sony. CDs are 4.7 inches in diameter and can hold up to about 80 minutes of music.

Cover version, cover song, or cover—a new performance or recording of a song of previously released commercially by another artist. As part of the balance in copyright between an individual's right to benefit from their work and society's right to use it, the composer has the right to determine who records a song for the first time. Once it has been recorded anyone can record their own version, as long as they pay for a mechanical license, usually administered through the Harry Fox Agency.

Digitization, or sampling—the process of analog-to-digital conversion. Once an audio file, book, picture, or any other artifact is converted from its original analog form to a series of binary numbers (samples) it becomes easy to store, copy, and transmit it.

Disc Jockey—a term coined in the 1930s for a person who played records at parties, often switching seamlessly from one record to another in order to keep the music going. Over time, the activity became associated with radio personalities who introduced new records on the air. In the 1960s, Jamaican sound system culture applied experimental playback techniques to prerecorded music and remixes which was taken up by hip-hop culture in the 1970s in New York City. The turntable turned into a musical instrument in the hands of turntabalists such as DJ Kool Herc, Grand Wizard Theodore, and Afrika Bambaataa.

Disklavier—a digitally-controlled acoustic piano manufactured by Yamaha.

Focus group—a small group of people selected from a target audience who discuss their reactions with trained moderators, which then becomes the basis for picking which songs are added to playlists for commercial radio stations.

45—The 45 was a record format introduced in 1949. They were 7 inches in diameter, and could hold up to 4.5 minutes of music per side, with the song with the most potential on the "A" side and an additional song on the "B" side. The format got its name from the fact that they are played at a speed of 45 revolutions per minute.

iHeartMedia, Inc. (formerly Clear Channel)—founded in 2008, it functions as both a music recommendation system and a network of radio stations. iHeartRadio produces concerts as well.

iPhone—Apple's smartphone introduced in 2007 combining a phone, music player, and Internet device with a touch screen keyboard.

iPod—a line of portable media players introduced by Apple Inc. in 2001.

iTunes Store—an electronic store on the Internet developed by Apple to sell digital music, TV shows, movies, books, and movies. It opened in 2003 and provided a legal alternative to peer-to-peer file sharing for its users, and since 2010 has been the largest vendor of music in the United States.

John Hammond (1910–1967)—talent scout, record producer, and music critic, and one of the most important figures in 20th-century popular music. Hammond was a key player in developing the careers of such artists as Bob Dylan, Benny Goodman, Billie Holiday, Pete Seeger, Aretha Franklin, Leonard Cohen, and Stevie Ray Vaughn.

LP ("long play")—was a record format introduced by Columbia Records in 1948. They were 12 inches in diameter and could hold up to 20 minutes of music on each side.

(Compulsory) Mechanical License—created in the Copyright Act of 1909. It was originally created to set the royalty rate for paying composers of songs when they were copied on a piano roll, and has since been applied to audio recordings. A mechanical license is needed whenever someone records (or "covers") or makes a copy of someone else's song.

Media cross-ownership—ownership of multiple media businesses (i.e., newspaper, magazine, radio, TV, movie, music, etc.) by the same person or corporation.

MIDI (Musical Instrument Digital Interface)—A system of hardware and software protocols developed in the 1980s to allow communication between synthesizers and computers made by different manufacturers.

MP3 format—a form of audio coding of digital audio designed by the Motion Picture Expert Group that uses data compression to significantly reduce the size of audio files, typically by a factor of 10. The .mp3 extension is added to filenames in order to indicate this type of encoding.

MTV (Music Television)—an American cable and satellite TV channel launched in 1981 to play music videos.

Napster—a peer-to-peer file sharing system developed in 1999 by Shawn Fanning, a college student at Northeastern University.

Payola (pay + Victrola)—undisclosed money that is paid under the table to get music played on the air. Federal law requires broadcasting employees to disclose such payments so that the audience will know who is paying to get the music heard.

Peer-to-peer (P2P file sharing)—a decentralized communication system in which each user can request files from any other user's shared files. The Napster software made it easy to search and find the songs, which were then quickly copied from from one user's computer to another.

Player piano, or Pianola—a self-playing piano powered by foot pumping or electrical motor. Air drawn through holes punched in paper rolls activates the keys.

Piano roll—a roll of paper played on a player piano, with punches indicating which key on the piano will be played at what time.

Piracy—illegal copying and distributing copies of a piece of copyrighted music or video. This can be done by copying CDs or DVDs, or electronic files over a network.

Playlist—a list of songs telling a DJ what to play.

Ragtime—a genre of syncopated music developed by African-American musicians in the 1890s, usually played on the piano.

Record label—a company that produces, manufactures, distributes, markets, and promotes recordings of songs.

RIAA—The Recording Industry Association of America is a trade association that works to protect the intellectual property of artists and music labels.

Rotation—the repeated playing of a limited set of songs at a radio station. Hit songs are put in "heavy" rotation and played many times during the same day so that listeners will catch their favorites, regardless of when they tune in. Disc jockeys at independent and college radio stations have more choice as to what is played.

Record store—a retail outlet that sells recorded music such as CDs and vinyl records.

Scott Joplin (1868 ?, Texarkana ?—1917, New York City)—An American composer and pianist known as the King of Ragtime. For more information visit http://scottjoplinarchive.org

Sheet music—sheets of paper printed on one or both sides with music. Popular music may be published this way, as either single songs or collections, and includes the melody, lyrics, and an arrangement for piano accompaniment.

Streaming—playing music (i.e., with Spotify) and video (i.e., YouTube) over the Internet rather than downloading it and having your device play it back from its stored memory.

Telecommunications Act of 1996—one of the most important federal laws of our time, reducing the FCC's regulation on cross ownership, and allowing large corporations to buy up thousands of media outlets across the country, reducing the diversity of information in the United States and around the world.

360 deals—a kind of record deal in which the record label gets a percentage of income that comes to an artist from any direction, including touring, sales of merchandise, songwriting, and acting. Labels have resorted to this to make up for profits lost from CD sales.

Tin Pan Alley—a section of New York City on West 28th Street between Fifth and Sixth Avenues that became the center of music publishing and songwriting.

Transistor radio—the transistor was developed by Bell Laboratories in the late 1940s. The Regency TR-1 transistor radio was the first transistorized consumer product and sold out almost immediately.

WAVE format—the Waveform Audio File Format developed by Microsoft and IBM to encode audio files in a high-fidelity uncompressed form, indicated by the .wav filename extension appended to filenames.

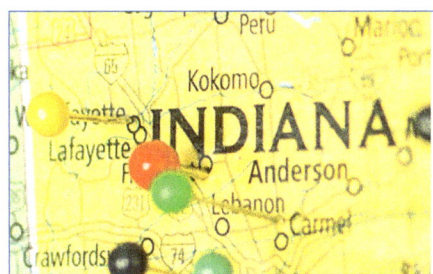

CHAPTER 2

The Artist's Team

Topics

The Artist
Manager
Lawyer
Agent
Business Manager
Tour Manager
Social Media Manager
Marketing
Promotions Director
Sales Manager
Public Relations Manager
Webmaster
Producer

Main Ideas

- A wide number of skills and efforts are needed to reach and maintain an audience.
- Each role requires different competencies.
- Independent musicians should get as many of the roles covered as possible in order to develop their business.

See the book's companion website for supplemental information, updates, and links: http://willshare.com/mmb

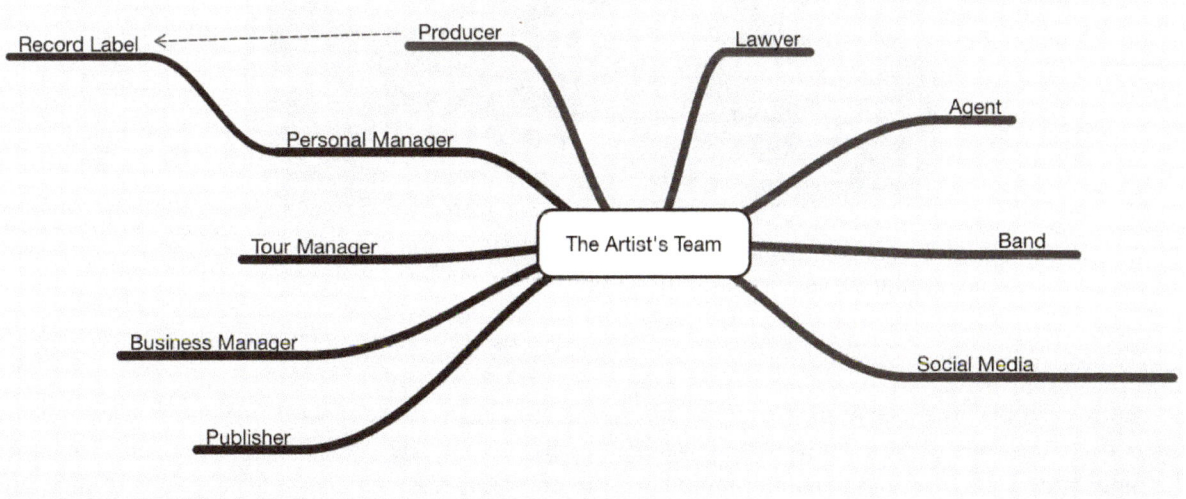

A mind map showing the key members of an artist's team.

Introduction

As with any complex enterprise, the music industry is an interconnected web of professionals with a wide range of skills. In this chapter, we look at some of the key members of an Artist's team and what each one contributes. As you read, make a list of jobs ordered with the ones you find most appealing at the top and the least interesting at the bottom. The increased awareness gained from taking a personal inventory can help you in whatever career you choose, whether or not it is related to music and entertainment.

Before you start reading, make a note here of what percentage of income you imagine an Artist has after paying the other people on their team.

The Artist, with a capital "A"

The two ends of the performer spectrum are occupied by the Artist and the Band. An Artist is a performer, usually a singer, who is recognized by an audience separate from the musicians that provide accompaniment. As an Artist, more things get done your way and you get most of the attention from the fans, but you have a heavier workload and it can be lonely at the top.

Elvis Presley was an artist, so is Taylor Swift. Michael Jackson, the King of Pop, was the one that audiences tuned in for during the intermission at the 1993 Superbowl. Most wouldn't remember his guitar player, despite her big hair and hair-raising solos. I know that it was Jennifer Batten played for Michael that day, and on his three world tours from 1987 to 1997 because I was a fan of hers starting back in her formative days, when she played with tasteful restraint in a small funk band in Del Mar, California. I will never forget the day a friend brought her over to jam with our band. She went on to tour with Jeff Beck, and may well be a star herself someday, if instrumentalists can get back into the limelight they enjoyed in the Jazz Age.

Everybody recognizes Taylor Swift. Does anyone know her guitar player's name?

Bands are at the other end of the performer spectrum—groups that have evolved with more or less the same players over time, but who are known to the general public as a unit rather than as the individual members. The more famous the band becomes and more fanatical their fans, the more aware fans become of their individual members. For example, Beatles fans know the names of all four members of the group and usually have a favorite, but they are still referred to as a unit. The membership of some famous groups is less important to the general public than their collective impact, such as Led Zeppelin and Coldplay.

More people can recognize Coldplay's music than name of the members of the band.

Some groups are somewhere in the middle, with an identity as a band and a recognizable leader, such Mick Jagger in The Rolling Stones, or Sting in The Police.

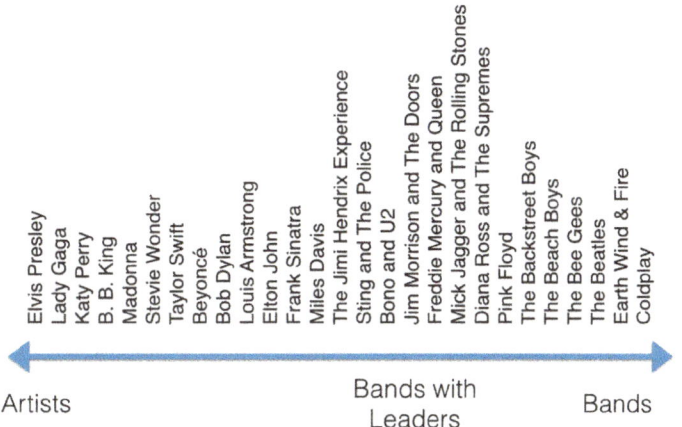

The performance spectrum. Artists on the left could play with any group of sidemen. Bands on the right are recognized as a group.

An Artist preparing for a tour may rely on a trusted partner who has been with them for years to be their Musical Director, and put that person in charge of coordinating the rest of the musicians with whom they have little contact. Some of these sidemen are contracted for the duration of the tour, or picked up for performances along the way.

We'll refer to musicians collectively simply as Artist at times in this book when things apply more or less equally to Artists and Bands, such as in the following description of members of their team.

Manager

An Artist may work with three different types of managers. The person who is most involved is the Personal Manager, or simply, the Manager. They carry a huge amount of responsibility and guide all aspects of the Artist's career. Some of the things a manager does for the Artist include:

- Developing an image and a story.
- Representing, and hyping them.
- Helping with business and creative decisions.
- Collecting fees for each engagement, and creating and executing a strategy to help them earn more money each year.
- Helping develop the team and making sure that everyone is doing their job, and working hard to promote the Artist's success.

A manager typically gets paid 10–20% of the Artist's gross income. When an Artist is just starting out that isn't worth much, so a family member, friend, or fan may take on the role. As an Artist's career grows, they may feel that they have outgrown a manager who lacks the experience and contacts to take them to the next level. Efforts made on the Artist's behalf may not pay off for a few years, so a "sunset clause" may be added to the contract so that the manager continues to receive a diminishing share of the Artist's income if they get dropped when the Artist's career starts to take off.

Lawyer

Some people say that the lawyer is the first person an artist should pick, in part in order to get their advice and benefit from their contacts to choose a manager. They typically charge 5–10% of the Artist's income for their services, or may work for an hourly rate. Music entertainment law is a specialized field as there are many issues unique issues. Music entertainment lawyers are also aware of the deals that other Artists are getting and can help structure one that is favorable to their client. They can help an Artist set up legal protection, like forming an LLC, which may be a good idea once they start to tour. In the case a fan is injured and sues, they will only be able to go after the LLC's assets.

It is difficult for an Artist to get a record label to listen to their demo tape. There are too many people making music today, and no one has the time to listen to the flood of mediocre material in order to find a gem. Entertainment lawyers and managers are in a better position to shop an Artist for a record deal, since just the fact that their services have been retained acts as a filter, demonstrating that their client is working successfully in the field enough to pay for their services, and they already have relationships with people who are in a position to make a decision.

Agent

An agent (also known as a Talent Agent, or Booking Agent) looks for work for their clients—actors, athletes, authors, directors, models, musicians, or anyone else in the fields of entertainment or broadcasting. A typical day for them is spent communicating with promoters and talent buyers on the telephone and writing emails to negotiate deals and plan tours for their clients. They need to be good multitaskers, with good organizational skills and attention to detail. Agents work independently or for an agency, and get about 10% of the work they find.

Business Manager

A business manager is usually one of the later members to join the Artist's team as there is not as much to do at the beginning when there is less money to manage. They handle the Artist's money, and help reconcile tour expenses, asset and capital management, investments, and income and sales taxes. They generally get a 5% share the Artist's income, or work for an hourly rate or flat fee. No license is required to do this job, and there are many stories of family (and nonfamily) members mismanaging an Artist's money, so special care should be taken when choosing someone to do this job. As an Artist gets bigger and busier, their team and payroll grow.

It is important that the Artist understands the role of each member of their team, and the best experience is if they have done the work themselves before hitting the big time. Remember, half or more of the music business is business, and watching the books is the bottom line.

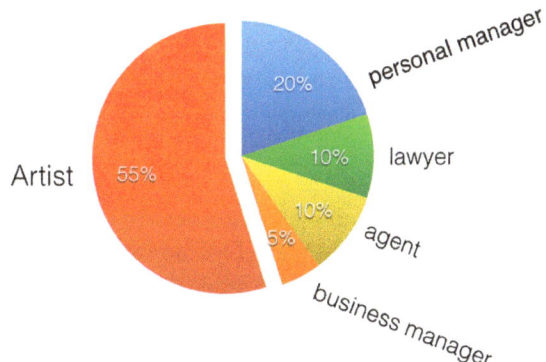

The Artist pays about half their income to the first four members of their team.

After paying these four team members the Artist is left with only about 55% of the money that they are paid. Refer back to the number you wrote down before you started reading this chapter. Was your estimate higher or lower than that?

But wait—we're not done yet! Let's continue with a number of other additional people that need to be paid in order to keep the business going.

Tour Manager

It is vital that someone is there on a tour to manage the transportation, schedule, and finances. When bands are starting out on a small tour and aren't earning enough to hire a tour manager, it is a good idea if one member serves as the point person to work with venues and watch the time. For a medium-sized tour, a Road Manager may need to be appointed to keep the band on course.

As the scale and complexity of a tour continues to grow, a higher level of skill and responsibility is required due to the effect success or failure has on the Artist's career, and because of the significant sums of money involved. Enter the Tour Manager. They get involved earlier than a road manager would, take the routing developed by a booking agent, and create a budget based on calculated costs for rehearsals, projected income from shows, musician and crew salaries, hotels, per diems, transportation, and lighting and sound systems. It is vital that the Tour Manager have experience with this process in order to determine whether the amount of projected equipment to be transported and the method of transportation are well-matched, and that the costs of personnel have been realistically anticipated so that a profit, rather than a loss, is shown at the end. Once the trip begins, the Tour Manager travels with the musicians and stays in touch with staff at upcoming shows in order to make sure that proper arrangements are being made.

We will learn more about the Tour Manager and live performance in Chapter 8. The remaining roles are likely to be filled by people at the Artist's record label if they are signed to a contract.

Social Media Manager

The Social Media Manager coordinates social media for the Artist or label, and has control over posting content on all their social media outlets. A Social Media Specialist works under them, produces content, and helps with analytics.

We will cover social media and analytics in Chapter 4.

Marketing

Marketing begins with defining a brand and choosing target markets based on an analysis of consumer habits and methods of purchasing, which we will return to discuss in Chapter 3.

The Marketing Manager is responsible for developing plans and strategies and presenting them to label executives. As this person is responsible for managing the marketing team, they are likely to have a college degree in marketing and/or related experience.

Marketing Analysts compile data gathered from consumer groups, previous campaigns, and target markets, and suggest techniques that would be effective considering the situation.

Marketing Representatives (Reps) communicate sales figures to radio and TV stations and trade publications in order to help build a buzz, deliver and set up promotional displays, organize radio station contests, help coordinate tours, and stay in touch with stores to make sure they have enough product.

As with many aspects of the music industry, much of the activity in marketing has moved to the Internet. Whereas marketing in the past led to campaigns on radio, TV, and in print, today's Website Marketing Manager takes advantage of opportunities on websites and social media. Most of the work now is in digital form—social media, video, and other content for cell phones. A record label may have a New Media Manager who is responsible for managing company social media accounts, video websites, and any other new forms of media. They are expected to be alert to changes in the industry and to suggest when the time has come to adopt a new technology.

© Elnur/Shutterstock.com

Changes in technology will continue to drive the evolution of the music industry.

Students can get experience in record label operations by working as a Campus Rep, in order to help promote Artists through social media and campus events. It may be a volunteer position or carry a small salary, but in either case it's a good opportunity to work with a variety of people and make industry contacts.

Promotions Manager

The larger the business, the more likely it will be to have a Promotion Manager. They work at high level—brainstorming, developing, directing, and implementing a campaign for a label or Artist. They coordinate with the Merchandising department, and decide how and when a record should drop, arrange interviews, TV and radio appearances, and press conferences. It is a management position and requires someone with a lot of experience and awareness—someone who can put together and monitor a team to execute a campaign successfully and achieve departmental goals.

The job of a Promotional Staffer or Assistant includes answering questions from clients, proofreading outgoing communications, contacting radio station program directors, setting up interviews and on-air performances, and to take key personnel from radio stations out to eat and drink and/or attend a show at a club in order to demonstrate their Artist's ability to attract, entertain, and engage an audience.

Sales Manager

The Sales Manager monitors album sales to wholesalers and retailers, and carries out sales campaigns to meet company goals. They also hire and fire employees in the Sales department. A degree in business or finance or commensurate experience is required in order to handle the details.

A Sales Representative (Rep) is the liaison between the record label and outlets for its record sales. A Retail Sales Assistant helps process orders.

Public Relations Manager

Publicists work to get positive representations of their clients in front of the general public through campaigns including press kits, press releases, show previews, and concert reviews. The Public Relations Manager is expected to contribute new ideas to help the company grow. They act as a liaison between the company and media outlets.

A Website Content Provider produces content to be distributed online.

A Public Relations Assistant is an entry-level position that involves such activities as maintaining databases, creating press kits, and other office duties. As with many positions, it can be a high-pressure situation where much is expected, you get the blame if anything goes wrong, and you don't get credit when things go well.

Webmaster

It's important to have a website that acts as the hub for all, an Artist's or label's social media. It's the Webmaster's job to make and maintain an attractive site that is easy to navigate, and to handle its interactive aspects (i.e., search, purchases, mailing lists, etc.). Major labels have someone on staff to do this work. Independent Artists and labels are more likely to pay someone a flat fee or hourly rate. The website needs to have new content regularly in order to stay fresh and keep fans coming back. Independent artists save money if they have a site that someone with less skill than the Webmaster can update.

Producer

There are two types of Producers. The first is the traditional type, who does anything necessary to deliver a marketable master recording that is commercially viable. This type of producer takes a holistic approach, guiding the project through the three stages of preproduction, production, and postproduction, and they have a big impact on the Artist's overall sound. The producer needs to have good taste a and great set of ears in order to guide the Artist to create something the public will want to listen to. Quincy Jones is an iconic example of this type of producer, with 79 Grammy nominations and 27 Grammy Awards.

In the old days, producers worked for record labels. Now they are almost all independents and work a fee and/or for percentage "points" from royalties.

Quincy Jones could do
it all—perform, arrange,
conduct, and produce.

The second meaning of Producer comes from hip-hop culture, and applies to electronic musicians and artists who make beats and background tracks with their own equipment. This type of producer is sometimes referred to as a Beat Maker or Programmer.

The legal issues involved with sampling in hip-hop are explored in Chapter 5, and the roles of Record Producer and Engineer explained in greater depth in Chapter 6.

Review and Preview

In this chapter, we have introduced a few of the key roles and duties of the members an Artist's team. There was not enough space to list all the related professions and services they provide for performers, such as photographers, videographers, hair stylists, makeup artists, wardrobe designers, choreographers, vocal coaches, chiropractors, and psychotherapists, nor the many contributions of families and friends, street teams, and super fans who spread the word and help develop a community.

A major record label has the resources and staff to fulfill these positions and cover their associated job responsibilities. All the jobs are important and each contributes to the Artist's success. Things continue to change in today's music and entertainment world, however, and the jobs can be done in different ways. The most important thing is that the different aspects are all covered. An independent band may be able to divide up the work among the members, whereas an Artist has to do everything themselves, or find someone to help with the things they don't have the time, interest, or skills to do.

Another thing to consider when forming a team is to balance out strengths with people who have complimentary qualities, who can fill in gaps where others are weak. It helps to have people on the team with different skills on the team who can come up with new ideas and get things started, see the big picture, define problems, evaluate performance, find practical solutions, solve problems, and get results. Most people can't, or don't have time, to do it all.

We end this chapter with a return to the mind map presented at the beginning, this time replacing the job titles with some of the basic underlying functions:

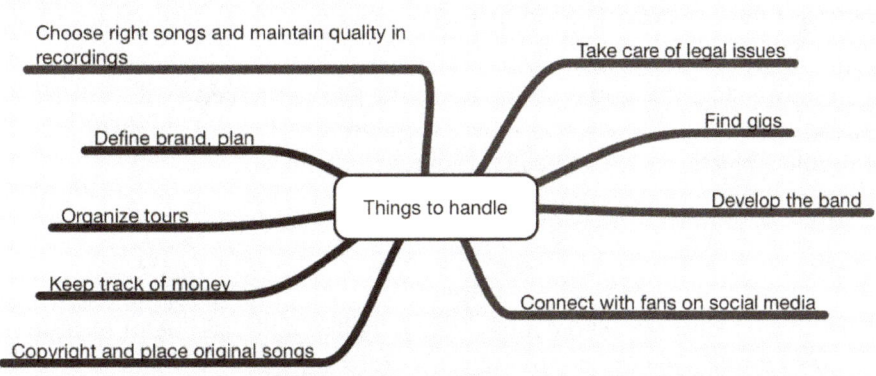

A mind map showing the range of the things that an Artist has to handle.

For Further Investigation

1. Interview a musician that doesn't have a team. Find out what they or their partners are doing to cover the duties of the jobs covered in this chapter. How do they decide where their energy is best put? What skills do you have that could help fill in the gaps?

2. Give an example of three types of groups whose music you like—an Artist with backing musicians, a band with a prominent leader, and a cohesive group without a famous star. How intense is your emotional connection with each? How far in front of the rest of the musicians does the singer in each case stand? Which of the three types do you tend to prefer? Ask the same questions of a nonmusician, and of a musician who is not a vocalist. Do you think people's reactions might be influenced by whether they are musicians themselves, and if they can relate to instrumentalists equally well as vocalists?

3. Pay attention to the acceptance speeches on awards shows like the Grammy Awards and the People's Choice Awards. Write down the names mentioned by the winners—their roles and companies. Do some research and find out more about those people that work behind the scene and what each contributes. How long have they been in the music business and who else have they worked with?

4. If you were an Artist, would you choose a manager just starting out in their career who loves your music and has lots of ambition and energy but lacks experience, or an experienced manager with other clients, who may be too busy to give you a lot of attention? Explain the reasons for your decision. What would be the advantage of the alternative choice?

5. Where is the office of the nearest attorney to where you live that has experience in music entertainment? What sort of services do they provide?

6. Write down a marketing message that has reached you in the last 24 hours. How was it delivered to you? What relevance does it have to you, your friends, and the group of people that you identify with? What was your reaction to it?

7. Are you interested in being an Artist? If so, which of the duties described in this chapter would you be able and interested in taking care of? Which would you need to find partners to help you with?

8.   Which kind of producer would you rather be in a recording project—someone who coaches the musicians to get the best possible performance, or one that makes beats and background tracks? What skills do you have could be applied to either or both?

9.   What skills do you have that could be applied to the jobs performed by the other members of the Artist's team discussed in this chapter? What experience do you have supplying the services they offer to other people? Which would you be most interested in doing?

Do It Yourself

1.   Find a band in your local area whose music you really like, and that doesn't seem to be very busy. Ask them if there's anything you can do to help them get more gigs.

2.   Attend a show by a band. Take notes of the things you like best about their music and delivery, and a list of things that you would suggest they consider doing differently if you were their producer. What one do you think would help the most if you were only going to make one suggestion? Approach it as a person looking for a solution. For example, instead of saying you thought they were too loud, be specific and suggest that they play softer in a particular song or section.

3.   Add some constructive comments to a song on YouTube or SoundCloud by a band in your area.

4.   Seek out someone doing one of the jobs covered in this chapter, and ask if you can shadow them for a couple of hours. Find a way to be useful.

5.   Find an entry-level position doing office work at a publishing company, booking agency, studio, advertising agency, or other enterprise. Be a good observer and prove your passion and competence. Learn from within and build your network of connections.

6.   Find a beat-selling website and create an account to license some of your material.

Vocabulary Review

Agent, Talent Agent, Booking Agent—finds gigs for an Artist and fits them into a schedule.

Artist or Solo Artist—The "star" of a group, someone that the public recognizes and focuses on during a performance.

Beats—rhythm tracks that rappers build on top of in hip-hop music. The people who make them are sometimes called Producers, Beat Makers, or Programmers.

Buzz—excitement about something that people are talking about.

Demo—a demonstration recording showing what a band's songs and performance sound like. It is used to help get a gig or a record deal.

Drop—releasing a new song or album to the public.

Gig—a paid performance or other type of job.

Hype (from "hyperbole")—to promote intensively, to make claims that are not be meant to be taken literally. Managers need to be able to hype the importance of their client, what they are doing, and how they are catching on.

Per diem—daily food allowance for musicians and crew when they are on tour.

Sideman—contract musicians who play on the side, and do not get a lot of attention from the audience.

Studio, or Session musicians—an elite bunch of Ninja performers who are hired for recording sessions and live shows, who can pick up a song by ear or by reading sheet music and play it flawlessly the second time through.

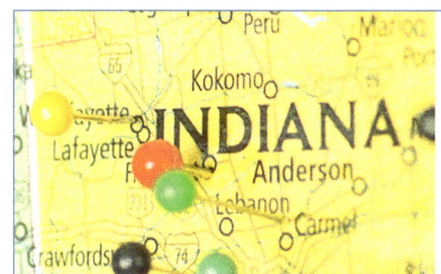

Topics

Brand
Elevator Pitch
Slogan
Tagline
Logo
Press release
Flier
SWOT analysis
Review and Preview

Main Ideas

- A brand identifies a product or service.
- A slogan is a mini mission statement.
- A tagline may be more about being memorable than giving a reason to buy.
- A flier is a small advertisement designed to catch a passerby's attention.
- A press release helps journalists get your message out.

See the book's companion website for supplemental information, updates, and links: http://willshare.com/mmb

Introduction

Marketing is the job of every employee. In addition to communicating with clients and solving problems, it's important to be able to articulate the value of products and services. The more you understand what your customers are looking for, the easier and more natural it will become. As Daniel Pink wrote in *To Sell Is Human*, "The average person spends 40% of their life trying to move others. We're persuading, convincing, and influencing others to give up something they've got in exchange for what we've got."

In today's sped-up world, however, it is getting increasingly difficult to get and hold a customer's attention. We are bombarded by marketing messages throughout the day, and at the same time our attention spans are decreasing because of many distractions and our media-rich entertainment options. It used to be that people could concentrate for about 20 minutes. Today, according to a study by Microsoft, our attention span has dropped to about 8 seconds, less than that of a goldfish.

One of your goals as a marketer is to catch someone's attention, and to hold it before they swim away. If they stop and listen, you may be able to go into more detail.

In this chapter, you'll learn how to create a brand, slogan, tagline, logo, press release, and flier in order to get your message across quickly and clearly. In Chapter 4, we'll apply these traditional marketing tools to the world of social media.

Brand

Branding can be traced back to the ancient Egyptians. In order to establish ownership, a mark was burnt or cut into the skin of animals, a practice that was continued in the United States until modern times by slave owners and cattle ranchers.

Today a brand is an essential marketing tool. Respect for a brand enhances a company's competitive strength, creates customer loyalty, makes it possible to charge more, and increases customer loyalty and repeat business. When defining a brand, consider the two types of characteristics of the target audience. *Demographics* include gender, age, income, and educational level, and aspects that can define populations such as Baby Boomers, Millennials, and Generation Z which depend on the year one is born. *Psychographics* deals more with culture, and is a study of personality that includes attitudes, values, interests, and lifestyles. These two factors are used in dividing consumers into subgroups and target advertising campaigns according to their common needs, interests, and lifestyles, so as to maximize profit and growth.

The brand statement needs to be delivered in a compact form so that it can be stored in consumers' long-term memories and recalled when considering future purchases. It should emphasize the best qualities of a company while staying reasonably honest. A brand is a promise of quality and consistency, and if the company can't live up to it, consumers may hold it against the company and stop buying their product.

McDonald's is one of America's most successful brands. Whenever you see the Golden Arches on a sign you know exactly what type of food awaits within, whether you are in your own neighborhood, on a cross-country trip, or in a foreign country. The company has perfected its process and products to reduce costs, making it possible to serve customers faster and more cheaply. However, there are a lot of other fast-food options with low-priced dishes. The reason McDonald's has been able to sell over 99 billion hamburgers is due to the place in consumers' minds they occupy, and the habits they have created in them to return for more. The company delivers the same brand experience 68 million times a day, and pays special attention to hooking children by offering play areas and toys in their "Happy Meals."

McDonald's customers have an emotional bond with the brand, even after they grow up.

Consumers pass through three stages of brand awareness. The first phase, *brand awareness and recognition* is a measure of the percentage of people can identify a product or service from its logo or tagline, for example, being able to recall what McDonald's offers when prompted by a picture of the Golden Arches. Children demonstrate brand awareness as early as the age of two. The primary goal of advertising a new product is to turn it into a "brand name" or "household name," one that is recognized in a great majority of households. The first time a consumer buys a product they are likely to pick a recognizable brand as they may be afraid of being disappointed and wasting their money.

Consumers demonstrating *brand recall* have a deeper connection. They are able to recall a brand when asked about a product category, for example, when asked for an example of a fast food chain, and one of the examples they come up with is McDonald's.

The best situation for a company is when the customer arrives at the third stage—*loyalty*, and always buys the same brand when needing more of a product instead of trying the competition. Picking one's favorite brand is a natural thing to do as it requires less time, energy, and thought. It reduces cognitive load, like relying on categorization and stereotyping.

Elevator Pitch

It can be useful to have a condensed form of your brand statement on hand that can be communicated anytime an opportunity presents itself. One form of this is "The Elevator Pitch"—a description of your product that you could say to someone should you find yourself with a quick opportunity to get your message across. It gets its name from one particular situation—sharing an elevator traveling between floors. It should be a short and persuasive speech lasting 20–30 seconds and designed to spark interest about what you or your business does. This may be all the time you have to get your idea across to someone in a position to help you, so practice it in front of a mirror until you can deliver it smoothly. After trying it out on friends and getting feedback from mentors you'll be ready to use it with the public. You should have a shorter version lasting under 8 seconds in case you realize that you have less than 20 seconds to talk, or find yourself underwater with a rich goldfish.

There are a number of things you can do develop your pitch. If you're in a band, it should include the style of music you play, and examples of familiar artists that are in the same vein. Here is a mind map with four of the main popular music styles in the middle, with subgenres branching off them:

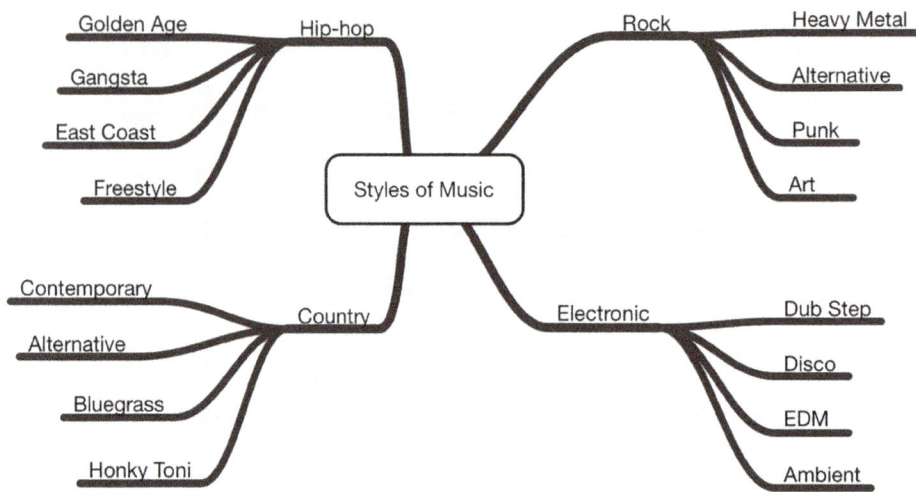

Four popular styles with examples of subgenres for each.

Another way to generate material for the pitch is to list adjectives that describe the group. Describe who the music is and isn't for. Not everyone is going to like what you do, and getting clear on who would love it will make it easier to market. Define the band's audience. Are they tech savvy? Where do they go, what do they spend their money on? What are their favorite bands? How old are they? Describing the audience may help you understand the band better, too.

What is the band's story? What can you say that reflects the band members as people and performers? What is unique about them that will allow them to connect with fans in a new way? Penn Jilette said that he loved music and that his major influences were Bob Dylan and The Rolling Stones, but he didn't want to repeat what they had done or try to do it better, so he became a magician instead. Where is an opportunity for you to stand out?

Research the competition to get more ideas. One good place to get inspiration is the South by Southwest (SXSW) festival's listing of artists. Here are a couple of excerpts:

"Using music like her own personal diary, she penned songs as gritty as her surroundings, which led her to become one of the premiere lyricists on the underground rap scene in New Orleans."

"The band shows their roots in blues, with the immediacy of post-pop punk hooks and sing-a-longs you find in all the best road trip anthems."

"Combining punk abandon with tightly-coiled dance music is part of the band's DNA. It's this core plus their growth and mastery of songwriting, that has allowed them to grow lyrically and sonically from album to album."

"Two of the most compelling new voices in North American Roots music."

"An international London-based trio playing quick, loud, bold, edgy garage tunes."

Each band's listing includes a little blurb, a photo, and links to their social media. Another good place to conduct research are the descriptions of CDs by independent bands on CD Baby:

"Beautiful soothing melody-driven jazz played with precision, nuance, and grace."

"A remastered version of the iconic 1969 release from the most cerebral of the Haight Ashbury bands."

"The band triumphantly returns with 10 new original compositions that feature amazing melodies, soulful playing, and all the fire and grace that they are known for."

"It turns out, the members of this comic pop-rock vocal band are all secret superheroes, creating music, poetry, harmonies, and humor that will rock your socks off!"

Once you have done some deep thinking about your core services and distinctive features, you are ready to begin to think of a way to distill them down in order to describe what you do in the most compact form possible.

Slogan

"Slogan" is an ancient Gaelic word for "battle cry." A slogan or motto is like a mini mission statement that sums up a company's brand and characteristics. It has the power to grab the consumer's attention better than the sight of a product or the name of the company. Walmart distilled their essence down to "Save money. Live Better." Motel 5 advertises their rooms as the "Lowest price of any national chain." The simpler a slogan is, the easier it is to understand and remember.

McDonalds' mission is "To be the best quick service restaurant experience. Being the best means providing outstanding quality, service, cleanliness, and value, so that we make every customer in every restaurant smile." The form of their slogan has changed over the years. It began in the 1960s as "The Closest Thing to Home," which effectively combined two messages—that there was a franchise near to where you lived, and that the food there was the next best thing to mom's cooking.

Some slogans for bands include:

"Greatest Rock Band in the World"—The Rolling Stones

"The King of the Blues"—B. B. King

"The Bad Boys of Rock and Roll"—Aerosmith

Tagline

A tagline takes a different approach to branding. Instead of expressing the core of a company's business like the slogan does, it is intended to be fun and/or memorable. Nike had a hit with "Just do it" in 1988, even though that didn't have anything particular to do with tennis shoes. In the 1990s, Apple tried to differentiate its system from Microsoft's with "Think different." The California Milk Processor Board launched "Got milk?" in 1993 in order to counter the rapid rise in fast food and soft drinks. That tagline, and the images that accompanied it were intended to transform milk into a more exciting product. Amazon's vision is to be "A place where people can come to find and discover anything they might want to buy online." Their tagline states a broader view: "Work hard, have fun, make history."

McDonald's has used a number of taglines over the years. Their response to the pace of life picking up in the 1970s became one of the best known of the century: "You Deserve a Break Today." Once the disco era arrived, their advertising team switched to "Get Down With Something Good." After that craze passed, and people became a little less concerned with how they looked in tight polyester outfits, it was time to let out the belt a notch and enjoy a Big Mac: "Two All-Beef Patties" on a sesame-seed bun with secret sauce, lettuce, cheese, pickles, and onions. Since the early 2000s we've had their new message hammered into our long-term memory: "I'm Lovin' It," a campaign that was kicked off with a song written by Pharrell and sung by Justin Timberlake.

Alliteration with or without humor can be effective. Some taglines for bands include:

"Will Work for Food"—New Kids on the Block

"The Fab Four"—The Beatles

"That Lil' ol' Band from Texas"—ZZ Top

"The Godfather of Punk"—Iggy Pop

Logo

A logo is a graphic mark or symbol that is used by businesses, organizations, and individuals to trigger the public's recognition. Today a company's logo is often used across the board with their trademark, brand, products, website, and social media outlets.

A logo's font and color of text should complement the meaning of the text and the image of the brand. Gold lettering is a natural choice for L'oréal's tagline "Because you're worth it" in order to create an image of exclusive beauty products. Hallmark's logo consists of their name written in an ornate typeface with a crown above, which combines perfectly with the tagline "When you care enough to send the very best." Look at the following examples printed with a variety of fonts available in Microsoft Word. Pay attention to whether your experience of each line changes depending on the font. Afterwards, read each line out loud in tone of voice that reinforces the feeling:

Here's an example in Lucida Bright

Here's an example in Matura MT

Here's an example in Rockwell Extra Bold

Here's an example in American Typewriter

Here's an example in Bradley Hand

HERE'S AN EXAMPLE IN HERCULANUM

HERE'S AN EXAMPLE IN STENCIL

Here's an example in Apple Chancery

The font something is written in affects how you feel about it.

There is a huge variety of fonts available on the Internet, and many free tools for experimenting with them, such as the website dafont.com:

Try your text in a variety of fonts and sizes.

The other important consideration for a logo's text is deciding what color best complements it. In one study, researchers discovered that 90% of snap judgments about products are based on color. There is no absolute correspondence between fonts, colors and the emotions they trigger, since they are affected by personal experiences, cultures, and time period. Here are some common associations, and companies that use the colors in their logos:

Color	Associations	Companies
Yellow	optimism, caution, cheerfulness, cowardice	Subway, Best Buy, McDonald's
Orange	friendly, energy, warmth, health, invitation	Amazon, Fanta, Firefox, Hooters
Red	excitement, power, violence, passion, sex	Coca Cola, Target, Xerox, CNN
Purple	creativity, wisdom, royalty, supernatural	Yahoo, Taco Bell, T Mobile, Barbie
Blue	trust, loyalty, peace, trust, cleanliness, cold	Dell, Ford, Facebook, Twitter, Skype
Green	peaceful, soothing, natural, greed, profit	Sprite, Xbox, Starbucks, Tic Tac, BP
Grey	calm, balance, subtlety, formality	Apple, Honda, Wikipedia
Brown	rustic, earthy, warm, romantic, depth	UPS, Hershey's, Cracker Barrel
Black	power, sophistication, formality, elegance	HBO, Sony, Comedy Network
White	purity, simplicity, innocence, cleanliness	Adidas, Under Armor, Canon
Multi	Friendly, fun, playful	ebay, Google, NBC, Disney, Apple

Logos may be as simple as the name of the business in a particular design, or a combination of the name and an image. In addition, the company's slogan or tagline may also be placed underneath or to the side:

ROBERT WILLEY

POWERED BY WONDER

Plenty of room for improvement here! How would you change the layout, and the proportions of size between the company name, logo, and tagline? What options for the color of the hand would you consider?

Press Release

It can be fun to try out different slogans, taglines, fonts, and colors for the designs for logos. A different form of creativity is engaged when writing press releases, which serve a different purpose and function, as they are meant to be read by editors and writers rather than by the general public. A press release is a written statement sent to the media to announce a news item, such as an upcoming event, award, or release of a product, and provide an opportunity for the company to tell their story and promote their brand. Whether or not you actually distribute the press release, writing one can be a great exercise and way to clarify in your mind what is special about your project. It used to be expected that if you poured a lot of money into advertising, a mediocre product you would see sales increase. In today's saturated, revved-up world you can't wait to start thinking about marketing until after the product is finished. Part of the preproduction work for a recording project or tour could include writing a press release for the finished product, laying out clearly what will be newsworthy, and communicated to an audience when it is done.

Your job as a publicist is to write a press release in a way that makes the editor or writer's job easier, so that the best features stand out, and that it is written in an appropriate style that won't require a lot of rewriting. You're in competition for space in the publication with other events. Don't expect that the editor will go to the work of figuring out what the angles are, and what would be of interest to their audience—that's your job. The investment of time writing the release may be rewarded by their distributing your message to the public at no cost to you.

Start with your name and contact information in the upper left-hand corner of the page. This will not be seen by the public, it is for the media people to contact you if they want more information.

Next comes a headline. Put it in an active voice, and answer the reader's question "What is this story about?" You may want to come up with the headline last. Make it clever. Write it as if it were going to be on the front page.

The rest of the release should be double-spaced in order to make it easy for the recipient to edit. The first paragraph should cover only the "5 Ws"—who, what, where, when, and why, if it's not apparent. This is the critical information that every press release needs. Include a phone number for the public in case someone has a question, like "Will there be wheelchair access?" or "Do you have to be 21 to attend?" Each subsequent paragraph should then go into more depth and cover a different aspect that will be of interest to readers.

The part that most beginners have trouble with in writing press releases is to make it sound objective. It is important to maintain a factual tone throughout. The only place you should include opinions and colorful language in your release is when you quote someone. It's OK to use sensational language and unsubstantiated claims there because it is still a fact that someone said them.

Look for a variety of examples on the book's companion website to see common style features and get ideas. The interesting part of the process is thinking like a marketer. The main obstacles you face in getting someone

An unmovable object awaiting an irresistible force.

to come to your event are attention, time, and money. To be effective, it helps if you understand what type of person might want to come, and to figure out ways to interest them and make them want to attend when they have little time and so many options for entertainment. You've got to deal with reality as observed by Sir Isaac Newton and expressed in his First Law of Motion: "An object at rest will remain at rest unless acted upon by an unbalanced force," especially when the place of rest is as comfortable as a couch, and there are a bowl of chips and a remote control involved.

Today our lives are impacted by new technologies, resulting in new situations codified in Willey's Marketing Corollaries: "A person seated on a couch will tend to remain on the couch until they run out of snacks" and "A person on their phone will tend to remain on their phone until it's too late to do something more constructive or the battery runs down." The publicist's job is to be the unbalanced force Newton referred to in his law (which unfortunately puts them at risk of becoming even more unbalanced themselves). You have to give a potential audience member a very good reason to summon the energy to push them into motion, and to move at the right time in the desired direction.

Each paragraph in a press release needs to stimulate interest and stoke the reader's energy. The fun part, if you find publicity work fun, is to figure out what is in it for the consumer, and what the optimal sequence of bits of information would be. Make an outline before you start to help you get organized and stay focused. Here's an example of one showing one possible ordering and content of paragraphs for a press release about a CD release party:

1. The 5 Ws.
2. Style of music: metal core. Quote from fan about how much they love the way the band plays.
3. Theme for event: the band's drummer is getting married. Quote from bass player about why they are throwing a party in her honor.
4. Story behind the CD's title track, and what went into its YouTube video.
5. Contests: (1) person who came farthest; (2) best submission of wedding anecdote.
6. First 10 to arrive get free autographed CD and T-shirt.
7. Band will be opening for The Lazy Lizards on their upcoming promotional tour. Quote from lead singer about how hard working they and the Lizards are.

When you're finished, check your work to make sure each paragraph accomplishes its goal. The logic of the outline may be clear to you, but be sure that the content gets it across to a reader. Always check your spelling and grammar and tighten everything up so that you don't repeat words and ideas. Have someone else that writes well look it over and help polish it up. Send your press release to appropriate publications. There's no use sending this one about a new metalcore CD to the Orchid Club Newsletter. Send it in a few weeks in advance to give them time to add it to the calendar. Newspapers increasingly want you to upload your information via their website.

A shorter form of a press release can be submitted as a Public Service Announcement to radio stations. Make sure the text sounds good when spoken, so that they will want to read it on the air.

Flier

The effort done to define your brand, design a logo and slogan, and brainstorm about what will draw an audience will make it easier to create a poster or flier. You should include the same 5 Ws that you led off with on the press release, but it doesn't have to maintain the same objective style. Its main purpose is to catch a passerby's eye, and to be so visually appealing that they will want to keep a put up on their wall and/or share on social media.

SWOT Analysis

Performing a SWOT analysis is another popular tool to deepen an understanding of a product or service, formulate a strategy, and make plans for the future. There are four parts to it, each with its own questions to be considered.

Internal Factors Within Your Control	
What is your reputation? How much capital and existing customers do you have?	
Strengths	Describe the positive attributes of your company. What advantages do you have over others? What do you do better than the competition?
Weaknesses	What disadvantages to you have relative to others? What could you improve on? What should you avoid?
External Factors Outside Your Control	
What factors about your location affect you? What is the general perception of your business? Are opportunities ongoing? How critical is timing?	
Opportunities	What trends are you aware of? How can you capitalize on changes in technology? What opportunities can you exploit to advantage?
Threats	What obstacles do you face? What suppliers do you depend on? What does your competition do better? What limits your audience in supporting you? Is there an unfavorable trend that may lead to decreasing revenues?

The most important factors revealed in the process of answering these and other questions can then be summarized in a grid:

INTERNAL	**Strengths**	**Weaknesses**
	1.	1.
	2.	2.
	3.	3.
EXTERNAL	**Opportunities**	**Threats**
	1.	1.
	2.	2.
	3.	3.

Review and Preview

The perspective you gain from performing a SWOT analysis can be used to revise your brand statement and to take another look at your logo and slogan to see if they are the best representation of the image you want to convey for your company. It is worth taking time to get the logo right since you will probably want to stick with it. Self-study and adjustments to changes in your situation and that of the market should be an ongoing process.

The understanding you have of branding developed in this chapter can be applied in the next chapter, where we will see how to market a brand through social media.

For Further Investigation

1. What is the brand for your school or company? How did you learn about it, and why did you decide to join? What is the brand for your department?

2. Make a list of 5 bands that play different styles of music and list 5 adjectives for each. What style and subgenre does each play? Who does each one remind you of? In what way are they different, and similar? Why is it easier to promote a band that plays one style of music rather than a variety of styles?

3. How would you define the brand of your favorite band? What graphical elements are associated with them? What ideas and images do you associate most with them? What would you tell your friends in order to interest them in listening?

4. Make a collection of your favorite logos. What do they have in common? How are they different? What do you like about them? Which is your favorite? Why?

5. Pick a large Midwest city. What gives its music and entertainment scene an advantage to attract music fans over other cities in the region? What places it at a disadvantage relative to others? What economic, technological, and/or social circumstances in the environment there could be exploited to its advantage? What elements in the environment could cause trouble?

6. On a scale of 1–10, how important is it to you to be *fascinating*? Take Sally Hogshead's test "Discover How the World Sees You." What did it report for your primary and secondary ways that you fascinate people? In what ways do you agree and disagree?

7. The next time you buy something, try a different brand from what you usually pick. Notice the thoughts that go through you mind as you consider your options, and then again when you begin to use it. Examine your feelings and thoughts as you decide whether to stick with the new brand or return to your old one. It may be hard to catch what's going on, since people often make up their minds in a fraction of a second.

Do It Yourself

1. List three adjectives that best describe different aspects of you. What is your brand? What would you tell someone about yourself in less than 8 seconds?

2. Perform a SWOT analysis of your business, or one that you would be most interested in starting.

3. Describe the types of customer that you believe would be interested in your business or service. Describe the type that would not be interested in it. What demographic features are you considering in your description? Which are you leaving out?

4. Define your company's brand. Who or what are you influenced by? Evaluate your website and social media outlets and change them as necessary to be consistent with your brand.

5. Create a slogan and tagline for your company. Make sure the slogan expresses the core of your business, while the tagline entertains.

6. Design a logo. Try a variety of fonts and colors for your company name, slogan, and tagline to go with it. Which combination of font and color best communicates your message and the feelings you want to get across? Try them out other people and ask how each makes them feel. Make both a color and black and white version of your favorite. Add one to your website and social media outlets, and begin using it consistently in all your marketing materials.

7. Create a press release for an event you could sponsor or be a part of following the guidelines presented in this chapter. Remember to maintain a factual tone, saving opinions and strong statements for one or two quotes.

8. Design a flier for the same or different event. Include your logo and the 5 Ws. Make sure whoever sees it will understand what is going on and what to expect if they attend. Minimize the number of words and increase the size of what's left so they are legible at a distance of 6 feet or more.

9. Learn how to silk screen posters and T-shirts. Make some hand-printed posters for your event, and get the band to sign them in advance, or at the merch table during the event.

10. Come up with a measureable and achievable marketing objective for your business or service. Implement it and evaluate its success. What did you learn? What will you do differently next time?

11. How can you make your website more useful and informative for visitors? By what date can you make the proposed changes? Explain your plan for updating it regularly with fresh content so that people will keep coming back. Make a schedule for doing that, and examples of the subject of new material.

Vocabulary Review

Brand—an identifying mark or expression of a product from a specific company.

Elevator Pitch—a 20–30 second speech that explains an idea for a product or service.

Flier—a small handbill advertising an event.

Logo—a symbol or design that identifies a product.

Merch—merchandise that musicians sell at shows.

Press release—a public relations announcement sent by the organizers of an event to the media in hopes of getting free coverage.

Slogan or **motto**—a short, memorable phrase used in advertising that represents a company's essence or approach.

SWOT analysis—a compact overview of strengths, weaknesses, opportunities, and threats.

Tagline—a short statement designed to inspire or entertain the audience. Note: some people use it synonymously with slogan.

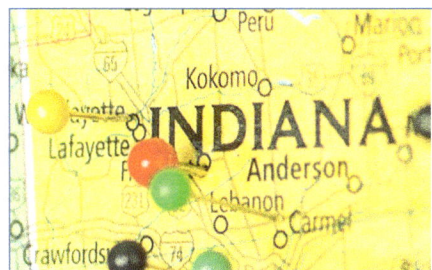

Digital Marketing

Topics

Touchpoints
Website
Email
Blog
Social Media
Analytics
Electronic Press Kit

Main Ideas

- Social media has become one of the strongest influences on our daily lives and one of the main avenues for marketing in music and entertainment.
- A website links together all of an Artist's online resources.
- An email list is one of the most important tools for marketing music.

See the book's companion website for supplemental information, updates, and links: http://willshare.com/mmb

Introduction

In Chapter 3, we covered the traditional marketing tools of brand, pitch, slogan, logo, press release, and flier. The move from print to digital marketing doesn't mean those things are no longer worthwhile. It is still important to define a band, represent it graphically, and be able to be able to express what is noteworthy about a product. In this chapter, we will apply the concepts learned in Chapter 3 to technology-based communication using digital platforms such as websites, email, blogs, and social media.

With all the emphasis these days on social media and cell phones, many musicians don't feel it's important to have a website anymore. However, a website lets you control your message and serves as the hub of your social media presence. In this chapter, we will begin with the components of a website and their associated email lists and blogs, and see the advantages they have to texts and posts on social media.

We will then cover the functions of the main social media platforms and how to get the most benefit out of using them.

The chapter ends with a look at electronic press kits.

Touchpoints

A touchpoint is any place where a customer has an interaction or comes into contact with a business. It is there that a consumer experiences a company, and learns about the brand and the benefits it may appear to offer. Each encounter helps them form an opinion about the business, which then shapes their future decisions about whether or not they want to buy the company's product or service. Touchpoints can involve person-to-person contact, like meeting a member of a band, or talking with the person working at their merch table. They also are also encountered when visiting websites, watching television, listening to the radio, using social media apps, or reading publicity printed in magazines and newspapers.

Touchpoints influence decision-making in three main stages of consumer behavior. During the **prepurchase phase** it is difficult to bring attention to the company's brand because of all the noise in the market place. Consumers are overloaded with information and advertising, and everyone is vying for their attention. The challenge for an unknown brand at this point is to get anyone to notice and remember it. Major record labels have a big advantage over independents because they have the marketing resources to put a new artist repeatedly in front of the consumer in a variety of channels to create recognition.

During the **purchase phase**, the challenge for the brand is to be familiar and keep satisfying expectations, while remaining relevant in a world where tastes are constantly changing. Humans like things that are similar to what that they already like, but at the same time we are wired to notice change. At some point, we may get bored with what we had been happy with and look for something new. During this phase, it is important that touchpoints be consistent with the image of the brand that the consumer has identified with it, and to offer as frictionless an experience as possible so that they don't change their mind during the process of making a purchase. Amazon has streamlined the purchase phase for their customers with "one-click" shopping. Many online shopping carts are abandoned as consumers change their mind and put away their credit cards before paying. Prospective customers may be turned off if you appear to trying too hard to sell. Instead, offer exciting products and make it easy for people to buy them. Approach it as if you are providing a service to help them get what they want, instead of trying to pressure them into purchasing your product or service.

During the **postpurchase phase**, companies use touchpoints to stay in contact with customers in order to develop lifelong relationships. An easy way for musicians to do this is with a newsletter or blog. Some companies have "loyalty programs" that give customers incentives to come back and purchase more. Bands can do this, for example, by handing out coupons to those who attend their shows for discounts on merchandise. The cost of fan acquisition is high, whether it is accomplished by marketing or performing. One of the rewards from the effort and expense required for touring is to increase the number of fans, one person at a time. It is in a band's best interests not to lose a consumer once they have turned into a customer. The quality of the music and performance becomes an integral part of their brand and image, and determines whether the customer will return to a performance or buy merchandise. The ideal situation for the band is to have the size of their audience increase due to their fans sharing their enthusiasm with others.

Website

A band or artist's website serves as a hub for their social media and the rest of their online touchpoints. In the following diagram, we see common elements on the left side, and the main the social media platforms they can connect to on the right:

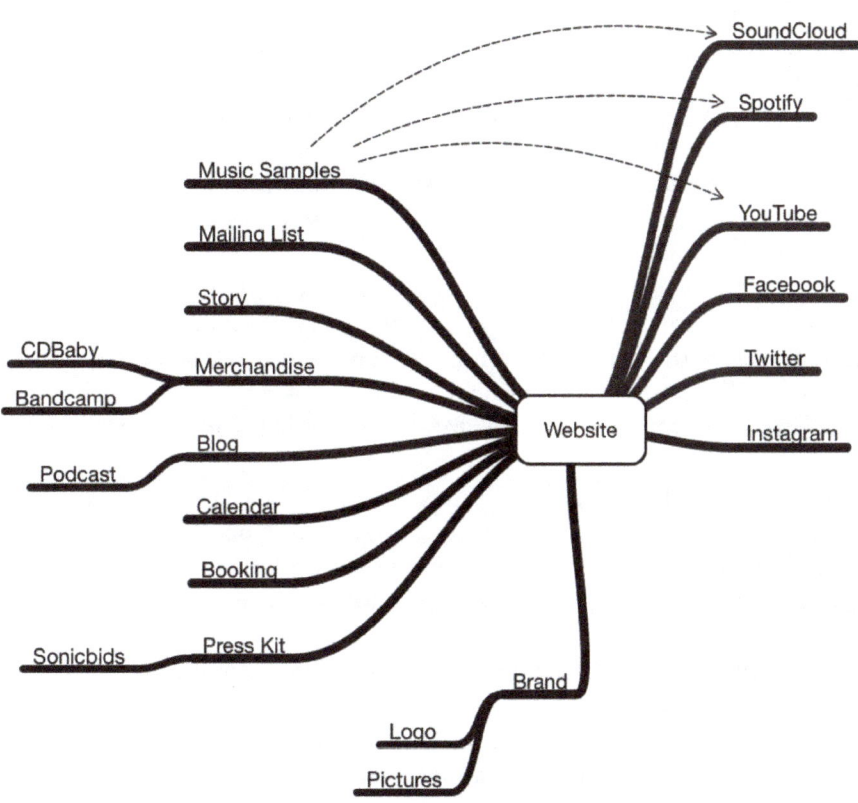

The website ties together all of an Artist's online resource.

There are a number of elements that bands and artists commonly include on their website. Each serves a one or more subsets of their potential audience—listeners, audiences, bookers, press, sound crews at venues, and tourists. Most websites include tabs that divide up the content on separate pages. It is recommended to put the most important information at the top of each page, and to limit the amount of content so that the user isn't slowed by having to scroll up and down. Make sure all pages load quickly, or your visitors may get frustrated and click off to another destination. You can embed samples of audio recordings and videos on the pages of the site itself, or link to a service like SoundCloud, Spotify, or YouTube to take advantage of their interface, storage, and bandwidth. The risk with that is, however, that once they leave they may not come back. Include a contact email address or a form so that anyone who wants to can reach you. When you get to the point of having a manager and booking agent you may provide their contact information instead in order to filter out the business requests.

People want to know who you are in order to better understand your music, and many musicians satisfy this curiosity by including a bio in which they tell their story. Beginning yours by recounting a love of music from an early age followed by testimonials from family members who recognized your talent and passion are instant tip offs of an amateur at work. Professionals focus more on industry credits and current activities. Bookers who are considering hiring you for a gig don't care about how the band was formed—they want to know how you successful you've been lately, and what you have to offer their customers. It is sometimes hard for an artist to tell their own story because they are too modest, don't see themselves objectively, or use too many vague superlatives. In that case, it can be helpful to hire a professional or enlist the help of someone who writes well and who can provide evidence of accomplishments that speak for themselves, leaving the reader to come to their own conclusion about their value.

A group's website is also the best place to direct fans to where merchandise can be purchased. Some website hosts like Squarespace have integrated stores making it easy to display products and collect payments. An alternative is to use a third party service to fulfill online orders. The drawback in that case is that the design of the online store will not be consistent with the rest of your website. Wherever you end up selling, the merchandise should include the group's logo and reflect your brand.

There are two types of calendars to consider. One is to let your fans see when and where you're playing. Its purpose is to make it easy for fans to see the date for each venue, its address, location on a map, and phone number, as well as the names of the other groups who will be performing that night, and how much it is going to cost. The second type of calendar is for booking agents and club owners to see when you are available. It blocks out the dates you are already performing, and any others on which you are not available to work.

Bookers will also be interested in what style of music you play, where you've played in the past, testimonials from fans and venues, pictures, and fliers that they can use for promotional purposes. It will help to get media coverage if you have a collection of good-quality pictures in both color and black and white at a high enough resolution to be printed as well as displayed electronically. Publishers are going to be careful not to print pictures without approval, so get written permission from the photographers and credit them by name. Some bands include a stage plot of their setup and an audio input list to help the sound crew at a venue understand their requirements in advance.

The URL for the website should include the name of the band, like Katy Perry did with katyperry.com. This allows a fan to just type the name of the artist into the search bar. In order to raise the site's ranking in a Google search, the name of the group should also be in the text of the first and second paragraphs of the home page, as well as in the title and metadata description.

In order to strengthen the connection between the parts, it is best to use the same style and design on all platforms, and to consistently portray the group's brand, such as a common color palette, font set, style of language, and logo.

The website serves as a hub by linking to all of the various social media platforms that a group uses, such as Facebook, YouTube, Twitter, and Instagram. Each of those sites should also link back to the website, so that a user of one platform will be able to easily navigate to all the others.

© stoatphoto/Shutterstock.com

Email may be the most important marketing tool.

Email

Perhaps the most important function of a group's website is to provide a place to sign up for their mailing list. The focus of attention of audiences today seems to be on social media, but studies show that well-written email communications is more likely to generate results than a tweet or Facebook posting. Remember that Facebook uses an algorithm to decide who will see your message. Only about 10% of the people who are friends or following you will get it. If your email address list is clean and up-to-date, everyone will get a copy. Facebook controls the format of your content on their service, but in an email you get to decide the style and how things are laid out. Email is one of the best drivers of merchandise sales. Once you have a fan's email address you can engage them on a one-to-one basis and reuse the address over and over. Answer as much of your fans' emails as possible.

Consider this possible new strategy for surviving in music and entertainment field in today's world of vanishing record contracts and low-paid gigs:

1. Give your music away in order to get people to come to your shows.
2. Give a great show and do everything possible to turn people into fans.
3. The way you make money is to get fans to buy your merchandise.

Your website should include one clear call-to-action. Probably the most important thing you can ask visitors to do is to sign up for your newsletter, so position the invitation in a prominent location, and make it clear what they will receive in exchange, like "Sign up for our monthly newsletter and get a free download of our latest single." That could be distilled down to make it even simpler and more direct. Include some text on the page that indicates that you have a newsletter, and have recorded a great new song, and then when you get to the all-import call-to-action simply write "Sign up to receive our latest single". "Buy now" is probably about the most focused you can get, unless you go overboard and hit them with a blinking button labeled "Buy!" Think like an entrepreneur and add value to every situation you're in. You should always give something away for free as an incentive for them to sign up for your monthly newsletter, such as giving them a free audio file, souvenir PDF, or other exclusive content. The gratification they get for signing up should be instant. Show your appreciation.

Once you get someone to sign up for your email list you want to keep them. By law, however, you're required to make it easy for them to unsubscribe, and you have to respond to such requests within 10 days. Always be looking for ways to save them time and provide value.

Most email services allow you to prepare a thank you and welcome message that is automatically sent out to each new subscriber. Some allow you to include a download link or attach an audio file as a surprise bonus. Growing an email address list and using it effectively can be a crucial part of your success. You may have gotten into the music business because you love to play an instrument, but the business is as important as the music if you want to be able to afford to put gas in your car and drive to places where you can perform it. In many cases, building a mailing list, engaging your community effectively through email and social media, and designing and selling merchandise is what is going to keep you in business.

When you send an email, you must be accurate in the return address you use in the From: field. Use relevant subject lines so that people will know what to expect if they open your mail, and avoid language that will get your message sent to their spam box. You should also build your email list through people opting in, rather than you simply adding them without their permission. The most thorough way to do this is with a double opt-in process, in which a person signs up for your list, and then a follow-up email is generated and sent back asking them to confirm that they want to sign up. This prevents a mischief-maker from signing someone up for a newsletter without their permission. Under this system, a person isn't actually signed up for the list until they respond to the follow-up mail. The risk of going through this additional step is that you may lose some people who change their mind, don't notice the follow up, or ignore it.

Companies such as MailChimp offer free services for a limited number of subscribers that is sufficient for a band that is just starting out. In addition to handling the mailing, they automate the subscription process, provide attractive templates, include a system to automatically handle requests to unsubscribe, and clean out invalid addresses. Your Internet service provider may not allow you to mail to large groups of people, since the traffic may look to them like a spam operation. When you use a email service you create a mailing list and a master single copy of each of your messages on their site. When you are ready, you activate the campaign, at which point their computer sends a copy your message to each person on your list.

Many people are already concerned about the amount of email they get every day, and may not want to sign on for more. Mailboxes are overflowing, and their owners often feel overwhelmed by all messages piling up asking for their attention. Think about how your email will be received by a busy person, and what it will contain that will be worth their time to read. At shows, collect zip codes along with email addresses so that you can separate recipients by geographical area. There is little point in sending an announcement of a gig that you're playing in Madison, Wisconsin to one of your fans in St. Louis, Missouri since there is more of a chance that they will unsubscribe as a result than to attend. Remember the adage "Less is more." Send mail regularly, but not frequently, and keep each message short. Provide links to your blog or other information sources for those just those readers who want to find out more. Another good feature of mailing list services is that you can create campaigns when it is convenient for you and schedule them to go out at the optimum time for readers.

The goal of a mailing list is to deliver a newsletter.

Create a newsletter and send out updates periodically to the people on your mailing list. It doesn't have to be a long magazine-type publication, in fact, it's better if it's short, simple, and literally a letter with news. Polish each one like a mini press release. There needs to be something newsworthy, otherwise there's no point in interrupting your audience and imposing on their time and attention. The power of using an email service is that your one letter can reach hundreds of thousands. If a thousand people spend a minute to read your message that's nearly 17 combined hours of human attention. Invest your time and energy to make your message worth that or more. For example, you could include a link in your email to some special content and don't let people know about it any other way besides the email. Proofread and edit each communication before sending it out. Think about how your message will appear to the reader, what they will see as the value for them, and what will leave them with a positive feeling that will turn into a habit of opening future emails from you. Don't look at this as manipulation, but rather as a way to streamline the transfer of a potentially positive experience. If you're not in the music business to make the world a better place, you're probably in the wrong line of work.

Give more than you get. If you just send out announcements of new products for readers to buy they may get tired of it and unsubscribe from the list. Decide on the balance you want between stories about you, your fans, bands in your area that play the same style of music, and other interest your readers. Ariel Hyatt recommends that about 40% of your posts should be for cross-promoting, talking about what other people are doing, and sharing links that you think your fans would enjoy. Another 30% should be responding to and conversing with your fans. Twenty percent should be of photos of what you do as a musician, especially those aspects that fans don't get to see at a show. After that Hyatt says that leaves 10% to talk about yourself. It may be the most interesting topic to you, but it only becomes important to your fans after they've become so interested in everything going on in your world that they want to know more about the person behind it.

Will the benefit of your newsletter to the reader be money or love?

Put yourself in the shoes of the reader—how is reading your newsletter going to help them make more money or find more love? What will they find so remarkable in it that they will feel an uncontrollable urge to tell other people about, and in the process, do your marketing for you? Think about the times you've known a secret, and remember how hard it was not to tell others about it. That's the sort of energy you want to create. It's not just about getting people to sign up for your email. That's important, but the real benefit is to give them what they want so that they will keep coming back for more.

You can also create hand-picked addresses for special lists, like V.I.P. fans and media contacts. Send them pre-announcements and special offers before you send out announcements to your general list, so that they feel special, and have time to take advantage of the advance notice.

Your website is not the only place to get addresses. Look for opportunities at your shows to get people to sign up. This can be done by having someone circulating with the signup sheet, or directing people to a clipboard at the merch table. Carefully inspect each one to make sure that their handwriting is legible, or use a service like Nimbit to collect them directly from your fans via text messages. Offer something as an incentive like you do on your website, like a discount on a shirt or CD, guitar pick, poster, autographed picture, or sticker, or enter them into a drawing.

Blogs

Planning and building a website can be a time-consuming process, and afterwards comes the challenge of maintaining it and adding new content so that visitors will want to return. The easiest avenue to adding new material is through a blog, which can be updated without touching the rest of the site. Blogs also have the advantage of archiving old material which rolls off the bottom, but can always be explored by a new fan who missed your earlier work.

People read blogs when they are curious or want to learn. The design doesn't have to be fancy. What's more important is that you post on a regular basis and include interesting content like reports on shows, touring, or progress on recording projects, with photos and videos that are visually engaging. Tag postings with relevant keywords to increase their chances of coming up in a search.

Some website hosts have blogging capabilities built in. If not, you can connect your own website to an external service such as Blogger, WordPress, or Tumblr. Take advantage of tools that automatically embed your latest blog post into your website so that the content appears on your website without you having to go in and edit it each time by hand.

Some platforms support subscriptions and maintain an RSS feed that delivers each post to readers in sequence, like a podcast. Services such as Google Feedburner help you get the URL for your feed and analyze your subscription rates. Like a blog, a podcast is a series messages, typically video or audio files that fans can subscribe to. Getting someone to subscribe is a good thing since they will then continue to get each future episode automatically instead of them having to go back to the website each time, which they are less likely to do. Some platforms allow fans to sign up to get an email each time you publish a new post.

Read blogs by other writers and bands, and comment on the postings that you like from them. It's important to establish a relationship before you ask them to report on your work. At some point, they may be curious about what this interesting reader (you) is up to and check you out. Let them arrive at the idea on their own of doing a review. Many bloggers are looking for content and may incorporate something you've written, or invite you as a guest commentator.

© Scanrail1/Shutterstock.com

The proliferation of social media platforms has reinvented the way marketing is done.

Social Media

Social media is powerful marketing channel that has become increasingly embedded in our daily lives, making it possible to reach a large number of people in a cost-effective way. If you only use it to announce shows and new products, however, you are wasting the opportunity it provides to listen to fans and find out what they want. Remember that your website should be your communication hub. It should link to all your social media platforms, which in turn link back to it. The default call-to-action on social media postings should be to visit the website and sign up for your newsletter.

Facebook has over a billion users.

Facebook is the place where people go when they feel lonely, so use it for what it's best at, to connect with people. Facebook's mission used to be "To give people the power to share and make the world more open and connected." They have since decided to focus on developing a social infrastructure that can be used to build a global community that works for everyone. Bands are missing an opportunity if they don't use it to have a two-way conversation, and enlist their fans in passing information on to their friends. Engage visitors, ask for their opinions and answer questions, like what their favorite song is, and which song they'd like your band to cover or perform. It should be a co-creative process where customer preferences are communicated to the musicians, who take that information and use it to improve their performance.

Brian Wampler's boutique guitar pedal effects company is run out of their headquarters in Martinsville, Indiana. He attributes his success to a fanatical dedication to supporting his tribe of users, instead of trying to reach a mass market. He is a perfect example of someone who has harnessed the power of Facebook and other social media outlets to focus on what his customers want, rather than watching and responding to competitor's products. He sells about 4000 pedals a month to quality-oriented guitarists, including many of the players in top country bands. In addition to designing the electronics of the equipment, he and his team communicate through Facebook and a newsletter and are constantly creating demos, lessons, and how-tos on their YouTube channel. The way he sells $200 pedals in competition with inexpensive Chinese imports is by building something good, and by being different and better. He tries to care more, listen better, and market better, and uses social media as the way to have a dialog with his customers and ask for their opinions and what new products they would like to see. Every member of his team has their own brand, and each is active on Facebook and Twitter interacting with customers. He hires based on what a person can contribute, and their ability to support the community.

Shorter posts usually get more attention on Facebook, so try to limit yours to under 80 words. Add a picture or video as visual components catch a reader's eye. Stay on a single topic. Don't post more than twice a day. Monday is not a good time to post as there are so many reports coming in about what happened the previous weekend. Instead, send yours out in Thursday through Saturday in the afternoon or early evening. You may want to write your postings when it's convenient for you and then schedule them to go out at opportune times.

Ask people to tag you and report on shows they attend. Interact with them so that you will start to appear on their friend's walls. Thank people for friend requests and compliments. It's equally important to address negative Facebook comments so that they don't go unanswered and leave a reader with a bad impression.

Facebook and Google are taking over the world of advertising. Buying some micro-targeted ads for a specific demographic suited for your brand can be cost-effective. Never before has it been possible to send messages to people who have demonstrated by their histories that they are especially good prospects. No one can predict where the music and entertainment business will be in 5 years, but it seems likely that data mining and tailoring ads and entertainment products to each customer's tastes will become increasingly common.

© Soundaholic studio/Shutterstock.com

YouTube turned video into a personal viewing experience.

YouTube is where people go when they are bored or want to be entertained. In his book *Hit Makers*, Derek Thompson says that average number of tickets to movies by adults dropped from 25 in 1950, to 4 in 2015 as a result of the proliferation of television sets, and that the world's attention is moving from infrequent, big, and broadcast to frequent, small, and social. A billion hours are watched by users around the world each day, mostly on the small screens of their cell phones. The prime demographic for advertisers is 18–34 year olds, and they are watching YouTube more than any television network. To hold the audience's attention, make your videos interesting and less than three minutes in length.

Using proper commenting and tagging techniques will help your videos come up higher in searches. Tag your videos thoroughly with appropriate keywords to make it easier for people to find your music. Research AdWords in Google including the word "video" in order to find out what people are searching for. After you upload your videos, be sure to give them descriptive titles. Put song titles in quotes. It's important to have a good title and description, and to pick a custom thumbnail that shows the most appealing frame of your video. Repeat the title, again in quotes, in the description field. Use less than 66 characters and be descriptive. Put the most important part at the top so it will visible even when the description field is minimized. Always include a call-to-action in the description, and supply the link to your website to help viewers discover more about your music.

If you cover someone else's song, include the original artist's name. List related artists in a way that connects with your work so that people who get to your video when searching for their name else will understand the connection and won't feel like they've been tricked. Comment on other people's videos. Answer comments on your videos, and if you have time, do it with a video response. Include introductions to your songs where you explain what the song is about, and why it has special meaning to you.

© solomon7/Shutterstock.com

Knowing how to write tweets, and
the best time to post them, helps
increase engagement

Twitter gives people a quick lift and an update on current events. The best time to post is in the afternoon between 2:00 and 5:00 p.m. when blood sugar levels start to dip. Be as informative as you can with the 140 characters you are given to work with, and link to a video or blog post to continue the story.

Find keywords or hashtags that are relevant to your style of music, and use the @ sign to connect with other users' names. Adding a # hashtag for phrases will attract followers who are searching for them.

If you want to grow a following, spend some regular time following new people who are influencers in the music industry using a tool such as Tweepi or ManageFlitter. Thank any real person who follows you, and unfollow those whose comments you don't want to see in your feed, for example, if theirs looks like spam.

© rvlsoft/Shutterstock.com

Instagram is considered by many to be the best
social media platform for customer engagement.

Instagram is the ideal way to communicate the day's highlights, and due to its visual nature suits the way that humans prefer to gather information. Some elite trendsetters had prerelease versions and posted examples processed with its useful filters before its launch in 2010. It caught on quickly and has become a powerful marketing tool. It is a simple app to use and is ideally suited for use on-the-go with cell phones, but then you probably already knew that and switched to Instagram a long time ago when your grandparents took over Facebook.

Hashtags can be added to posts to link photos to related content and trends. Users can connect accounts to their other social media accounts. Video sharing was added in 2013, followed by a variety of other features. Twice as many Instagram users are female than male.

To increase your success on Instagram, determine what accounts your audience is following and the hashtags they are using to better understand what they are looking for. Find your niche and what is unique about your brand. Use the service for images and light commentary. In a call-to-action, ask your audience to turn on post notifications, using bold and colorful text with a big arrow pointing towards the settings button. Consider adding geolocation to mark the location of shows. Thank people who follow you, and reward them by giving them access to exclusive content or discounts on merch. Post great photos that are consistent with your brand and use the same filter each time for a consistent image. Use a color palette that is similar to your website.

Like with other platforms, start following and commenting on other people's pictures who use hashtags related to your type of music. Use the @ sign to tag your picture to other users, and the # hashtag symbol for categories. Create an account with your band name in it so that people understand who is posting.

In addition to considering what you are posting, help your fans post to their accounts about you. In the days before cell phones, autographs were popular. Audiences today seem more interested in selfies with an artist than getting their autograph. Create photo opportunities tailored to cell phones, and situations where it will occur to your audience that "This would look great on Instagram! My followers will like this!" It's all about the visuals. What will you be wearing, what props will you have, and what will be in the background? People want to show off that they are living an exciting life, so create a special moment that they can brag about.

Analytics

Social media is crowded and competitive. Use the digital fingerprints that visitors leave on the electronic touch-points on social media platforms to help you understand how they are engaging with your content. Analyzing the data from their behavior can help you make more efficient use of social media platforms in the future, and give them more of what they are looking for. It is important to test and track the results when designing an effective strategy.

"Insights" is a powerful tool built into Facebook that page administrators can use to track the number of active users, how many people are talking about a posting, what type of messages are most popular among an audience, and determine most effective time of day and time to post. You can also get a report on how many people spread the word about an individual post, and the age group and location of people who clicked the "Like" button. However, the number of "Likes" doesn't really tell you much, other than the number of people who prefer to give you a little pat on the back than take the time to write a comment. What's more important is to know how engaged readers are, and to try to trace that back and account for it analyzing the posts that got attention. For example, you might want to know what the subjects were of the posts that got shared the most, and check the writing style of the ones that didn't get liked so you can make changes to your style in the future.

Additional, more granular information over a longer time period can be downloaded in spreadsheet form. The report is delivered in multiple tabbed sheets, each looking at a different aspect of the data, such as "Daily Like Source", "Daily Page Stories by Story", and "Daily Reach Demographics."

	A	B	C	D	E	F	G	H	I	J	K	L	M	N	O	P
1	Description	Date	F.13-17	F.18-24	F.25-34	F.35-44	F.45-54	F.55-64	F.65+	M.13-17	M.18-24	M.25-34	M.35-44	M.45-54	M.55-64	M.65+
2	Daily: Total Page	3/22/17		38	8	7	18	5	3	1	18	12	8	38	8	3
3		3/23/17		222	30	8	20	9	10	1	105	28	9	14	7	2
4		3/24/17	2	56	9	2	2	5	2	1	32	7	2	3	5	1
5		3/27/17	1	127	16	7	10	5	2		78	29	4	6	9	1
6		3/28/17	1	99	14	6	8	9	2		110	42	5	11	4	1
7		3/29/17		27	3	2	7	4	2	1	38	8	2	6	2	2

A section of the Total Page Reach sheet showing the age and gender of readers of each day's postings.

You can find out from email services such as MailChimp how many people opened a newsletter, clicked on links, forwarded it, and how much time they spent reading. Based on this information, a different approach can be taken the next time with the same group of people to see if it gets better results. There are tools for Twitter like Trendsmap that show realtime local trends in tweets. Twittercounter.com and klout.com offer services to measure engagement.

It could be useful to know which posts on Twitter, Instagram, and Facebook are being favorited the most and forwarded. Which of your followers are commenting the most? Which social media platform is returning the best results? Knowing that can help focus efforts on the platform that is delivering the best results.

Electronic Press Kit

In the old days, people sent out press kits on paper. The cost of printing and mailing and the time it takes to deliver was cut once people switched to using electronic versions instead. These have the added benefit for the recipient that they do not take up any physical space and can be accessed anywhere, and at any time.

One thing that hasn't changed is the need to produce high-quality materials. Remember, you only have one chance to make a first impression. Your electronic press kit (EPK) will speak for you when you are not there, so it should be compelling and easy to read. Sonicbids is a commonly used service that bookers are familiar with. Remember, the people who are in a position to help you are busy, and will pass over anything out that appears to be a waste of their time. Stay focused and put your best foot forward. Edited and well-polished content is a sign of professionalism and an indicator that you are serious.

Here are some common elements to include in a press kit:

- Contact information. Be sure that the phone number you provide is set up for voicemail and doesn't fill up with messages to the point where no more can be left. Check it regularly and return any calls and texts promptly.

- Your story. You may need professional help to do this objectively and with style. Unsupported claims are meaningless and only serve to bore the recipient and tip them off that the band does not have anything better to talk about. What style of music do you play? How big is your fan base? Who have you opened for? Where have your biggest shows been? Whenever possible, provide objective and specific details that lead the reader to form their own conclusions about the band's prospects. These become opinions that matter.

- High-resolution photos that are ready to use for promotional purposes. Save the informal and goofy shots for Facebook and Instagram.

- A recording of three songs. Remember to put the best one first. It's more impressive if these have been publicly released and can be shown to have attracted some attention. One of the main things that recipients are looking for is evidence that the band has a following.

- A video from a live show demonstrating your stage presence and the enthusiasm of a crowd. A video with a sparse and unresponsive audience is going to ruin your chances of getting hired. Another advantage of having an electronic press kit is that you can have the media embedded right into the package rather than having to include a physical CD or DVD which depend on them going to the trouble to put it in a player.

- A well-produced five-minute informational video about the group.

- Press clippings and reviews. These can be distilled down to quotes accompanied by links to the full stories.

- Links to your website and social media outlets.

- A schedule of recent and upcoming shows, and a calendar of any dates that you're not available. This should demonstrate that the band is succeeding in a relevant market.

Review and Preview

We began this chapter with a discussion of the importance of a website serving as the hub for all of a band's social media, including a blog and email. Much was made over the importance of collecting email addresses and sending informative and interesting newsletter content to those who sign up. Remember, the acquisition cost of fans can be very high. You only need 1,000 super fans to support yourself. You have to win them over one-by-one, and once you've established a relationship it's important to not waste all your efforts.

The second half of the chapter covered some of the main aspects of top social media platforms. Maintaining a social media presence is not enough. Without an understanding of the results it is producing, you may be wasting your efforts on content that your visitors are ignoring. Learning how to review analytics, and making the time and effort to experiment with changes in approach can help make social media efforts more productive and rewarding.

An EPK is a standard booking and marketing tool that lays out all the elements in one place for someone considering hiring or publicizing a group.

For Further Investigation

1. Sign up for three band mailing lists. Analyze the process you go through. What incentive does each offer to get you to give up your email address? How easy is it? Is there a double opt-in process? Keep track of the content you get over the course of a month and analyze it. How does it compare with other bands? What parts did you find most interesting? What aspects interested you the most? Unsubscribe when you're finished.

2. Subscribe to email newsletters by authors and marketers Bobby Owsinski and Arial Hyatt. Learn from the content, and the way they have designed its delivery. Read the interview with Ariel on the book's companion website. How does their approach and content compare with the experience you had doing the last exercise with the bands?

3. Listen to Bobby Owsinski's podcast. How does it complement his newsletter and website? How do you like his approach of starting off with news of the day, and then having an interview with an industry expert?

4. Find YouTube playlists that you like. What were the best ways you found to discover them? Ask your friends what they are listening to. Compare and discuss. Analyze the use of titles, descriptions, and tags.

Do It Yourself

1. Create a fan page for your band or business. Add all your information to the profile for the account to make it easier for people to find you. Set up autoposting from your band page to your own page. Maintain a section for the press and link to your full electronic press kit. Stay active and thank each person that asks to be a friend. Ask friends and the members of your band to follow you in order to start to build your audience. Track the growth of your reach using Facebook Analytics.

2. Look at the number of followers you have on Twitter and how many are retweeting your messages. Keep track of how your engagement changes from month-to-month and try to figure out what you are doing, or not doing, that is driving engagement up or down.

3. Register for a Gmail account if you don't have one already. This will create an associated YouTube account, since YouTube is part of Google. Log in and create your own channel and playlists. Title, tag, and describe your content appropriately to increase your search ranking. Drive traffic to and from your website and share your videos on your social media. Respond to any comments.

4. Create a full-blown, full-featured website. Start with a simple version of it with the most important elements. Gradually add more of the most important remaining features. Link to and from your social media, and regularly feature a call-to-action there to visit it.

5. Create a mailing list for fans, and offer them some exclusive content that they can't get anywhere else if they sign up. Make a V.I.P. mailing list for super fans and influencers. Make another for press contacts and publications for press releases. Once a month, send them an announcement of an interesting event you are participating in. If they mention you, be sure to send them a thank you note.

6. Start a newsletter and send it out to the people on your mailing list. If you use a service such as MailChimp, you'll be able to see how many people opened it. An email newsletter is the best place to start marketing a new product since readers are expecting to find news there.

7. Create a blog and regularly share interesting stories about what you, your band, and others are up to.

8. Follow new people on Twitter and Instagram and engage with them.

9. Create playlists on Spotify and YouTube of your music, and others for bands that you are influenced by. Share them with your fans.

10. Limit yourself to a single call-to-action in each of your emails and social media. Ask your fans to follow you on Spotify and review your material on SoundCloud, iTunes, and YouTube. The more you are mentioned, the higher you will come up in searches.

11. Try out some of the analytics tools linked from Chapter 4 section of the book's companion website.

Vocabulary Review

Book—to hire someone for an event.

Call-to-action (CTA)—a direction to a reader to do something specific, like telling them to sign up for your mailing list, or to follow you on Twitter. Notice on public radio stations that they get around not being allowed to have call-to-actions.

EPK (Electronic Press Kit)—A single, compact set of resources that efficiently and creatively communicate an entertainer's story and abilities.

Gig—slang for "job".

Merch (merchandise)—Items bands sell after shows or on their websites, usually with their name and/or logo displayed.

Reach—in Facebook Insights "reach" is the number of people your post may have reached, including friends of your fans.

SEO (Search Engine Optimization)—techniques used to increase the ranking of a website or YouTube video in a search.

Touchpoint—any place that a consumer comes into contact with a business.

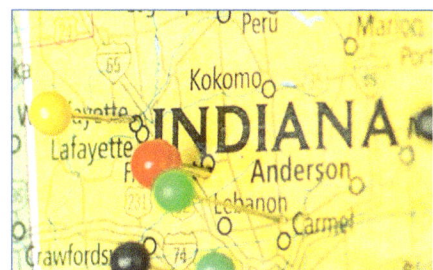

Songwriting and Copyright

Topics

Main Ideas

- Copyright law tries to maintain a balance between the interests of the creator and of society.
- Copyright law has not kept up with advances in technology.
- Legal precedents established in court cases over sampling put the brakes on the evolution of hip-hop in the 1990s.
- The benefits from copyright have moved predominantly to the side of creators and owners.
- Creative Commons has provided an environment in which sharing may take place.

See the book's companion website for supplemental information, updates, and links: http://willshare.com/mmb

Introduction

The music business has two main streams of revenue—the song business and the artist business. In this chapter, you'll look at the process of songwriting, how songs are copyrighted, what rights are covered, and for how long.

Songwriting

The music and entertainment industry is driven by hit songs. The major record labels have the resources to inundate the general public with their songs and set the conditions to make them popular through repeated exposure on radio and other media. The best way for a song to be accepted is to be similar to what people already like, while adding just enough surface difference to catch the listener's ears and attention. We like to hear old songs played in a new order, but at the same time get bored of any one of them because each is fairly simple and doesn't have enough complexity to stand up to constant repetition.

An insatiable desire for new songs exists. The challenge is to make *great* new songs. More people than ever are making music, and the tools to produce recordings of them has come down in price to the point where everyone and their friend can afford to make them. The market is glutted with mediocre material from amateurs, and neither the record companies or even the general public has the time to sift through everything that is being produced in order to find what's outstanding. Record companies no longer accept unsolicited material since they don't have the staff to listen to everything that comes in the mail. People learn about new music from their friends, and audiences are formed around lesser-known groups and fragmented into subgenres. Unknown songwriters depend on people with industry credibility like well-known lawyers and managers to bring their songs to the attention of record labels, or make a name for themselves from the buzz they have built through social media and attendance at shows.

Songwriting can be a rewarding pastime. Even if you don't sell your songs, it can be an inherently satisfying activity and form of self-expression. According to the Positive Psychology movement, "flow" happens when someone becomes hyperfocused and fully immersed in an activity over which they have control. It's important to have immediate feedback, such as happens while listening to the song's progress, and to feel that success is achievable. You need to be challenged so you don't become bored, but not so much so that you become too frustrated. You know you're "in the zone" when you become so engrossed that you forget about yourself and your environment.

Songwriting can also be a craft. One useful exercise is to analyze your favorite songs and rewrite the hits. Make a spreadsheet and list the different sections of a song in the columns, and all the instruments you can hear in the rows. Listening with good headphones or speakers helps with the discovery process. Then color in the cells where that instrument or sound is heard, and add notes if necessary. Here's an example of an analysis of "Chained to the Rhythm" by Katy Perry and Max Martin. It shows how different sounds are heard in different places in the arrangement, which helps maintain the listener's excitement and interest.

	A	B	C	D	E	F	G	H	I	J	K	L	M	N	O
1		intro	verse 1	verse 2	pre-chor	chorus	chorus	break	verse 3	pre-chorus	chorus	chorus	break	chorus	coda
2	# bars	4	16	16	8	16	16	2	16	8	16	16	18	16	16
3									tone deaf						
4	piano chords	filtered							filtered						fade out
5	bass	filtered							filtered						fade out
6	claps	filtered							fade in						
7	kick drum														fade out
8	guiitar														fade out
9	pad bass														
10	pad chord														
11	piano octaves														

In this spreadsheet analysis, the shaded cells indicate where instruments are heard at different points in the arrangement. You could make the width of the columns relative to the number of measures in order to get a better impression of proportions.

In his book *Outliers*, Malcolm Gladwell popularized the idea that it takes about 10,000 hours to master a challenging activity in most fields, such as practiced by surgeons, chess players, pilots, or concert violinists. According to this model, if you devote two hours of every day to songwriting you will have racked up 728 hours in a year. At that rate, it will take you about 14 years to become a master. You can speed up or slow down the process by being more or less deliberate. The activities that require the most hours are the ones that require repetitive practice, so that the skills become so second nature that you don't have to think about them, and can rely on them when you're tired or distracted.

The good news, I think, is that you should get some transfer credit for some of the experience you've had as a musician and a music lover over the years. In addition, a new Princeton study shows that deliberate practice is not as important in fields where the rules change more often than they do in surgery or chess. In fields that don't have super stable structures, practice accounts for only a small percentage of differences in performance. Songwriting is an example of the type of activity that lends itself to insights and breakthroughs. Classical composers like Bach, Mozart, and Beethoven each spent a lifetime honing their craft, and would have continued to grow had nature not called. On the other hand, Sid Vicious could hardly play the bass but became a breakthrough sensation in the band Sex Pistols. Practicing is not a guarantee of success in popular music. You need to be remarkable in some way and be in the right place at the right time to take advantage of opportunities.

Some people have a flash of inspiration and sit down and write a song in short order. Bob Dylan claims to have written "Blowing in the Wind" in 10 minutes. Other songs evolved over a series of rewrites and changing the words as he went along and responded to what he heard during recording sessions. Leonard Cohen was known for writing whole sets of lyrics for a melody before he was satisfied. Usually a song can be improved upon and edited just like any other form of communication. In his book *On Writing*, Stephen King describes his practice of writing a first draft and then setting it aside long enough so that when he returns he has enough objectivity to be able to rewrite it. I suggest that if you want to be a songwriter that you don't wait for inspiration. Become a great observer and keep a notebook of phrases that you read and hear that catch your attention. Sit down and start doing the work and inspiration will come. As you become more experienced, you will have more frequent and longer sessions in the flow state. Make a portfolio of 40 or more songs so if you get someone's attention that's in a position to help you'll have a body of work to work with. Get feedback from professionals and the public and see what resonates with other people. One tried-and-true approach is to put a band together to present the songs in a complete arrangement in public.

Writing with one or more partners can be rewarding, especially when each person has different skills and brings out the best in others. Many hit songs today are written and produced by a team as the style is to have a highly produced and hyper-polished sound. During these meetings, you will often see each person recording the session on their phone in order to document their contribution, in case it becomes necessary later to negotiate their share. It is good to have partners draft a songwriting agreement so that it is clear who owns what percent, and whether one person can use the lyrics or music for another project should the song not succeed, or make placement deals without asking the partner's permission.

Intellectual Property

> Legal disclaimer: I am not an attorney. The information presented in this book, including in this chapter, should not be taken as legal advice. It may help you become aware of issues and formulate questions to investigate more further. Copyright laws in the United States and abroad are complex and you should always consult with an attorney to discuss your situation.

Property is something that is owned by someone. Examples that usually come to mind first are things you can see and touch—such as clothes, cell phone, car, and musical instruments. A category of property that you may not be as familiar with is intellectual property, which refers to creations of the mind, and includes such things as musical, literary, and artistic works, as well as inventions, symbols, and designs. Intellectual property rights give creators exclusive rights to their creations, and provide incentives for them to develop and present their work, and it is believed that this motivation has significantly contributed to economic growth. Economists estimate that two thirds of the value of large businesses can be traced to the value of their copyrights, trademarks, patents, and trade secrets, all of which fall under the category of Intellectual Property. Songs, and the videos of them, are the main forms of intellectual property in the music industry, and they can be tremendously valuable for their owners. We go to see artists perform, but we often go in order to hear them sing *those songs*. Songs also have a life of their own apart from the performer, and are the main generator of income for the composer and their publisher. As we will see in Chapter 7, it is usually the songwriter in the band that makes the most money.

Intellectual property laws are designed to promote "progress of science and useful arts." At the same time, they strive to provide a balance between the private needs of copyright owners (i.e., publishers, artists, composers, and writers) and the interests of copyright users (i.e., consumers). They give the right to the individual or a company to profit from their creations and to retain creative control over them for a limited time, and at the same time recognize the public's interest in building and creating new works based on what is learned from existing ones. The effects of changes in technology and our media-driven society have made this balance harder to maintain.

© BrAt82/Shutterstock.com

Copyright laws and the judges that interpret them try to maintain a balance between the copyright owner's right to profit from their creation and the public's right to use it for the benefit of society.

A patent is a form of intellectual property that can be registered for any new or useful product or process, and give the owner the exclusive right to make, sell, use, and offer it for sale. In order to get a patent, you have to explain in great detail exactly how the product is made or the process is done. It costs about $2,000 to file, plus $5,000–10,000 in attorney fees to do the patent search and prepare the papers properly. Once awarded, a patent lasts for 20 years. After that time, anyone can use the information that was filed to create a copy. This happens, for example, with generic drugs. The company that does the research to create a drug patents it and then becomes the only one that can manufacture it for 20 years. When the patent expires anyone one else can follow the process to produce a cheaper substitute that is chemically equivalent.

A trademark identifies and distinguishes one product from another. A word, symbol, logo, picture, phrase, color, shape, or sound can be trademarked as long as it is distinctive. Unlike a patent, a trademark lasts for an indefinite period of time. It costs about $1,000 to do a search to make sure no one already has already registered it. The "TM" symbol can be placed next to a logo to indicate that the company is using it as a trademark. Once it has been registered with the U.S. government the "®" symbol can be used. A trademark must be renewed and defended if other companies start to use it, otherwise the company that owns it can lose their exclusive rights. For example, at one time "escalator", "dry ice", "trampoline", and "zipper" were trademarked by the companies that introduced them, but they allowed them to fall into common use without complaint.

A trade secret is a formula, design, or pattern of information that is not generally known. Unlike patents they last indefinitely, and don't require disclosure of what they contain. Companies must try hard, however, not to let their secret be revealed to the public or other companies by employees, reverse engineering, or industrial espionage.

Coca Cola covers its intellectual property in multiple ways. The name, logo, and design of the bottle are all trademarked. They claim that the formula for the beverage is the world's most guarded trade secret, and keep it in a special vault in the company's headquarters in Atlanta.

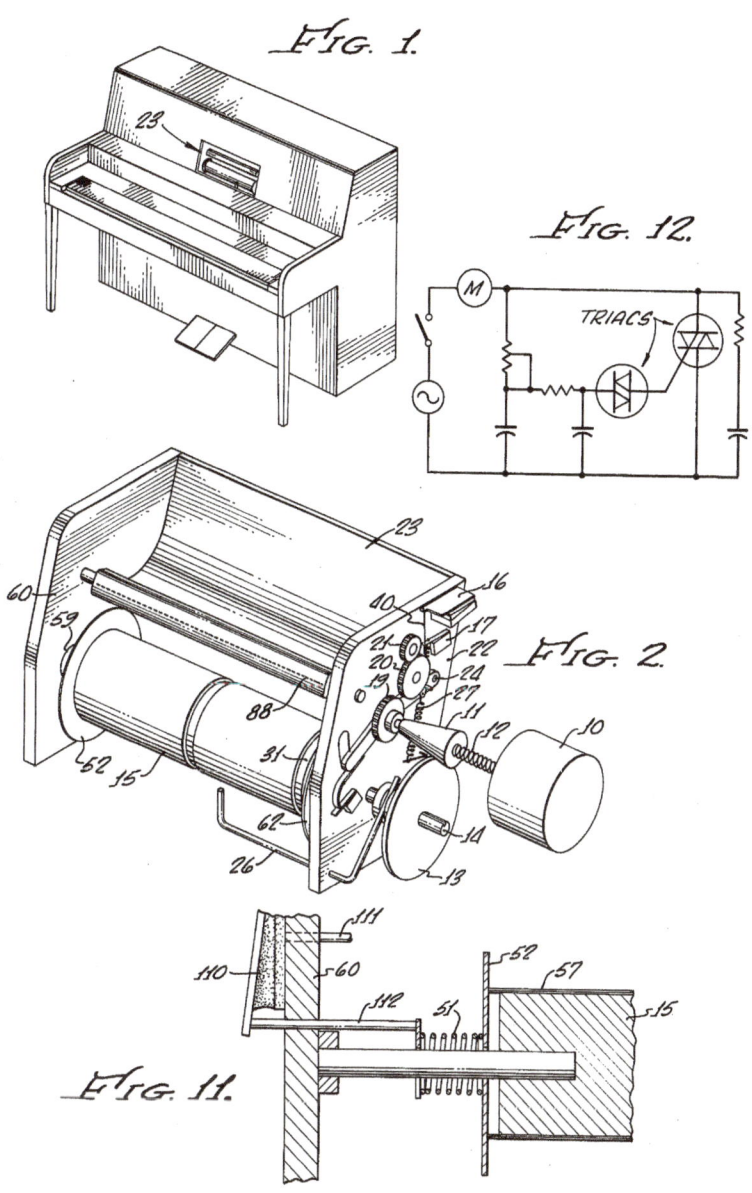

Diagram from a patent application for a player piano mechanism.

Copyright

Copyright is the form of intellectual property that most concerns musicians, especially those who are songwriters. A copyrighted work must be original in some way, and not just consist of information that is common. Copyright does not protect facts, ideas, methods of operation, familiar names, short phrases, symbols, or designs. Copyright protects such things as original literary, dramatic, musical, choreographic, photographic, and artistic works such as poetry, novels, sculpture, movies, motion pictures, other audiovisual works, sound recordings, computer software, architecture, and words and music in songs. The copyright for works for hire is owned by the creator's employer. It is a federal offence to violate any of the rights provide by copyright law to the owner, and it is enforced by the FBI.

Three Ways to Copyright a Work

You can copyright a work in any or all of the following three ways:

1. Save the work in a fixed, tangible form. Copyright protection begins as soon as a work is created in a form that is sufficiently permanent or stable. It is "tangible" when it can be touched. Thinking up a song and singing it does not constitute a copyright. If you notate it on a piece of paper or burn a recording of it on a disk, however, it is then in a fixed form, so it is copyrighted. That's all you have to do. No publication or further action is required.

A phrase of a song notated in lead sheet form, which has the melody, lyrics, and chord symbols. A song is copyrighted once it is written down on paper, or recorded in a fixed form like on a CD.

2. Give Notice. Giving notice informs the public that the work is protected by copyright, identifies the copyright owner, and shows the year of first publication. Giving notice is not required, but is something that can easily be added to the fixed form of the work, and should there end up being a lawsuit, the defendant will not be able to claim that they did not know that the work was copyrighted if they had access to your work with the notice on it. The form of the notice should be the copyright symbol "©" (or the word "Copyright" or abbreviation "Copr"), followed by the year it was copyrighted and the name of the owner of the copyright.

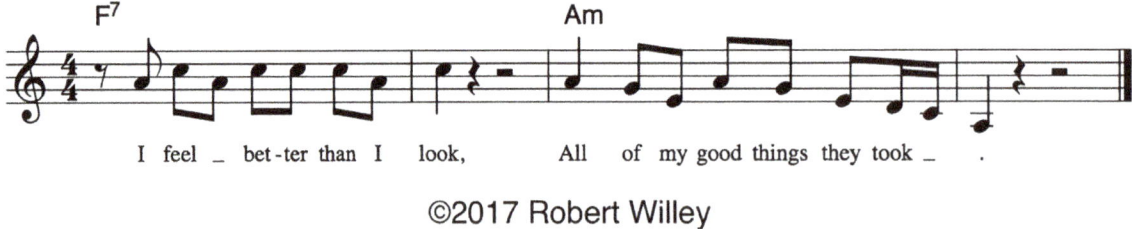

©2017 Robert Willey

The notice "©2017 Robert Willey" has been written at the bottom of the lead sheet.

The copyright notice for a sound recording begins with the symbol of the letter "P" in a circle, followed by the year it was first published, followed by the name of the owner of the copyright.

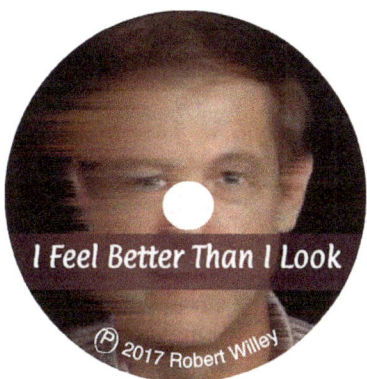

The notice "℗2017 Robert Willey" placed on a CD indicates that this sound recording is copyrighted.

3. File forms with Library of Congress. This is the gold standard and best protection for copyright, and gives the owner the best chances to prevail should there be a lawsuit. The online filing process starts at https://www.copyright.gov/registration/performing-arts/ and costs about $45. You can save money by copyrighting a collection of songs in one filing.

The Library of Congress has copies of most works published in the United States.

Six Things That Copyright Covers

Copyright is a bundle of rights. The owner has exclusive rights to do the following six things:

1. Copy. This is probably the most important right granted by the Copyright Act, and the one that musicians are most concerned with. Only the copyright holder may make reproductions of "substantial and material" parts of the work such that it can be read or perceived directly or with the aid of a

machine or device. Examples of unauthorized copies include making photocopies of a book, copying software, putting Mickey Mouse on a T-shirt, or using part of a copyrighted song from one composer in a song by someone else.

2. Distribute. This includes making the work available to the public by sale, rental, or lending. The copyright holder has control over the first distribution of a particular copy, but no say what happens to it after that. For example, the copyright holder can decide where a copy of their book is sold, but after that the person who buys it a copy can sell or rent their copy. Congress has added several limitations to the "first sale" doctrine, including a ban on the rental of software and CDs, since it is so easy for a borrower to make an identical digital copy.

3. Perform. When you think of "performing" you probably imagine someone playing a song in a live situation, but "performance" in copyright terms covers any situation in which the song is heard, whether played by musicians in the same room or on radio or TV. The Copyright Act states that performing a work means "to recite, render, play, dance, or act it, either directly or by means of any device or process." This allows the owner of copyright to decide when a musical, literary, dramatic, choreography, pantomime, motion picture, or other audio-visual recordings is performed in a place open to the public or in a place where a substantial number of people outside a normal circle of family and its acquaintances are gathered. Playing a copyrighted song at a backyard wedding with friends is not a violation of copyright, whereas playing the same song in a train station full of strangers would be. A performance is also considered to be public if it is transmitted to multiple locations beyond the place from which it was sent, such as on television or on radio. We will see in Chapter 7 how licensing is done to allow groups to perform in public and record songs composed by other people.

4. Display. In this case, the copyright covers a "display" rather than a performance. In music, it covers the printed lyrics, composition, and arrangement, but not the sound recording. The definition of what constitutes a public place is the same as for a performance—a private display to a small circle of family and friends is allowed, but not a public display in a museum, television show, or Internet transmission. For example, a person who buys a lawfully made copy can display a copy of a painting on a wall in their office.

5. Adapt. The technical term for this is to make a "derivative work." According to the Copyright Act, this is a work based upon one or more preexisting works, such as a translation, musical arrangement, dramatization, fictionalization, motion picture, sound recording, art reproduction, abridgement, condensation, or any other form in which a work may be recast, transformed, or adapted. Examples of derivative works would include making a movie from a novel, or creating a new version of a computer program.

6. Transmit digitally. Copyright owners have the exclusive right to perform a sound recording publicly by means of a digital audio transmission. The royalty rates paid to the owner for broadcast depend on whether the service is interactive or not for the user, for example, whether they can request or skip a specific song.

Each one of the six rights can be licensed individually. For example, the owner of a copyright could make an agreement to let a Dutch company sell up to 10,000 copies of a recording of their song in Europe over the course of the next five years.

How Long Copyright Lasts

The length of time a work is copyrighted has changed over the years. All works published before 1923 are now in the public domain. Works published between 1922 and 1978 are protected for 95 years. Works created since January 1st, 1978 are protected for the life of the author plus 70 years. If there is more than one author, the 70 years begins after the last author dies.

For an anonymous work or a work for made for hire, the copyright lasts for 95 years after its first publication or 120 years from the year of its creation, whichever ends first. There are a number of other fine points that must be understood by those wishing to use published works created before 1978.

Public Domain

A work that is in the public domain is not protected by any copyright or other restriction. It therefore is owned by the public and can be used by anyone for any purpose without asking permission or paying a royalty. The Constitution guarantees protection to authors for a limited time period, and most works enter the public domain because their copyright or patent has expired, for example, early silent movies or generic drugs, or anything else published in the United States before 1923. It can also occur when a work that was never copyrighted to begin with, either because copyright does not protect that type of work, or because the owner deliberately placed it in the public domain to begin with, by including a statement such as "This work is dedicated to the public domain" instead of using the standard copyright notice.

Because of legislation passed in 1998, no new works will fall into the public domain until 2019, when the copyright on works created in 1923 will expire. In 2020, works created in 1924 will enter the public domain, and so on. Works created by an individual will enter the public domain 70 years after their death. If a work is created by a team, it will enter the public domain 70 years after the death of the last surviving member.

Fair Use

Fair use, like public domain, is an area that was set up to balance the individual's or business's right to profit from their inventions with society's interest. Don't think that something is allowed just because it seems fair to you, like sharing something with someone as long as you acknowledge the source and don't make any money off of the transaction. Fair use is a copyright principle that allows the public to freely use limited parts of a copyright work for specific purposes such as commentary, criticism, news reporting, teaching, scholarship, and parody. For example, if you are writing a review of a record you can quote a few lines of the lyrics. If an artist is coming to town the local news agency can show a clip of them performing as part of their reporting. A teacher can copy a few paragraphs from an article for their class. In the case of parody, some part of a well-known work can be imitated and ridiculed.

The risk with claiming Fair Use protection is that the owner may not agree and take you to court. The outcome of that process will be subjective, considered on a case-by-case basis, and depends on the skill of the lawyers and the interpretation of the judge. You may be liable for damages if you lose your case. In these cases, the judge considers four factors:

1. The purpose and character of the use. When considering this factor, the judge considers whether the use is for a purpose such as parody, research, or education, and whether the user just copied the original, or transformed it and added value by including new information or insights.

2. The nature of the copyrighted work. You have more freedom to copy from a factual work like a biography than you do from a fictional work such as a novel. You also have more freedom to copy from a published work than an unpublished work as the author has the right to control its first public publication.

3. The amount and substantiality of the part that is used. The less you use, the more likely you will be excused. It may be OK for a history teacher to show a scene from a movie as part of a lecture in class. However, if the part you take is the "heart" or most memorable part of the work you may lose your case. For example, if you quote the line "He's tellin' me more and more about some useless information" from the Rolling Stones song "Satisfaction" you are less at risk than if you use the opening guitar riff and chorus line "I can't get no satisfaction."

4. The effect on potential income for the copyright owner. A teacher may not show the whole movie at the end of the semester as a reward for good behavior, since the students in class would then be less likely to rent it themselves to watch at home.

Creative Commons

As you have seen, copyright is a bundle of six rights, and they all are automatically included when you claim copyright for something. The creators of Creative Commons believed there could be a situation in which rights holders might wish to claim "Some rights reserved" rather than "All rights reserved." They set up a nonprofit organization to make it easier for creators to allow others to legally build upon their work and to share it with others. The licenses that can be generated on their website are easy to understand and don't require the involvement of lawyers or time-consuming negotiations. Since 2016, over a billion works have been issued with Creative Commons licenses.

© Yuriy Vlasenko/Shutterstock.com

Creative Commons logo and license
indicators.

The double "CC" in a Creative Commons notice replaces the standard © symbol. It is followed by one or more icons that represent the combination of conditions that the author has chosen to add. "BY" indicates that users must give the author credit. "NC" means "Noncommercial" and allows for any use as long as it is not sold. "SA" stands for "Share Alike". In this case, users are allowed to copy, distribute, display, perform, and modify the work as long as what they end up making is then made available to the public under the same terms. An electronic form of the license is clickable and contains additional information. One of the advantages of the Creative Commons system is that it facilitates sharing and growth. The problem for most unknown creators is not that people are stealing their work, but that they are unknown. Creative Commons helps you use the power of the Internet to leverage your work and reach a wider audience.

Sampling

The word "sampling" is the common term for the process of "analog-to-digital conversion" in which the changes in voltage of a continuous audio waveform are repeatedly measured at short intervals of time and turned into a stream of binary numbers, which can then be stored in a computer's memory or transmitted over the Internet. A "sample" of a recording usually then refers to the audio clip that has been digitized.

Sampling reached the peak of its popularity in popular music during the Golden Age of hip-hop, as practiced by groups such as Public Enemy, A Tribe Called Quest, and The Beastie Boys. At first the recording industry did not take much notice, but once hit records started coming out a number of court cases were filed. Rulings went in favor of the record companies, and by the end of the 1990s recording artists were required to obtain rights for every sample used, no matter how short it was or how unrecognizable it became after it was processed and added to a mix.

Two licenses are needed to use (or "clear") a sample. First, a Master Use license must be paid to the owner of the original sound recording, which is usually the record company, and allows the sample of the recording to added to someone else's song. In addition, a royalty must be paid to the composer of the recorded song from which the sample was taken. In order to save money, recording artists will sometimes rerecord the song and use that (called a "replay") so that they don't have to pay the record label for a Master Use license. In this case, the only royalty they have to pay is the royalty to the publisher that represents the composer of the song.

In 1989, The Beastie Boys released their album *Paul's Boutique* which incorporated samples from 105 different songs. They paid about $125,000 to composers and record companies for the rights, or about $1,200 per sample. There is no statutory rate for licenses samples like there is for mechanical licenses to record copyrighted songs, and the rates that record companies demand for samples have soared since the precedent-setting cases of the 1990s. Today it costs about $10,000–$20,000 to clear a sample, and the fee must be paid in advance, before anyone knows if the song it will be used on will make enough money to recoup the investment. Only the most successful artists can afford to use samples, and when they do, it is usually just one or two per song. In their book *Copyright Criminals*, McLeod and DiCola estimate that if The Beastie Boys were to produce *Paul's Boutique* today they would lose $7.80 per copy after paying licensing fees.

Compulsory License

A compulsory license is a mechanism set up by the government that allows someone to produce a work or process without the consent of the owner. In the case of the music, this happens when someone wants to record another person's song. Mechanical licenses cover this use and are issued by the Harry Fox Agency. Once a song has been publicly published anyone else may pay for a mechanical license to record and publish their own version of it without the need to get the permission of the copyright holder. A mechanical license does NOT give you permission to sample the original recording of the song.

Safe Harbor

Have you noticed any copyrighted material on YouTube? Many of the 82 million videos that have been posted there are from users who are not the copyright holders of the content. Hopefully by now you understand that you can't upload something you don't own the rights to and make it OK by just adding a disclaimer notice in the comments section that you are not the copyright owner. It doesn't matter if you're not claiming you made it or that you're not making any money off of it. Remember that copyright includes the exclusive rights to copy, distribute, display, or make a work available for digital transmission.

So how does YouTube get away with hosting all the rampant copyright violation? Viacom sued them, in fact, in 2012 for $1 billion dollars for "brazen" and "massive" copyright infringement, claiming that YouTube had allowed users to upload and view over 150,000 videos that they own, such as episodes of SpongeBob Squarepants and The Daily Show. Viacom claimed this was done without their permission, and that their videos had been viewed more than 1.5 billion times. They claimed that YouTube had deliberately allowed users to build up a library of works in order to increase the site's traffic and thereby its advertising revenues.

After a series of appeals, it was finally settled that YouTube is entitled to "Safe Harbor" immunity under section 512 of the Digital Millennium Copyright Act. In addition to criminalizing production and dissemination of technology, devices, or services intended to circumvent copyright protection services such as DRM, the act limits the liability of online service providers for the copyright violations of their users.

YouTube now has artificial intelligence routines that scan content for copyright infringement and either take it down or route advertising revenue to the owners. Copyright holders who notice an infringing video may file a takedown request, and then YouTube is required to notify the alleged infringer and remove the file. Google, YouTube's owner, has had other challenges filed to their widespread sharing of copyrighted works. A series of court decision in the federal court system found that their program of scanning copyrighted books and making snippets available through Google Books was transformative enough to be allowed under the provision of fair use. The richness of content contained on YouTube and available through Google may be at the expense of copyright holders, but it is another way that the law can be balanced to offer a benefit to society. Future generations are likely to look back and see a sudden acceleration in cultural and technical progress that took place at the beginning of the 21st century due in part to easy access to this shared information.

Review and Preview

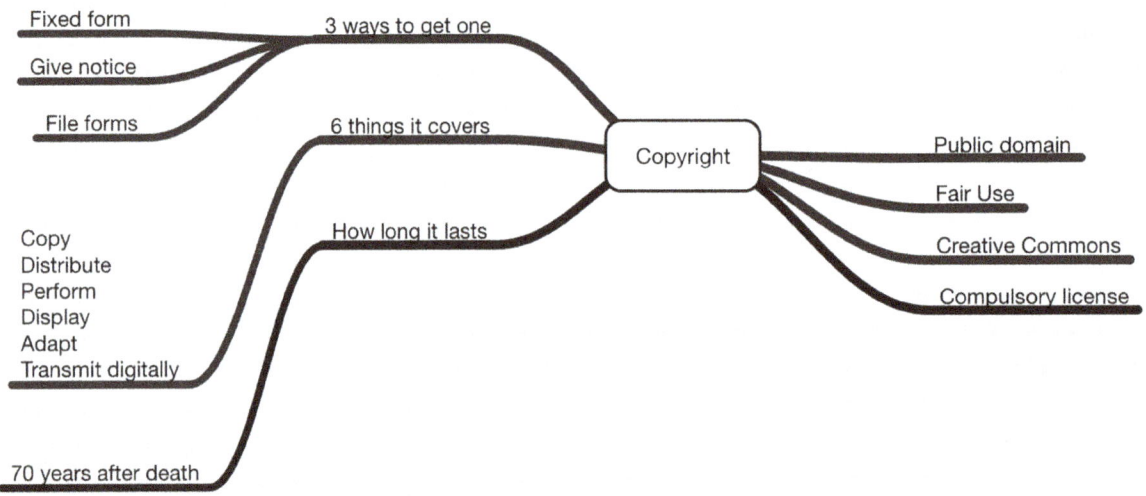

Mind map overview of main topics in Chapter 5.

In this chapter, you've learned about a number of aspects of copyright. Its comprehensive coverage and the long term that it covers mostly favors copyright holders such as composers, publishers, and record companies, but there are some provisions like the public domain, Fair Use, and compulsory licenses that guarantee some benefits for the public. We are overdue for a rebalancing of interests that takes into account changes in technology and communication. The pressure is mounting from people who want to reuse digital content, and the sharing of it should not be so tightly controlled for much longer.

In the next chapter, we will look at the process of making and selling recordings of copyrighted songs. In Chapter 7, we will come back to see how the rights to the songs are licensed by publishers, and in Chapter 8 how artists make money from performing them.

For Further Investigation

1. Watch the world's first open source documentary *RIP: A Remix Manifesto*. Watch for Lawrence Lessig, Cory Doctorow, Gilberto Gil, Dan O'Neill, and Jammie Thomas. The film was created over a six-year period and remixed by hundreds of contributors. How does that process of making the film itself align with the proposals presented in it for the future of copyright?

2. Study the writings of Lawrence Lessig on Creative Commons and copyright reform. What was the motivation of the founders of Creative Commons to provide an alternative to regular copyright? Where can you find material with Creative Commons licenses? Why did Lessig switch his efforts from copyright reform to campaign finance reform?

3. Read Cory Doctorrow's book *Content: Selected Essays on Technology, Creativity, Copyright, and the Future of the Future*. Why doesn't he think copyright management systems like DRM will work, and why doesn't he distribute his books on platforms that use them like Audible books?

4. Listen to records from groups from the Golden Age of hip-hop like Public Enemy, A Tribe Called Quest, The Beastie Boys, and N.W.A. What is your experience when you hear a sample of a song you know used in a new context? How does it compare to the delight one has when surprised during the telling of a joke, or experiencing a dream?

5. Watch the documentary *Copyright Criminals*. Do you think the current copyright laws strike a good balance between the rights of creators and the public? How would you change them so that bands like Public Enemy or artists like Girl Talk could incorporate samples?

6. Follow the links on the book's companion website to court cases involving copyright infringement. What are the pros and cons, and how did the judge explain their decision?

7. Listen to Girl Talk's albums. They are clearly incorporating lots of copyrighted material. Do you think the composer can claim Fair Use? Why don't you think the record labels that own the recordings sue him?

8. Start the process of uploading a video to YouTube and go as far as you can without actually uploading the material. At what stage do they ask if you own the material? What language do they use, and do you think most people understand or care? Do you think the language is a clear and strong enough deterrent to stop people who don't own the rights to what they are uploading?

9. Interview two or more people who create intellectual property. Ask them how they feel about people who expect digital copies to be free. Ask a recording engineer or artist how they would feel if people could use samples of their work without paying a royalty.

Do It Yourself

1. Make a spreadsheet analysis of several songs by your favorite artist or producer. See what common elements you find that define their style. Produce a song of your own that follows the same structure and see how closely it resembles the songs you analyzed. What is similar? What is left to do to make yours sound more like the ones you studied?

2. Pick an example of your creative work that exists in a tangible form. Apply a notice to it and fill out the online forms from the Library of Congress to cover it, whether you pay the fee and send them in or not, just so that you know what the procedure is.

3. Pick a piece of your work that you would like to release under a Creative Commons license. Remember that once you use that system you can't cancel it. Creative Commons is built on regular copyright law, so it still gives you the protection you choose, and can allow you to maintain exclusive rights to sell your work even if you let others use it for noncommercial purposes.

4. Watch the *Secondhand Sureshots* documentary. Find and sample some old records and create a sonic collage. You won't be able to distribute the result without clearing the samples with the publishers and record labels, but it may start you thinking in a new direction. Try recording some musicians playing instruments and transform those samples that you are now the owner of.

Vocabulary Review

Compulsory Mechanical License—once a song has been published and available to the public, anyone can pay Harry Fox for a mechanical license to rerecord their version and make copies. Congress has set the rate per copy.
Creative Commons—an organization founded in 2001 by Lawrence Lessig to simplify the process for authors who choose to share aspects of their work. Using a Creative Commons license, creators can easily decide which uses others may make of their work for free.
Derivative Work—a work based on one or more preexisting works which are transformed and adapted to make a new work, possibly in a different medium.
Fair use—excerpts of copyrighted works can be used without getting permission or paying royalties, as long as certain conditions are met and the uses are appropriate.
Intellectual Property—creations of the mind, including copyright, trademarks, trade secrets, and patents.
Public domain—works that were never copyrighted, or whose copyright has expired. Works in the public domain are available for public use without the need to pay any royalty.

(Public) Performance—the transmission or communication of a work to the public by any device or process, whether or not the public is in the same or separate places. Presentations at gatherings of individuals or families and their normal circle of friends are considered to be private and therefore don't require performance royalties to be paid.

Royalty—a payment made by one party, the licensee, to the owner of an asset.

Safe harbor—providers of online services are not held accountable for the copyright violations of their users.

Sampling—taking a snippet of an audio recording from an existing record to use in a new song.

Work for hire—a work prepared by an employee within the scope of their employment. The employer ends up owning the copyright.

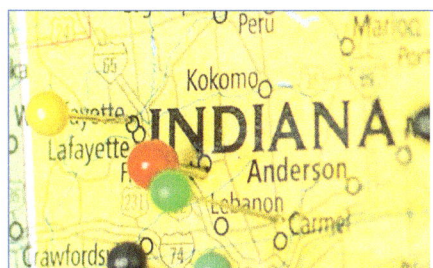

Topics

Main Ideas

- Music production work can often be accomplished in three phases: preproduction, production, and postproduction.
- The meaning of the job title "producer" has taken on a wider range of meanings in the record industry of the 21st century.
- A record label has large enough staff to cover all the different aspects of record production, marketing, and distribution. DIY artists should consider ways to handle as much as possible themselves.
- A recording advance is often the only money a band ever sees from a recording contract. Only the biggest hits generate enough royalties to pay back the money the band owes to the record company. Some musicians have decided it is more profitable to sell a smaller number of records themselves than to sign a contract with a label.

See the book's companion website for supplemental information, updates, and links: http://willshare.com/mmb

Introduction

This chapter covers a wide range of topics relating to the production of recorded music—beginning with the recording process and the people involved with it, record label operations, and royalties.

Studio Roles

Every studio needs an Engineer to operate the equipment. Before a session starts, they are responsible for choosing and positioning microphones, making all the connections, and setting up headphone mixes for the musicians so they can hear themselves and each other. Once the recording starts they keep notes, watch levels, and make any needed adjustments in order to capture the best possible sound. Some engineers specialize in one of the three main phases—recording the band ("tracking"), mixing, or mastering. Maintenance and repair work can be outsourced if the engineer does not have the time or expertise to do it themselves. For smaller projects when there isn't a big budget, the engineer may take on aspects of the Producer's role.

As described in Chapter 2, the traditional role of the Producer is to guide the musicians to create the best possible outcome, and come out with a marketable product. They have a similar responsibility as the Director of a movie. A good ear, experience with music, and excellent communication and interpersonal skills are essential. The Producer may help with creative decisions, book studio time, organize the schedule, coach the musicians, keep an eye on the budget, and oversee the editing and mixing. Another meaning of the word "producer" is in the hip-hop world, where producers do not handle all that administrative and supervisory work and are responsible instead for making beats and background tracks.

There are two basic types of musicians in studios. The first are those who regularly work with an artist and already know the music before the session starts. The second type are Studio Musicians who are brought in for the session to play from a musical score or by ear. Although they are valued for their ability to pick up new songs quickly, their number has decreased since the 1980s, as advances in technology allowed composers to build up tracks using synthesizers and drum machines. Full time work in this field only exists today in the main recording centers like Nashville, Los Angeles, and New York. A new type of studio musician has emerged in the last 20 years since the cost of technology has dropped to the point where independent musicians can afford to have a recording setup in their homes. They fulfill the requests clients who hire them to play an individual part, which is then delivered electronically and inserted into the mix, often in another city. Clients post their needs on websites like fiveerr.com, where composers, producers, mixing and mastering engineers, session musicians, and freelance musicians meet to collaborate.

The Three Phases of the Recording Process

The three basic stages of preproduction, production, and postproduction are common to a variety of types of media work, including audio recording, filmmaking, video production, radio production, animation, and photography.

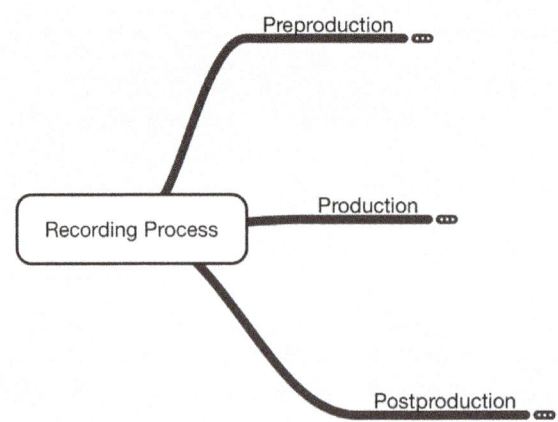

The three phases of production.

The goal of the **preproduction stage** is to get a sense of a project's direction and to prepare for its successful recording. There are a number of questions to answer in the process of developing a vision. Who is the intended

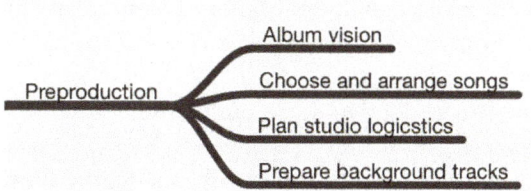

Preproduction.

Planning for the recording sessions is done during the preproduction phase.

audience? What feelings does the artist want to communicate? What elements are distinctive about it that can be used later for marketing?

The choice of music is usually decided during the preproduction phase as well. First, the songs to record have to be chosen. There may be differences in how the song is going to be recorded compared with how it is played live. What will the form be? What sort of introduction and ending? What will the tempo be, and what key will it be in? What instruments will be used? What role will they play in each section of the song? What will be consistent in order to make the listener comfortable, and what will change in order to hold their attention? These decisions become part of the arrangement of the song and notated in whatever form is most useful for the musicians. It can be helpful to make demos to test out the arrangement and to give the engineer and musicians an idea of the intended feel. Background tracks and beats can be prepared which will later be mixed in to the recording. The engineer can launch the recording software, set up and name tracks, and put in markers for the different sections of the song. Scratch tracks can be recorded if the song is going to be recorded in layers so that the first musicians to lay down their parts will hear the context of the song.

In addition to addressing the musical issues, this is also a good time to work out studio logistics. What studio will be used, and what hardware and software? Who will be the engineer? Who will perform? Will the musicians record to a click track? How are they going to hear each other? Will they all be together in one room, or will they be recorded separately in isolation rooms or at different times? What is the budget for the project? How many sessions will be needed?

The music is recorded during the **production phase**. The main tasks to be accomplished are to record the basic tracks and overdub any additional parts while the musicians are present. Editing can take place along the way or put off until the postproduction phase.

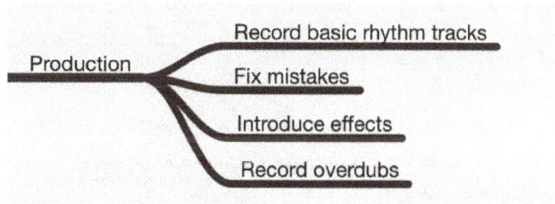

Popular music is often recorded in a series of stages.

Jazz and classical musicians often prefer to play together at the same time. In the case of classical musicians, all the parts are normally written out and it helps to have them getting feedback from each other and get a good blend. One of the key elements in jazz is how the musicians interact with each other, and so you wouldn't want to record the piano, bass, and drums first and then add a solo over them later, since there wouldn't be any interaction between the rhythm section during improvisatory sections.

In popular music styles such as rock and pop, the background parts are usually much steadier. The repeating patterns of those types of music allow them to be recorded in layers. A standard approach is to create the basic rhythmic foundation by recording the drums, bass, and parts of rhythm guitar. While the sound of the drums is picked up with microphones, the bass and guitar amps can be in isolation rooms so that their sound doesn't leak into the drum mics. The advantages of having a separate track for each instrument are that the tone and volume qualities can be controlled individually and, that if someone makes a mistake, they can go back and fix their individual part without affecting the recording of other instruments.

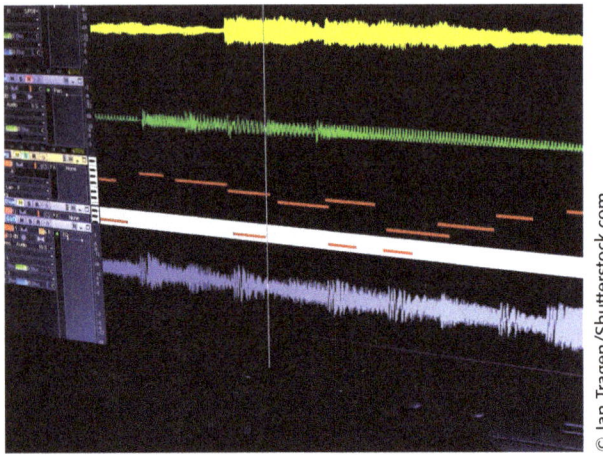

Each instrument is recorded on a separate channel, shown here as horizontal strips of audio and MIDI data.

One of the advantages of digital recording is that it is easy to edit the performances either by hand or automatically. Notes that are out of tune can be moved to the right pitch, and those that are played ahead or behind the beat can be time-aligned to tighten the groove. Some mistakes can be fixed by rerecording just a section. The process is called "punching in" since in the old days of analog recording the engineer would hit the record button just before the spot to be fixed, which caused the tape recorder to switch from playing back the old part to recording something new. Once the basic rhythm parts are recorded, solo, harmony, and vocal parts can be overdubbed on additional tracks. The Beatles recorded their albums in the 1960s on tape recorders with two, four, or eight tracks. Today's computer systems offer nearly an unlimited number of tracks, and it's not uncommon to end up with over 100 tracks.

In addition to music recording, the engineer can start to introduce audio effects such as EQ, compression, and reverb to inspire the musicians to give their best performance, and to start to get an idea of what the finished recording could sound like.

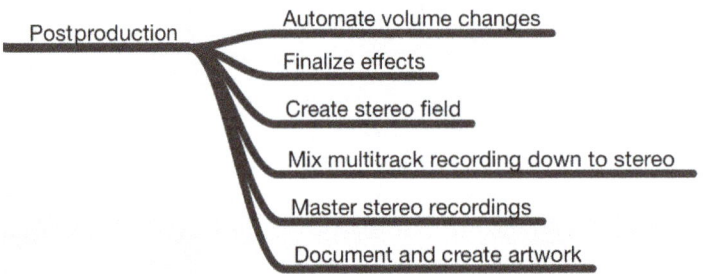

During the postproduction phase the recording is prepared for manufacturing and distribution.

Once all the musicians' performances have been recorded on separate tracks, the project moves into the **postproduction** phase. The mixing engineer balances the different tracks based on the importance of each instrument in the song, adjusts their tone, and pans them to the desired location in the stereo field between the left and right speakers. Reverb can be added to create depth. Changes in settings can be automated over the course of the song. When the engineer, artist, and producer are satisfied, the multiple individual tracks that were recorded during the production phase are mixed down to two channels—a left and a right track—so that consumers will be able to play them on their stereo headphones or speakers.

The various songs in an album may have been recorded and mixed at different times and on different equipments. The Mastering Engineer's job is polish the stereo mixes by adjusting the levels of the various frequency bands and to prepare formats for online delivery and distribution on disc. Often, mastering is done by an engineer who was not involved with the recording and mixing of the song so that they are able to be highly objective and compare the stereo mix with the best examples of music of the same genre produced by other artists.

The postproduction phase is also to time to compile documentation including the names and roles of the people who were involved in the recording. Designs and photography are laid out to provide the artwork and packaging.

Types of Studios

There is a wide variety of types of recording projects, and each method has its own requirements for facilities and personnel—from small single-room setups to large facilities that can hold an entire orchestra. Some projects can be done by one person, such as synthesized sound tracks or background music for jingles. A composer may create these with a keyboard loaded with a variety of instrumental sounds. Microphones are not needed here because the sound is generated by a computer.

It helps to have an isolation booth if a microphone is needed, so that the sound that the performer makes is not in the same room as the engineer listening to loudspeakers to judge what is being recorded. The doors and double-pane windows that create the acoustic isolation between the engineer and musicians allow the engineer to hear only the sound that is coming from the monitor speakers in front of them. If the engineer were in the same room as the musicians, they would hear the sound of their instruments in the room as well, making it hard to know what is being picked up by the microphones.

© tele52/Shutterstock.com

A control room acoustically isolates the engineer from the performers.

Today many musicians do a lot of their work at home, and rent out hours in a studio when they need a larger recording space, better microphone collection, outboard gear, access to a studio's collection of instruments, or professional assistance. This hybrid approach saves money by doing everything that is possible at home where there is no charge for studio time, and then to use the studio for just the parts that take advantage of its facilities and expertise of the engineering staff. A studio may also have better acoustic treatment and monitoring equipment, creating the conditions necessary to make more accurate decisions and end up with mixes that sound good in a variety of rooms. It helps if the walls, floor, and ceiling are treated so that the sound waves are partially absorbed instead of reflecting off hard surfaces.

Some independent label studios rival the facilities of major labels. The larger the scale of the operation is, the more isolation rooms and amenities will be found, like cooking and sleeping facilities. Live recording can be one of the more complicated types of projects as it takes place in the field during a nonrepeatable event and involves multiple instruments and cameras.

Major Labels

A record company is a brand for audio recordings and music videos. The word "label" comes from the round stickers that were put in the center of vinyl records to identify the name of the song, artist, record label, and copyright information:

© Oxlock/Shutterstock.com

Vinyl record with generic sticker.

Most record labels have an in-house publishing wing that handles development of new artists (A&R), production, manufacturing, distribution, marketing, and promotion. The number of major record labels has gradually gone down over the years.

Six companies: 1988–1999
>   Warner Music Group (United States)
>   EMI Records (British)
>   Sony Music Entertainment (Japanese)
>   BMG (Bertelsmann Music Group)
>   Universal Music Group (UMG) (American, owned by Vivendi—French)
>   PolyGram (Dutch)

5 companies: 1999–2004
>   Warner Music Group
>   EMI Records
>   Sony Music Entertainment
>   BMG
>   Universal Music Group (absorbed PolyGram)

(4 companies): 2004–2012
>Universal Music Group
>Sony Music Entertainment (absorbed BMG)
>Warner Music Group
>EMI

Big Three Today:
>Sony Music
>Universal Music Group
>Warner Music Group (absorbed EMI)

Almost all the massively successful artists are signed to one of the three major labels, since they are the ones with the organization to market and distribute on a worldwide scale. A "music group" is a corporate umbrella usually owned by an international holding company, which may be organized in multiple "divisions." The "Big Three" major record labels are conglomerates—large corporations that own smaller businesses—and control 95% of recorded music. A&R staff help new artists select producers, studios, musicians, and material to record, and supervise sessions. Albums can be altered or censored, and artwork/titles changed if label feels it will increase success. Artists often complain that they don't have control, but because there are so few options they usually have to agree to whatever terms the label offers.

Independent Labels

Independent labels can refer to either any label that is not one of the major three, or to smaller labels that release nonmainstream music. The abbreviation "indies" usually applies to the latter case. There was a resurgence of indies in the 1990s, when technology got cheaper and the number of home studios exploded. These companies have less influence since they don't have the financial power and infrastructure to control the market. They may be completely independent or have a business relationship with a major label. Many focus on nonmainstream music and specialize in niche markets that aren't served by the major labels. For example, in the 1980s major labels wouldn't work with punk bands, so the musicians made their own records. Some artists continue to own their own labels. They may start out producing their own music and later branch out to take on other groups.

Record Label Roles

The major record labels have large staffs and multiple departments to handle all the various aspects of the business. Since indie labels usually have less than 10 employees, each person fills more than one role. An independent artist has to do as much as possible by themselves and get additional help from whatever team they can assemble.

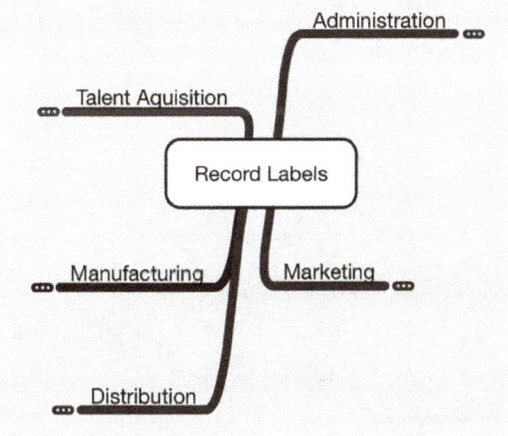

The top-level structure of record labels.

Talent Acquisition

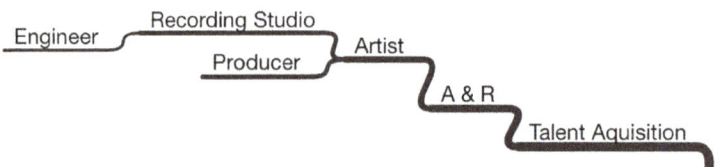

Talent Acquisition.

The front line of the acquisition department is the A&R (Artist & Repertoire) staff. "Repertoire" refers to the songs that an artist records and performs. In the old days, A&R reps would find material for them. Today, musicians usually pick their own material, and the main responsibility of A&R agents has shifted to finding and recruiting new artists, and to bring them to the label to sign recording contracts. The label then finances, manufactures, markets, distributes, and promotes an act's records if it feels that they have a chance of being popular. New talent is found with online tools like Google, YouTube, and Facebook. A&R reps also visit clubs, bars, shows, showcases, and listen to demo recordings and videos sent from artists, their managers, or lawyers. They may also get leads from other departments at the label, or try to pull bands away from other labels.

Administration

The attorneys in the Legal Affairs department write contracts and negotiate deals with artists and service providers. A recording contract is a legal agreement between musicians and a record label, in which the artist or band makes one or more records that the label can sell and promote. Artists who are "signed" to the label have entered into deals and agreed to the terms of recording contracts. Usually the label ends up owning the recordings, while the songwriters hold on to the rights to the compositions. In most cases, the artist cannot record for any other label while they are under contract unless they get their label's permission. You can see when an agreement like this has been made where the liner notes say that one of the artists on the record has appeared on the record courtesy of another label.

Manufacturing and Distribution

The main delivery system of physical copies of songs is the compact disc format. There are two types of compact discs. The ones that made by record labels are "replicated", meaning that they were manufactured using a glass master. The setup charges for this process are higher, but afterward the per disc cost is lower. They are usually

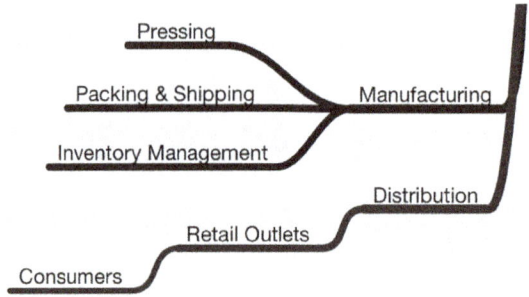

Manufacturing and Distribution.

made in batches of 1,000 or more and are long lasting and scratch resistant. Discs that are "duplicated" are burnt CD-Rs, which can be done one at a time with a personal computer. Companies like Kunaki offer on-demand manufacturing of duplicated discs complete with full color printing, inserts, and shrink wrapping, and handle taking payments from online shoppers, burning and printing copies, and mailing them out. This is very convenient for musicians since the arrangements doesn't require any up-front costs.

The next step is distribution—the process of getting records from the manufacturing plants into stores. Major labels control their own distribution like they do with publishing. Indie labels may work out distribution deals to have major labels distribute their records, or work with independent distributors. Songs can also be purchased through iTunes and other online vendors and downloaded over the network.

Marketing and Sales

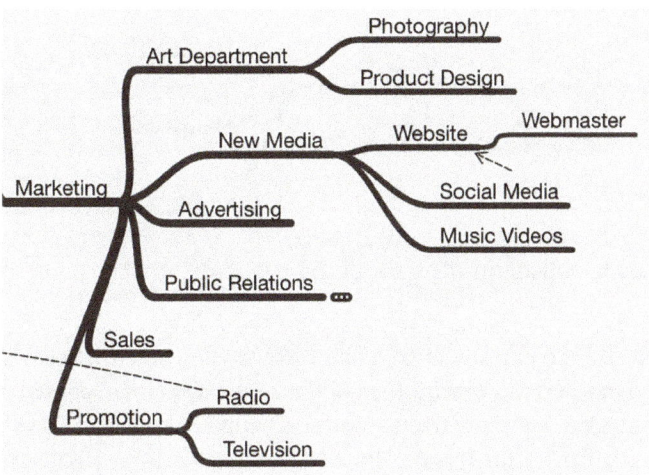

Marketing.

The Marketing department's job is to build demand for the company's records, which they do through a variety of activities such as analyzing the market, developing strategies to market records, and informing radio stations and trade magazines about growing sales and positive album reviews. One way to work into this position is to get an internship at a record label or work in a record store. **Sales reps** visit retail stores to make sure they have enough product, and stay in touch with them and online stores by making phone calls and writing email. **Rack jobbers** are independent wholesalers who provide racks of CDs, DVDs, and other merchandise in stores that are not primarily selling music, with whom they split the profits from sales.

Public Relations

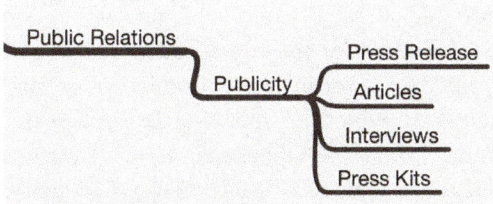

Public Relations.

The Public Relations department works to come up with a strategy for the promotion of a record and to implement it. One of the tools they use is publicity, which, unlike an ad, is free. The goal for a Publicist is to help an artist maintain and advance their image. To do this, they work to get their artist in the news as often as possible in order to give people a reason to talk about them, and by generating media attention through radio, TV, magazines, music trades, and blogs. Some of the things they do to attract attention include sending out promotional copies of new records and other material to the media, composing press releases, arranging interviews, writing speeches, and making arrangements for press parties.

More on the roles of marketing, promotions, sales, public relations, and social media management is covered in Chapter 2.

Record Label Income and Artist Royalties

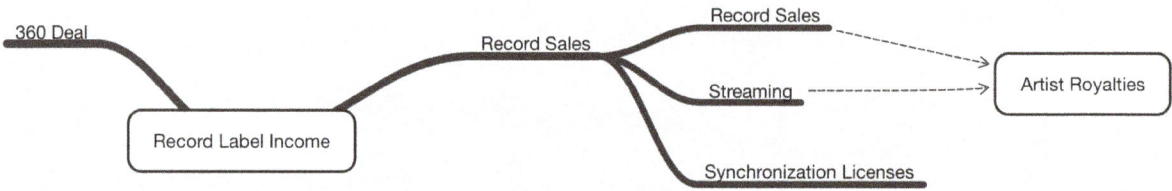

Record labels pay royalties to artists on the sale of their records.

A royalty is a payment made by the party who owns an asset to the party that created it for the right to use it. Record companies usually own the master recordings of the songs, which are copied and sold to the public. The deal an artist is able to get depends on their track record and what their lawyer is able to negotiate.

Some producers are paid a flat fee for their work, while others work for royalties "points" from record sales. This system gives them an incentive for taking a lower payment up front, when it is not known if the record will be a hit. One point is equal to 1% of the sale price. Unknown producers typically get 1 or 2 points, those who are well known can get 2 to 4, and superstars as high as 6 for an album. Sometimes the payment doesn't kick in until a minimum number of records are sold.

In an "all-in" deal, the artist is responsible for hiring the producer, who is paid out of the artist's royalties. The combined royalty for the unknown artist and their producer is in the 12%–15% range, 15%–17% for a mid-level act, and 18%–20% for superstars. The advance that they get in this case is against future royalties. For example, a producer might get a $20,000 advance and 3 points for doing an album, and then would not get any royalties until the label recoups the advance from the 3% they are getting from their share of sales.

Like the different tiers for royalties, there are also different categories for record prices. The USNRC rate applies to records sold at or near full price in the United States through normal retail channels. The royalty rate for "Mid-priced" records is around 75% of full list price, so if the royalty rate for a USNRC sale is 10%, the royalty for a mid-priced record sale would be 7.5%. "Budget" records are sold for 40%–50% of USNRC, for a royalty rate of 4.5%–5%. Records are usually sold outside the United States for 50% of USNRC.

The discounts taken on the artist's don't stop there. There are additional ones that reduce what they are paid for their records. Many copies are sold with a discount or given away. Record companies have worked out "free goods" deals with stores where up to 10% of the copies are given to stores to make their business more profitable, for which no royalties are paid to the musicians. In some cases artists may have to pay for packaging. There are other categories of products from which no royalties are paid to the artist, like promotional copies sent to broadcasters and journalists, and "cutouts"—copies that are left over when an album has been removed from a label's production line, which can be identified by a small physical mark or notch in the cover of an LP.

Major label record companies "advance" money to a band to produce a record, which is a type of loan against future royalties. The process of the record company getting this investment back is called "recouping."

The band's first album generates
$2,000,000 of income.

Let's look at a hypothetical deal, using round, hypothetical numbers, in which a label gives a band a $250,000 advance to record their first album. Let's imagine that it does quite well and sells 200,000 copies at $10 per copy. This generates $2,000,000 in income, and you might think that the band would start celebrating in anticipation of getting a big check from the record company.

When the band checks their contract, they may find that it says that they are due a 10% royalty of record sales. In this scenario, their share of the income would be $200,000, with the label getting the rest ($1.2 million). Well, it may not be all they hoped, but it still sounds like a nice chunk of change!

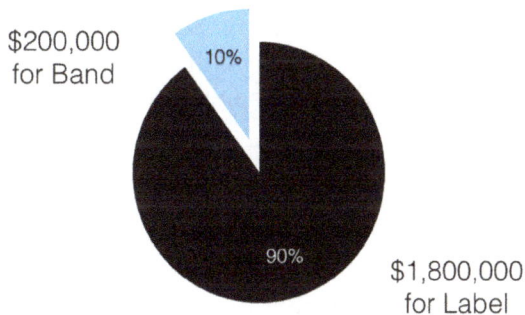

In this deal the musicians get a 10% royalty on
the records sold.

Unfortunately, the band won't actually get their hands on any royalty money until the record label has recouped what that they loaned the band to make the record. The advance ($250,000) minus the royalty from sales ($200,000) equals the new debt they have left ($50,000). Put on your thinking cap. How many more copies of the record is the band going to have to sell before they finally start to collect royalty payments?

Starting in the mid-70s, contracts began to specify a number of records a band would record rather than a length of time. A "four-album deal" means that the label has the option to release four of a band's records. If the first album or two don't do well, the group will probably be dropped before the contract is completed. In a multialbum deal, it is standard practice to include a cross-collateralization clause. This means that any money that a band owes from one album will be recouped from royalties on any of the other albums. In the case of the previous example, the band won't get any royalties from their second or third albums until they pay off the advances for them, and the $50,000 they still owe on their first.

In a 360 deal, the record label gets a percentage of what an artist makes from many sources.

The decline in record sales at the end of the 20th century prompted record companies to look for new ways to make money. This led to a new type of business relationship called a "360 deal" in which an artist agrees to give the record company a percentage of their income from a variety of sources including record sales in order to pay back advances and marketing, promotion, and touring support services.

Streaming

Streaming is now the main method for delivering songs to the public. There are two types of streams—interactive and noninteractive. Interactive, on-demand streams like Spotify allow the listener to request songs, which requires a larger royalty payment. Noninteractive streams like Pandora and SiriusXM offer a "lean back" experience like terrestrial radio stations in which listeners do not have any control over the order in which the songs are played, and they pay less as a result. The thinking is that listeners are unlikely to purchase a copy when they can place a request for a song whenever they want to hear it.

For each stream there are two tiers, one for premium paid subscriptions, and the other for free services supported by ads. Two different copyrights come into play regardless of the type of stream or tier. A sound recording royalty is paid to the owner of the recording (usually the record company), and a composition royalty is paid to the composer (usually through their publisher).

Digital broadcasters pay the sound recording royalties to SoundExchange, a nonprofit performance rights organization that was created by Congress, whose job is to take the money and distribute it to the artists and songwriters. When a song is played on terrestrial radio (i.e., AM or FM), only the composer and publisher get paid, whereas with a noninteractive service, 45% of the royalty for the performance goes to the lead artist, 5% to other featured performers, and 50% to the owner of the master recording, that is, the record label.

The record label collects the money from SoundExchange and pays the artist according to the terms of their contact, usually somewhere between 15% and 22%. This is why artists get upset by how little money they get for streams of their music. DIY artists use music aggregator services like CDBaby and TuneCore to get their music on streaming services. These companies charge a yearly fee and/or a percentage of the streaming royalty they collect on behalf of the artist from SoundExchange in addition to the flat fee they collect per song or album.

Review and Preview

We covered a lot of topics in this chapter, and you may want to go back and review the information to connect up all the parts of the process of recording songs, the functions of studios and record labels, and the roles of the people who work for them.

It was proposed in Chapter 2 that independent musicians have to consider how they will cover the many functions handled by an Artist's team. It may be beneficial to also consider who will take care of the services provided by recording studios and record labels. If you are a DIY artist, make an inventory of skills and identify where the use of your time and energy will produce the greatest return. Be smart about what you take on, and put together a team for the rest. Like Derek Sivers, founder of CDBaby said, "Do it yourself doesn't mean 'Do it all yourself.'"

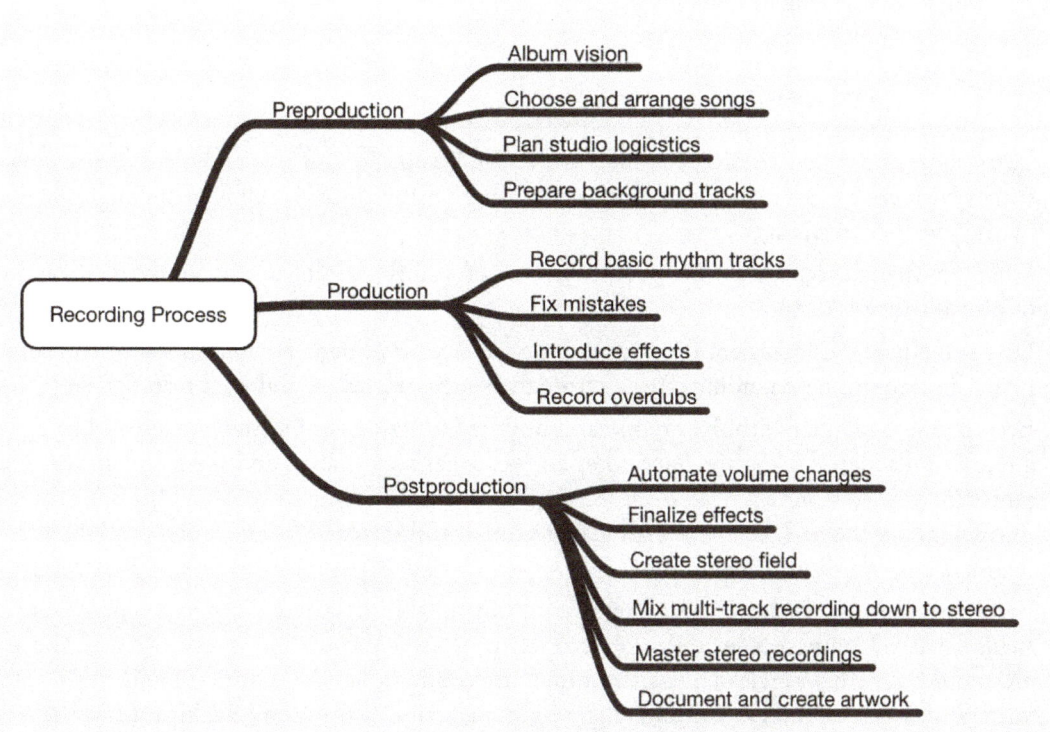

The three phases of record production.

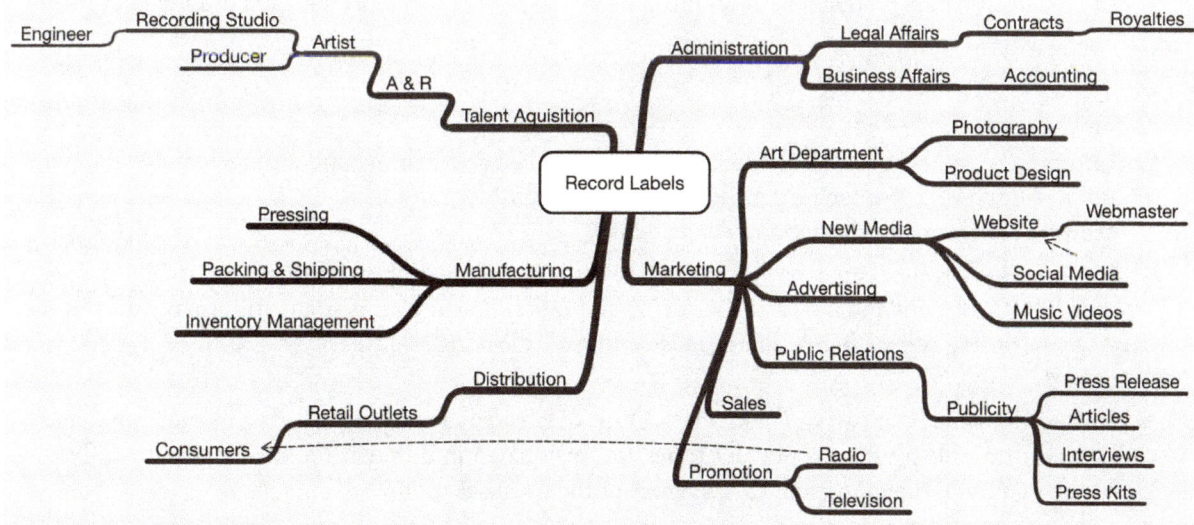

The structure of record labels.

Many have found it to be advantageous to produce their music themselves and end up making more money selling fewer copies themselves than they would if they took an advance from a label that they had to pay back. More artists should follow the lead of hip-hop artists, who have traditionally been more careful to hold on to their publishing rights than musicians in other genres. One sign of the tide turning happened in 2017, when Chance the Rapper became the first unsigned artist to win multiple Grammy Awards.

In the next chapter, we will look at publishing, and the main revenue streams for songwriters from royalties generated through the licensing of their songs.

For Further Investigation

1. Learn more about how recording studios work. See if you can visit one and observe a mixing session. It may be harder to arrange time during a recording session since the performers might be distracted by the presence of strangers.

2. Discover what studios are in your area, what sort of facility they have, who works there, and the type of projects they take on.

3. Find some new musical talent in your area. Consider your options for finding them. Try something new. Check out their recordings. Who wrote the songs, and where did they record them?

4. Become more familiar with the process and business structure behind the music you like. If you have a record collection, look at the liner notes and see what major labels and independents are represented. If you don't have any physical records, make a list of some of your favorite songs and do some research about them. Where was the music recorded and mixed? Who were the producers and engineers? Where was it mastered?

5. Become more aware of how music is marketed to you, and the forces that are pushing towards particular artists. Compare a few different reviews of the same project and interviews with the artist from around the time it was released. Can you find any common language, which might suggest that the writers were given copies of the same marketing material to work from? Make a list of the next 10 marketing messages you get about music. Often times campaigns are coordinated with album release dates and live appearances. Do any of them have to do with a new release or upcoming concert in your area?

6. Visit a record store in your area. If you don't have a dedicated outlet, look for the small display at Walmart, Target, or Best Buy. How are the recordings organized? What are the cheapest and most expensive records? Which products are most prominently displayed? Does anyone seem interested in them?

Do It Yourself

1. Improve the setup of your home recording facility. Make the lighting and arrangement of the space more conducive to producing your kind of music. Consider improving the acoustics with some DIY acoustic panels to absorb soundwave reflections.

2. Record a song you or someone else wrote. Do more preproduction work than you usually do, and see whether it turns out any better as a result. Spend more time and effort than you usually do and see if the recording sounds better. Put in more effort on the design and packaging and see if it gets more attention.

3. Record the same song two different ways. Once with everyone playing together in one room, and once with people playing at different times and/or isolated in different rooms. Notice any differences in the quality of the sound and cohesiveness of the musicians.

4. Start a record label and release some records. See if you can market them and sell some copies.

5. Get your music played on Internet radio and podcasts.

Vocabulary Review

360 deal—a type of contract in which a record label gets part of the artist's income from practically any income stream.

Advance—the money a label gives an artist to create their recording.

Amp (amplifier)—makes an audio signal louder.

Automation—the recording of the changes in settings during mixing so that every time the music plays back the same effects are achieved. This makes the process more efficient.

Click track—a regular click that a musician hears in their headphones while recording so that their idea of where the beat is agrees with the computer that is recording them.

Compression—automatic volume control. This can help make the loudest parts softer and the softest parts louder, so that the resulting music will sound good in noisy environments, like the in a car.

Cross-collateralization—a system where record labels take royalties from one record to recoup money advanced for another in a multialbum deal.

Demo (demonstration recording)—used by groups to work out arrangements, or to show music managers in clubs that are considering hiring them.

Download—songs that are copied to your local memory storage, as done with iTunes. Once they are on your local device you don't have to be connected to the network to play them anymore.

EQ (equalization)—the independent control of different frequency bands, such as the bass and treble controls on a hi-fi system.

Groove—the underlying texture in a song produced by the rhythm section (drums, bass, chords), in other words, everything behind the lead instruments and vocals.

Iso (isolation) **booth**—a small performance space that is acoustically isolated from the engineer in the control room.

LP (long play record)—a 12-inch vinyl record that can hold about 20 minutes per side.

MIDI (Musical Instrument Digital Interface)—a software and hardware specification adopted by manufacturers in the 1980s that allows computers, keyboards, and other equipment to communicate with each other.

Outboard gear—signal processors external to mixers and instruments, like compressors and reverb units. Today, many people use software processes inside computers to simulate the effects they provide.

Overdub—recording a new track over an existing background. Solos and harmony parts are usually overdubbed after the basic tracks have been laid down.

Pan—moving sounds left or right in the stereo field. The term began in the motion picture industry, where the camera pans across a scene that is otherwise too wide to see all at one time.

Points—a royalty on a recording project, equal to a percent of the sale price.

Punch in/out—begin and end recording at specific points in the music, activated while the music is playing back.

Rack Jobber (or rack merchandiser)—an independent person who sets up displays of music products in a store with whom they share the profits from sales.

Recoup—the process of an artist paying back money a record label has invested in their project(s).

Reverb (reverberation)—the resonance and prolongation of sound. The dimensions of an auditorium create longer reverberation times than those experienced in a small room.

Rhythm section—the instruments in an ensemble that provide the background beat, over which lead instruments and vocals are added. The basic elements are percussion, bass, and chords played by keyboards and/or guitars.

Streaming—music transmitted over data networks, as done by Spotify, Apple Music, Pandora, etc. You must be connected to the Internet to listen.

Studio Musicians—freelance musicians who are hired for a recording session, known for their ability to perform a song well after playing it once or twice.

Tracking—the process of recording the instruments and vocals before mixing.

USNRC rate—the Net Sales of Records as Top-Line Records through Normal Retail Channels in the United States. This is the highest royalty rate that a label will agree to pay an artist for sales.

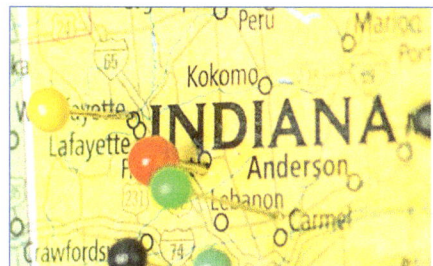

CHAPTER 7

Publishing

Topics

Songwriting Contracts
Mechanical Licenses
Performance Royalties
Master Use License
Permission to Sample
Synchronization Licenses

Main Ideas

- Publishers' main objectives are to acquire the rights to songs, and to license them to generate royalties which they divide with the composers they represent.

- Compulsory Mechanical Licenses are administered by the Harry Fox Agency and allow people to record and distribute copies of other peoples' songs. Congress set a statutory rate of 9.1 cents per copy for songs under 5 minutes in length.

- Performance Royalties are collected for composers by the three Performances Rights Agencies ASCAP, BMI, and SESAC from venues and broadcasters. The blanket license fees they collect are then divided up and distributed to the publishers in proportion to the frequency that their composers' songs were performed.

- To combine all or part of a song with a moving picture, a Synchronization License must be negotiated with the songwriter's publisher for the use of the composition. The fee must be negotiated.

- A Master Use license is required to place an existing recording of a song in a new project, for example, as part of the soundtrack of a movie or in a commercial. The fee must be negotiated and the payment goes to the owner of the recording, which is usually the record label.

See the book's companion website for supplemental information, updates, and links: http://willshare.com/mmb

Introduction

Most of the revenue streams that we look at in this chapter flow to the composers of songs and their publishers, the rest goes to record companies for the use of their recordings in new projects and for digital broadcasting.

After reading this chapter, you should appreciate why the ownership of a copyright for a song is so important. Members of a band do not share in the income generated from publishing unless a special agreement has been made that specifies that compositions are owned by the whole band and not just the songwriter.

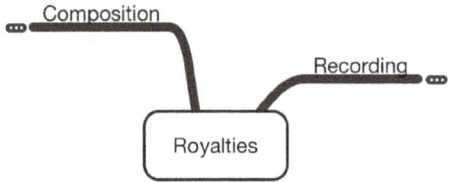

In most cases the royalties for the use of a song go to its composer. When a recording is used part goes to the record label.

Songwriting Contracts

Most composers are busy composing and performing songs and don't have the business connections to get their work used in commercials, films, and video games. In the old days, publishers made their money by selling printed copies of music in sheet or book form. Today, less music is sold on paper, and what publishers mostly do is to sign up composers and the rights to their copyrights for a limited times period, during which they look for opportunities to make deals using them. The money that comes in from these arrangements is then divided with the composers, usually in a 50–50 split. For example, under this arrangement, if a song is licensed for use in a movie the publisher would get 100% of the publishing share and the composer would get 100% of the songwriting share. Music publishing is one of the rare cases in mathematics in which the whole—the total income generated from a license—equals 200% instead of 100%. If there is a lyricist and composer, they are likely to split the songwriting share 50–50. In the same hypothetical soundtrack use, the publisher would get 100% of the publishing share, and the lyricist and composer would each get 50% of the songwriting share.

Here are the basic arrangements for four of the most common types of agreements between composers and publishers:

1. Individual and Exclusive Agreements: Under this agreement, the composer turns over the copyright to one or more of their songs to the publisher for a specified length of time. In return, they will receive a share of the income that is generated from any deals the publisher makes with companies who want to use their material. Under this type of agreement, songwriters receive a steady weekly or monthly

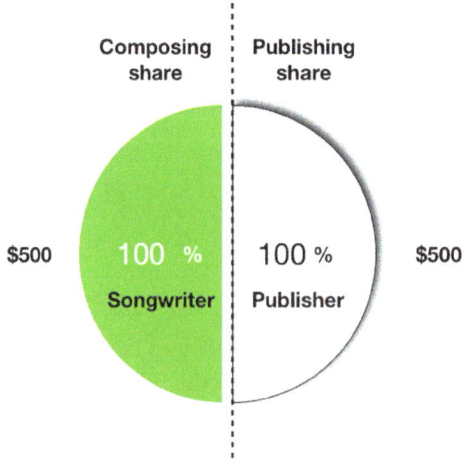

In an Individual or Exclusive Agreement, if a license for a song generates $1,000, the songwriter gets 100% of the composing share ($500), and the publisher gets 100% of the publishing share ($500).

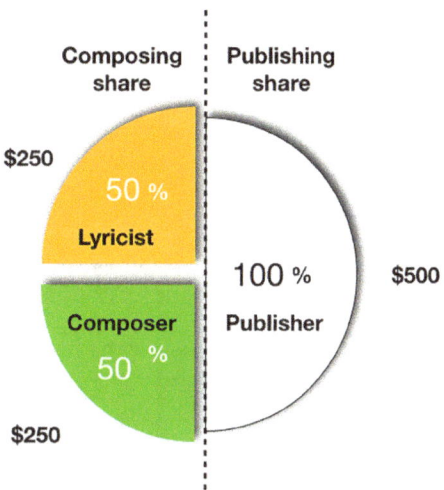

Lyricists and composers often split the royalty for composing 50–50. In that case they would each get 50% of the composing share ($250 each), and the publisher would get 100% of the publishing share ($500). An agreement must be arrived at when a team of songwriters is involved in order to specify what each member's contribution will be worth.

advance or "draw" like a salary against future royalties, which helps the songwriting continue to work on writing songs while waiting for the royalties to start coming back. The money that the publisher advances will be recouped when the songs begin to attract customers.

2. Co-publishing: This agreement allows the writer to co-own the copyright to their song. When it is used, they receive part of the publisher's share in addition to the composer's share.

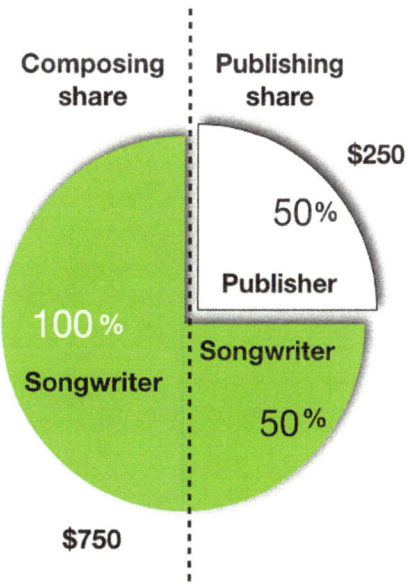

In this co-publishing deal, the songwriter is getting 100% of the composing share and 50% of the publishing share on $1,000 of income, for a total of $750. The publisher gets 50% of the publishing share for $250.

3. Administration Agreements: The publisher is put in charge of administering the licenses for one or more compositions for a specified length of time. In this deal, the composer retains the copyright to the song and is responsible for finding opportunities to place it for commercial use. Since less work is required on the publisher's part, the composer retains a larger percentage of income that is generated.

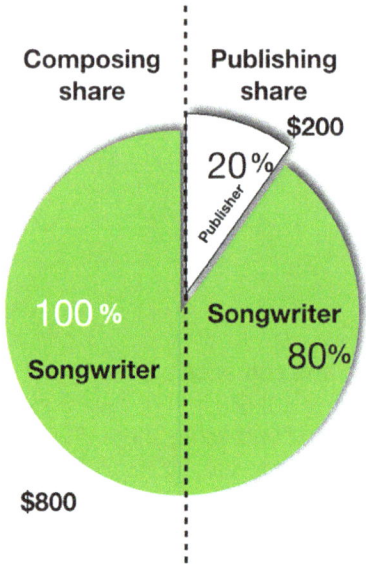

In an administration deal the publisher usually receives 10%–25% of money they collect on the composer's behalf. In this deal, the songwriter gets 100% of the composing share and 80% of the publishing share, for a total of $800. The Publisher keeps 20% of the license fees ($200) for administering the deal.

4. Foreign Sub-publishing Agreements: Many publishers don't have the necessary contacts in other countries to make deals abroad. The publisher may make an agreement with another publisher to represent their songs in another country.

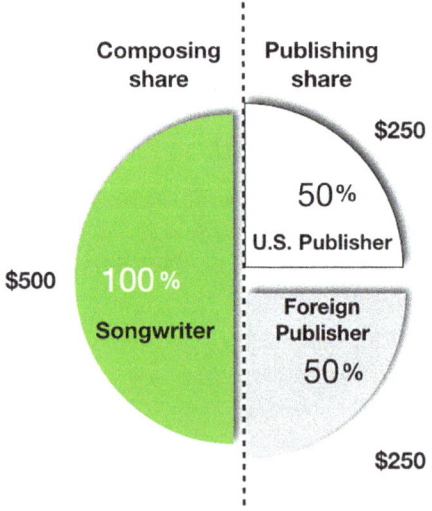

In this hypothetical Foreign Sub-publishing deal, the songwriter is getting 100% of the composing share ($500) from the use of their song, while the two publishers are each getting 50% of the publishing share ($250 each).

Since Chance the Rapper is not signed to a record label and owns his own publishing, if someone wants to use his song in some new production, he will get 100% of the songwriting share ($500) and 100% of the publishing share ($500), for a total of $1,000. That is good news for Chance, especially because the fee for one of his songs is going to be a lot higher than $1,000. Giving away his music in order to build an audience appears to have worked out very well for him indeed!

Mechanical Licenses

The term "Mechanical License" dates back to the 1909, when Congress passed a law to give copyright owners a nonexclusive right to make and distribute, or authorize others to make and distribute, mechanical reproductions of their musical works. As part of the process, they set up a 2-cent royalty on each player piano roll that was sold. Previous to that law, composers were paid either a flat fee or a royalty for printed copies of the scores of their compositions, but were not paid for what were viewed as performances of their songs by automatic instruments, in the same way that they weren't paid when live musicians played them.

Mechanical Licenses were later applied to phonograph records, and continue to be a big part of composer's income, even though there are fewer mechanical systems in use each day. Today a mechanical license fee is paid each time a copy of a song is made—on a vinyl disc, on a CD, or as a digital download from the iTunes store. Anytime the sound of the song is copied, even if it is just bits in a computer's memory, a mechanical royalty is paid to the composer through their publisher for use of the composition—the lyrics and melody—apart from any particular audio recording of it.

In Chapter 5, we saw how copyright law attempts to balance the individual's right to make a profit from their work with society's interest in being able to benefit from it. This principle can be observed in action in regards to mechanical licenses:

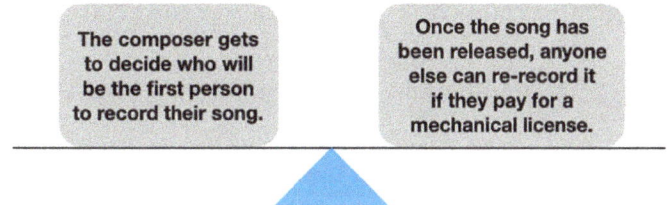

The balance between the composer's and the public's interests.

For their part, the composer gets to decide who will be the first to record their song, or in fact, if anyone ever gets to record it. Once the recording has entered the public sphere, however, anyone else has the right to work with, study, improve upon, interpret, or re-record it, so long as they don't change the song's basic melody, lyrics, or character. Congress worried that publishers might act in a monopolistic fashion, so they created a "compulsory" mechanical license to allow anyone to make and distribute a mechanical reproduction without the permission of the composer as long as they paid the rate that was established by law.

It would be inefficient if Mechanical Licenses had to be negotiated for every use. Imagine that you are in a band that wants to cover a song written by someone in another state. It would slow you down unnecessarily if you had to find out who wrote the song that you're interested in covering, track them down through their publisher, and then get them to fill out a Mechanical License and send it back to you. Some composers don't answer the phone, or may have changed their address. Also, if you want to just make five copies it's probably not worth their time to bang out a license upon your request.

This impediment to progress was solved in 1927 with the founding of the Harry Fox Agency, which now represents over 48,000 publishers. If you want to record someone else's song you go to their website, find the song that you want to cover in their database, and then pay 9.1 cents for each copy you plan on making or 1.75 cents per minute if the song lasts over five. Voilà, you now have a mechanical license!

If you want to use a sample of someone's song in a new song of yours, you will first have to get a mechanical license from the composer of that song for the right to use their composition. A mechanical license by itself does not give you the right to use the recording. For that you will also need a Master Use license from the record company that owns the sound recording. If you want to save money, you can pay the composer of the song for the use of the composition with a Synchronization License, and then hire someone to record a version of mimicking the sound of the original recording (called a "replay") and use that for your project in order to avoid having to pay for the Master Use license.

Performance Royalties

You may remember from Chapter 5 that copyrighting a song gives its owner the exclusive right to perform it. How does this square with your experience of hearing people perform songs that were written by others? How do they get away with that? The answer is due to a system of performance royalties that is administered by Performance Rights Organizations on the behalf of composers and their publishers. This streamlines the process of licensing the right to perform another person's song.

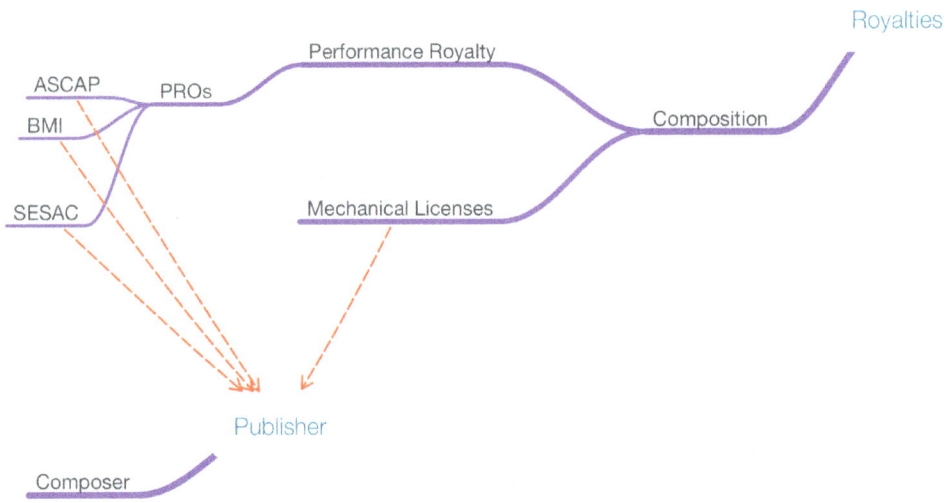

Royalties for compositions are in the two main categories: Performance Royalties and Mechanical Royalties.

We just saw how it would be impractical for musicians to have to track down composers every time they wanted to record one of their songs, which led to the creation of Mechanical Licenses and the rise of the Harry Fox Agency. Imagine how much more often the complication would arise if you had to get their permission just to *play* the song, which happens more often than recording it. In order to reduce the friction that would exist were that the case, a system was set up that does something similar to what the Harry Fox Agency does for people who want to record copyrighted. Groups called Performance Rights Organizations (PROs) collect blanket license fees periodically throughout the year from anyone who has music performed on their premises, including universities, bars, radio stations, television channels, and concert halls. The company holding a blanket license then has permission to play any song by any composer that the PRO represents, rather than having to negotiate on a song-by-song basis.

There are three PROs: ASCAP, BMI, and SESAC. Publishers pick one of the three to sign up with to represent them, although they all work about the same. Human representatives and computer programs from each PRO sample what songs are played around the nation, tally how many times each of their composers are having one of their songs played, and then plug the data into a formula that calculates what percentage of the license fees that should go to each writer. The more often your song is found to be played, the more money your PRO will send you.

Restaurants that play music from noninteractive radio, TV, cable, and satellite systems are exempted from paying performance royalties as long as they don't charge their customers to listen, are smaller than 3,740 square feet, and have fewer than four televisions. They don't get an exemption if the music is performed by others means such as by a band, cell phone, or CDs, have more than one TV in any one room, have a TV whose diagonal screen size is greater than 55 inches, if the audio comes through more than six loudspeakers (or four in any one room), or if there is a cover charge. The complete rules and fee schedule are even more complicated, but you get the idea.

The meaning of "performance" in the "Performance Royalty" is probably different than what you would expect. It can happen at any time is performed or broadcast, regardless of whether or not there are live musicians involved, in either of these two situations:

1. In the presence of an audience, in a place open to the public, or when a substantial number of people outside of a normal circle of a family and its social acquaintances gather together.

2. Via broadcast, by means of any device or process in separate places and at the same time or at different times.

In Case #1, music played by a DJ at a dance club would be considered a performance even though there are no musicians playing instruments. If the DJ took the same sound system to someone's backyard wedding for the same number of guests, it would not be considered a performance since it is not open to the public, and is a gathering of family and friends.

In Case #2, records played by terrestrial radio or Internet streaming stations would be considered a performance because songs are transmitted from one place to another. Streaming stations pay PROs for the right to broadcast copyrighted compositions and, in addition, pay SoundExchange for the right to broadcast copyrighted recordings. SoundExchange monitors what has been played, and in a similar fashion as the PROs, divides up the money they receive from broadcasters to make royalty payments to the record labels in proportion to frequency with which their songs were played. The owner of the recording (typically the record label) gets 50% of the royalty, 45% is supposed to go to the featured artists, and 5% to the nonfeatured musicians. However, musicians may receive less than that depending on the terms of their contract, and before they see any payment, their share will go towards recouping any advances they received from the label that have not yet been paid back.

Master Use License

In Chapter 6, we mentioned that one of the last steps in the postproduction process is mastering. Multitrack recordings are mixed down to stereo, and the final polishing is performed by the mastering engineer who prepares the final version for distribution. The final stereo version that will be copied to sell to the public is called the stereo master.

If you want to use the recording of a song in a project you will have to get a Master Use License from record label or whoever owns the recording. The record company is not required to grant your request, or even to give you an answer. If they are willing to consider your request, there is no statutory rate that they must accept.

Permission to Sample

If you want to use a sample of someone else's song in your record you will have to get a Master Use License from their record company for their permission to use the sound recording. You will also need a Mechanical License from the publisher of the song as well for permission to use the song's composition.

Since you will be creating a derivative work based on the original song, there is no standard rate for either of the licenses. It seems unfair that you can rerecord your own version of an entire song for 9.1 cents a copy, but if you want to sample even one second of the recording of it there is no such statutory rate, and could end up costing you hundreds or thousands of dollars.

In the 1990s record companies and their agents filed a series of lawsuits charging hip-hop artists with copyright violations. Judges ruled that it didn't matter how short a sample is, or how unrecognizably it is transformed—you still need to get the record company and composer's permission. This effectively put an end to the Golden Age of Hip-hop, and groups like Public Enemy, A Tribe Called Quest, and The Beastie Boys had to stop making complex sample-based recordings because it became prohibitively expensive and time-consuming to clear all the samples. These days only the most successful artists can afford to license samples for in their project, and if they do, it is probably going to be for just one or two, since the licensing fees have to be paid in advance, before you even know if the new song is going to be a hit and generate enough money to pay for the them.

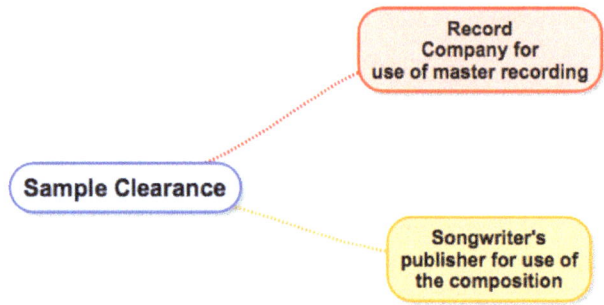

Two licenses are needed to clear a sample: a Mechanical License from the publisher, and a Master Use License from the record company.

It is unfortunate that sampling has become so locked down. The current climate wastes the potential of a huge amount of source material to create new works and ties the hands of creative people who would like to repurpose it, and prevents the new creations from reaching the ears of people who would enjoy hearing them. Whole wings of history have been locked up, as no one was there at the time gathering the signatures from the people involved to get the necessary release forms signed so that people could benefit from it in the future. Going forward, we can create a new repository of material for the benefit of society if Creative Commons catches on, but that will not address the problems of being denied use of everything from the past.

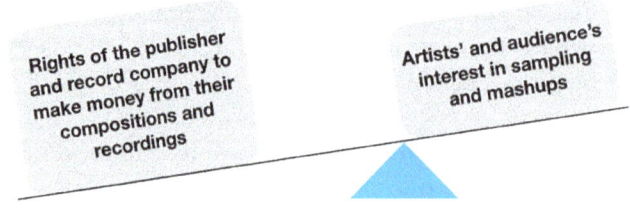

The balance in copyright law between the rights of owners and interests of users has shifted too far towards the owners.

Dreams and jokes delight us with the unexpected places they take us. We are missing out on similar experience when we are denied the opportunity to enjoy music and video freely mixed into new contexts by digital artists. The feeling of wonder begins with surprise and discovery, and hearing an old sample or seeing a snippet of video in a new context can do the same thing. The listener/viewer contributes value from the memories they maintain and recall, and it is the contents of their memory that makes it powerful. After being inundated with music, commercials, TV for many years as consumers, I believe we should be compensated in some way for all the memory space media and marketers have staked out. Why is it that Andy Warhol could put a Campbell Soup Can or Marilyn Monroe's image in his paintings, but a hip-hop artist can't mix in the Campbell Soup theme song from one of their commercials, or a bit of Marilyn's voice from a movie?

Synchronization License

You will need two licenses if you want to synchronize a recording of a song with a moving picture in a TV show, commercial movie, or video game—a Synchronization License from the publisher for the rights to use the composition, and a Master Use License from the record company for the rights to use their particular recording of it. Neither the publisher nor the record company is required to grant your request, and if they do, there is no statutory rate that either must accept. As it is with the Mechanical License, everything is negotiable. Factors that determine the fee include the project's budget, how much of the song is to be used, how important it is to the scene, whether it's playing the foreground or background, how much reliance is being put on it to elicit an emotional reaction, how well-known it is, and how famous the performers and composer are.

Often times you'll hear a familiar song in a movie and realize that the recording of it is not the original one you remember that made it famous. This is usually done in order to save money, since it can be cheaper to just pay the Synchronization License with the publisher for the rights to use the composition, and then hire someone else to record ("replay") the song than it is to pay for a Master Use License to whomever owns the original recording. The next time a song comes on in a movie, notice what effect it has on you, and whether it being the original version or a replay makes any difference.

Review and Preview

It is important to understand the income streams for publishers and record companies since that is where a lot of the money in the upper levels of the music industry comes from. When bands are developing their repertoire, everyone should understand who owns the copyrights to the songs, and what the ramifications of that may be in the future. A lot of musicians think that they should get some royalty money for helping with the creation of a song when they contribute a bass line, drum beat, or guitar riff during rehearsal or a recording session. One of the attitudes we have inherited from a European classical music heritage is the granting of higher status to melody and lyrics over rhythm. If our intellectual property law came out of an African tradition, we might value groove above all else, and be less concerned about imitating and appropriating parts of old songs, something that was common in the blues and jazz traditions.

You may need to go back and review the material covered in this chapter and in Chapter 5 in order to be able to remember and apply the process of copyrighting songs, know what copyright covers, and which type of license is needed to use them in different applications.

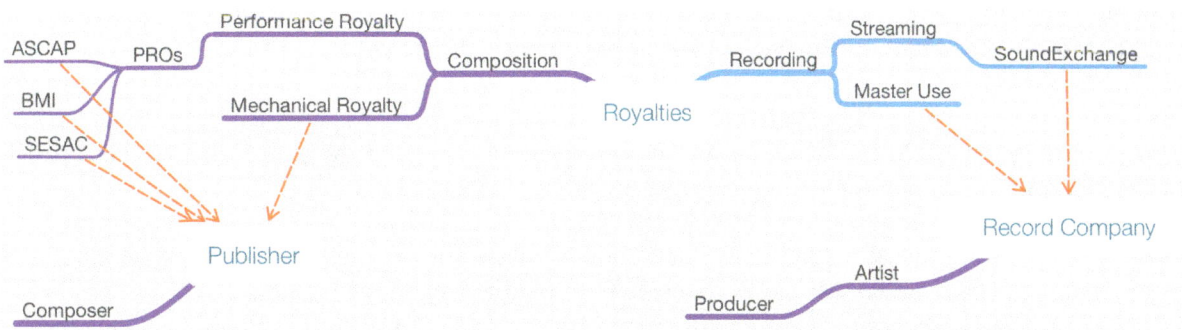

An overview of revenue streams that result from the use of compositions and recordings.

For Further Investigation

1. Visit the website www.whosampled.com. Find the original songs that are reported to have been sampled used in someone else's song. Can you hear what use was made? Would the new song have been the same without them?

2. Listen to recordings of sample-heavy projects from hip-hop groups from the 1990s like Public Enemy, A Tribe Called Quest, De La Soul, and The Beastie Boys. How does the texture compare with today's artists? Does the complexity of the music seem to call for a different level of wordplay?

3. Watch the documentaries *Copyright Criminals* and *RIP: A Remix Manifesto*. Listen to Girl Talk's albums with your friends, and discuss your reactions and favorite parts. Why doesn't he get sued? Role play a trial and take turns speaking on his behalf and representing the record labels who don't want him to sample their records.

4. Learn about the court decisions from the 1990s that led to a tightening of copyright enforcement, and an end to sample-rich projects. Ask your Congresswoman what she thinks about it.

Do It Yourself

1. Watch the documentary *Secondhand Sureshots*. Get a few friends people together, find some funky old records, and create new songs using samples from them. Remember to bop your head.

2. Listen to some experimental electronic music that uses sampling like "Williams Mix" from John Cage, and compare it with the results obtained during the Golden Age of Hip-hop. Listen to the Beatles' songs "Tomorrow Never Knows" on *Revolver* and "Revolution 9" on the *White Album*. Make a piece of your own sound art using the classic musique concrète techniques of pitch and time change, reversal, looping, filtering, and spatialization. You could do this with Audacity—a free computer cross-platform program that offers many built-in sound processing routines.

Vocabulary Review

Blanket License—venues that pay license fees to PROs have a blanket license in order to give them the right to play any song by any composer that they represent.

Clear a Sample—the process of getting permission from a song's publisher and the owner of the song's recording, in order to use a sample of song in a new production.

Compulsory Mechanical License—once the first recording of a song has been publically released, anyone can make copies of their new recording of someone else's music by paying for this license. The publisher cannot deny giving them permission, therefore it is *compulsory*.

Cover (song)—a "cover" is a recording or performance of someone else's song. For example, "cover bands" perform other people's music. To "cover" someone else's song means to re-record it yourself, or do your own version live.

Cover charge—a fee charged at bars, nightclubs, or restaurants which is collected at the door to pay for the night's entertainment.

Draw—the amount of money a songwriter gets per week or month from their publisher.

Exploit—music is one of the few businesses in which "exploiting" is a good thing. To "exploit" the copyright for a song means to find opportunities to license its use in order to generate royalties.

Harry Fox Agency—administers fees for Mechanical Licenses.

Master—Mastering is the final stage after mixing a song in which it is prepared for release to the public. The "master" is the definitive version that copies are made from to distribute to the public.

Master Use License—a license negotiated with a record label to use one of their recordings.

Mechanical License—allows the licensee to make a copy of their performance of someone else's composition.

Musique concrète—a school of electronic music begun in France in the 1950s led by Pierre Schaeffer, in which non-instrumental (concrete) sounds are organized to make music without the traditional parameters of melody and harmony.

Performance—in terms of publishing, the playing live or a recording of a piece of music in public for an audience of unrelated people, or broadcasting it over the air or network.

Performance Rights Organization (PRO)—an agency that collects blanket license payments from venues and broadcasters that perform music. They sample what is played in a wide variety of situations and pay the publishers who represent the composers whose songs were played, in proportion to the number times each song was presumed to have been played.

Player piano—a mechanical piano that plays back songs stored on rolls of punched paper.

Replay—the re-recording of a song to use in a new project, done in order to avoid having to pay a Master Use License for use of the original recorded version.

Repertoire—the choice of songs that a musician is prepared to play.

Sampling—taking a portion of audio from an existing recording song and mixing it into a new song.

Synchronization License—a license paid to the publisher of a song which can then be synchronized with a moving picture, such as in TV, film, or commercial.

Topics

Main Ideas

- Small clubs give bands the opportunity to practice their show and connect with an audience.
- Regional touring is a good way to build a fan base but not usually a great money maker. If a band is frugal and sells merchandise, they can at least cover their expenses.
- As royalties from the sale of recordings drop, live performance is the one reliable source of revenue for top acts.

See the book's companion website for supplemental information, updates, and links: http://willshare.com/mmb

Introduction

Record sales have been falling since 1999, and digital downloads and streaming have not made up the loss in revenue to record labels and performing artists. Today's audience is saturated with possessions and electronic diversions, and what they are increasingly looking for are experiences. For these and other reasons, live performance is growing as an important source of income for musicians.

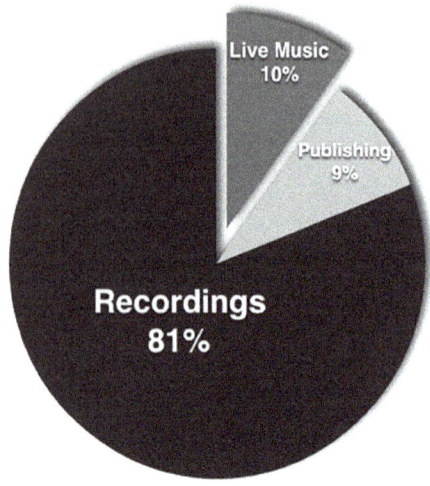

Percentages of music industry revenue in North America in 2000.

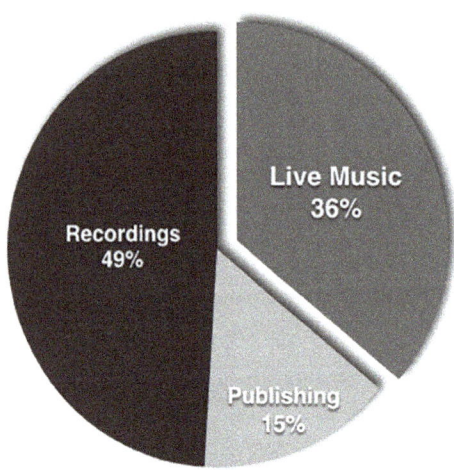

Percentages of music industry gross revenue in North America in 2003. In just 3 years, the importance of live music increased by 26%.

The big money is made by acts with major record label support. According to Forbes Magazine, Taylor Swift was at the top of the list of performers based on estimates of their gross incomes for the year between June 2015–June 2016:

Taylor Swift ($170 million)

One Direction ($110 million)

Adele ($80.5 million)

Madonna ($76.5 million)

Rihanna ($75 million)

Garth Brooks ($70 million)

AC/DC ($67.5 million)

The Rolling Stones ($66.5 million)

Calvin Harris ($63 million)

Diddy ($62 million)

Adele is unusual because she made most of her money from recording rather than performing, and because she has turned down every endorsement deal she's been offered. Taylor Swift was the highest paid entertainer of any type, despite the fact that she didn't release any new music that year. Instead she toured, wrote songs for Rihanna and Little Big, struck deals with companies like Apple, Diet Coke, and Keds, and created exclusive content for AT&T's new streaming service.

In this chapter, we will look at the realities for musicians at the bottom of the music industry economy. As you will see in this chapter, live performance for them is more of a break-even situation.

The first step in a band's career is to develop a local fan base.

Playing at Home

Most groups start out playing in their local community. If they are successful and have the time and energy, they later foray into the surrounding area. Many of the musicians at this level have day jobs and are doing music at night and on the weekend. These "weekend warriors" find that it is more affordable to stay close to home in order to save money that would otherwise be spent on transportation, food, and lodging.

The goals at this stage are to develop one's musicianship and a set of songs that are worth presenting to the public. During our interview (located on the book's companion website), Timothy Hays said "The question in the back of the musicians' minds at this point should be 'Why would someone want to come hear us when they have so many options for entertainment and demands on their time? What can we do that will make them want to turn out to hear us play?'"

You'll have an easier time developing a reputation if someone in the band can write good songs. The band should understand that it is the person who comes up with the melody and lyrics that will own the copyright. These and other issues should be worked out in a written band agreement before any money starts to come in, including how decisions will be made over repertoire, hiring and firing, and the ownership of equipment.

It's hard enough for two people to stay together in a relationship. When it comes to three or four in a group, the dynamics can get even more complicated. Bandmates end up spending a lot of time together and it's important to be friends, or to have at least have worked out how issues are resolved. Touring is more than just playing on stage. You have to support each other and put the wagons in a circle when attacked. Remember the Marine Corp's motto "Semper Fidelis" ("always faithful") and be loyal to the group and to each other. Watch each other's backs, and don't leave anyone behind.

Bands should set up in practice like they will during performance so that they can get used to the layout and make the best use of the space, since small clubs usually have tiny stages. Some groups reserve some of their rehearsals for just working on vocals, and practice not only the songs but the transitions between them, who will talk to the audience, and the gist of what they will say in order to reduce the number of gaps during the show that would cause a drop in energy that loses the audience's attention. Record your rehearsals and review them later to help get perspective on where your strengths and weaknesses are.

Pay attention to the audience's reaction and keep track of what works. During rehearsal focus on what needs to be most improved, and if you don't see a change in the audience's reaction, work on your musicianship or try a new repertoire and method of delivery. One of the most important things to do is to develop your skills as an entertainer. I realized during my years of performing that it mattered how we related to the audience more than how well we played. You can't slack off on the music, but it's critical to relate to the audience and engage them. Watch their body language. When do they pay attention? What gets them moving in time? When do they disconnect?

© JSlavy/Shutterstock.com

Humans, like other animals, have a herd instinct that inclines them to think and behave like the majority.

The first people you pull in are the hardest because of our herd mentality. Individuals are influenced by their peers to adopt certain behaviors and attitudes, and it takes some effort to get some people to take a chance on your music. When you're playing in a club that is empty it doesn't matter how great the band is playing. If someone sticks their head in and sees that no one is there, they will most likely back out and go somewhere else. On the other hand, if you're not playing that well, they will probably come in anyway if the place is half full. Nurture the beginnings of a herd. You are there to make their evening better. Talk with your fans during breaks and get to know them. Get ideas from them about where you can perform. Ask for testimonials that you can use in your marketing materials. Ask them to visit your website, sign up for your mailing list, and report your event on their social media.

The music business is 50% or more about business. Hone the definition of your brand and elevator pitch to describe it. Have several versions ready for different categories of people and situations you might meet them in. Start an email list using a tool like Mail Chimp. When you perform, get as many names and email addresses as you possibly can. Have a business card ready to pass out. Observe people who are more successful than you and figure out what they are doing that you aren't. Learn what you need to succeed. You become the people that you hang out with and the books that you read. Read trade magazines and music industry books. Attend trade shows like NAMM, SXSW, and Gear Fest.

One of the existential questions you face in the music and entertainment business is "What comes first, the rehearsals or the gig?" The more competent the musician, the busier they tend to be, and less interested in practicing a lot if there isn't a show on the horizon. On the other hand, how can the leader of the group convince a club owner to hire them until they have a demo tape and a set worked out? Look at it from the venue's perspective, and figure out what they are looking for. Their bottom line is that they have to make a minimum profit each night in order to pay their bills. It will be easier to convince them to hire you if you can demonstrate that you have a following on social media, have been successful at selling tickets in the past, have physical record distribution in the United States, press reviews, airplay, a history of touring, and a team on the ground to help with promotion.

One way to get exposure is to open for a better-known band. This puts less pressure on you to deliver an audience and fill up an evening, and you may get a few new fans from performing in front of people who like the same kind of music. Don't expect to have a lot of time for a soundcheck as the venue's priority will be to take care of the headliners. Simplify your setup and focus on getting on and off as quickly as possible.

There are as many ways to *lose* a gig as there are to get one. As we said, the bottom line for the venue's manager is how much money they pull in over the course of the evening. Many clubs don't have regular clients and it's up to the band to draw a crowd. For a room with a capacity of 300, you will be expected to attract at least 25 people on an "off night" (Sunday through Wednesday), 40–50 on a Thursday, and to fill it up on Friday or Saturday. Even if you're opening for another band, it's important to bring in your own thirsty audience for your set. Remember Willey's Law of Live Performance:

alcohol + music = money

You want to develop an image of a reliable brand that sounds as good live as it does on its demo, shows up on time, doesn't take long breaks, and delivers on its promises. A sign that you're overplaying a club is when your fans stop turning out, so consider avoiding playing at the same club twice in the same month. Some bands are lucky and latch on to a weekly gig for a while at the same establishment. If that happens, be sure to keep putting energy into it to keep it going, and be watching for other opportunities as it doesn't usually last for too long.

The manager is the band's customer—and boss.

Once you have a relationship with a bar or restaurant it's important to stay on good terms, so that you can have a regular opportunity to play there and use the gig as a reference to establish credibility with managers at other venues. Check out what is happening at the club on nights you are not there to see if you're playing the right style. It is less risky to play smaller clubs with lower ticket prices so that you can fill the place up, and easier to get a good turnout on Thursday–Saturday. Make your set as strong as possible and leave the audience wanting more. Get email addresses from people who show up and contact them when you're playing again. Enlist fans to help put up fliers and make announcements on their social media. Let the venue know what you're doing to promote the show.

Make every show a unique and special event like a CD release or birthday party, contest, a theme show, or a collaboration with another band. Wear costumes, use props, work with a DJ, dancers, or a local celebrity. Give it a creative name and offer prizes like gift cards, clothing, and CDs. An average band playing average music is not going to attract attention and fan loyalty. Be amazing!

Venues and Deals

The deals a group will get for a show depend on the location, date, and their reputation. One way to test the waters is to start at an Open Mic night where the audience takes turns entertaining each other. From there you might work up to playing for tips or a "door deal" where you get a percentage of the admission fee. As you attract a bigger audience you may be eligible for shows where tickets are sold and you can get a guaranteed fee for the night. Remember to always look at things from the fans' and club manager's perspective. How much money do they have to spend, and how will the evening generate a profit after paying salaries, utility bills, insurance, etc.? A band that is starting out will be lucky to make $100, some free drinks, and a place to stay, whereas an established band that brings in hundreds of fans might get around $1,500. It's important to be smart about routing and plan a string of engagements far enough apart geographically so as not to compete with each other, but not so far apart that transportation expenses will eat up everything you earn. At this point, what you should be focusing on is developing your music, how you deliver it to the audience, and growing your fan base.

There's no point in going on tour until you've built a local fan base. As Brandon Meeks said (see the complete interview on the book's companion website), the most important thing is marketing:

> "It's all about understanding business models, what genre and subgenre you're in, and the people who follow that and how to connect with them. That's the critical thing. You have to understand the target for what you're doing, and really hone in on how to get in front of those people consistently and build a community around your work. That determines success, more than whether you play an instrument or not. Of course the end product has to be good, but when it comes to the business side it's more about marketing and reaching people once you have the product."

There are many other venues besides bars where music can be heard, such as restaurants, wineries, weddings, workshops and clinics, corporate and community events, festivals and fairs, college, and performing arts centers.

© 3DMAVR/Shutterstock.com

Adventure awaits!

You should have promotional material to give the people who hire for these situations, including an audio demo tape, video clips, website, photos, set list, and evidence of past performances.

Touring

At some point after you've become a big fish in a small pond, you may want to try taking your music to another level. The band Twenty One Pilots was successful in Columbus, Ohio, but it wasn't until they took the plunge and went on the road that they became a sensation.

Not every band may be able to travel, due to the day jobs and family responsibilities of its members. It's hard work and a long shot. The prospects for touring are not much more profitable than playing locally when you are starting out. Do it because you love the music and want to cover your expenses, not as a way to get rich (there are many easier ways). You might hit the big time, but you'll probably be lucky to just break even.

On the other hand, you'll never know if it's possible unless you try. If you feel the call you may want to go for it and enjoy some exuberant moments of celebration. It's better to be doing something, and failure is not always a bad thing. If you look at a setback as an opportunity to pivot and reset your course, you'll probably end up with an opportunity that you didn't know existed at the outset. There is no better teacher than experience, and whatever happens, you'll test your resolve and develop grit, both of which are character building. Along the way it will become clearer who you are serving and how you can help them accomplish their goals.

The least expensive and most efficient way to experience is touring is to start out with a "Figure 8" or "Petal Pattern" tour. These are good for short runs where you can hit nearby cities between stops back home:

A Figure 8 travel pattern connects shows along loops on either side of your hometown.

A tour can be extended to include more cities in a "Petal Pattern."

You may need a booking agent to convince out of town employers that you can draw a local crowd. If you land a gig, make every effort to do well there so that you can contact them a couple of months afterward to see if they will book you again.

A contract clarifies what is being agreed to.

Contracts

It's a good idea to have a contract before a gig starts. For most situations, it's a one-page document that lays out the basics—the names of the group and the venue, address, phone number, the date and time to perform, how long you will play for, how big the stage is, what payment you will get, any deposit that has been collected, the number of names you can add to the guest list, how and where merchandise will be sold, the price of tickets, and details regarding security and safety. Unless thousands of dollars are on the line, it probably won't be worth trying to force a club owner to live up to it as you'll just burn your bridge for a repeat engagement. The main purpose is to put the essential elements in writing to help everyone understand what's been agreed to. Don't expect your booking agent or anyone else to stand up for you. There will be times when a club won't honor their agreement and will pay you less or nothing because business was slow. You will learn that a "guarantee" is a moving target and that you may receive less than you were promised.

A technical rider attached to the contract describes general stage requirements and lists any sound and lighting requirements that the band needs to put on a good show. It's a good idea to get a list of the equipment a venue has to offer, and to deliver a stage plot showing how you set up and how you connect your equipment to the P.A. system. A hospitality rider specifies the food and drinks you would like to have available backstage for the band and crew. Remember that everything you ask for costs money and reduces the venue's ability to pay you. It's better to stick with the absolute essentials and bring as much of what you need as you can yourself. Confirm the details of a show as the date approaches and review the information supplied in your technical rider with the staff. "Advancing" is the process of working out the arrangements, and should be done by a designated member of the band if there is no tour manager a couple of weeks before each performance. Find out the order of the groups that are going to perform that night, and research them to find out what sort of music they play. Find out what promotional efforts have been made and what is left for you to cover. Be prepared for surprises and don't expect that everything you ask for will be available when you get there. The more you know about the venue, the easier time you will have. Keep a folder for each club you play in with all the information about your show in one place, and leave a copy somewhere where you can access it in case you lose it. Make a Google Map marking the location of each one. Don't always trust your GPS. Get a map and learn how to read it.

If you don't have a tour manager, have a point person in the band that communicates with the staff at the venue when you arrive. Give them a guest list with the names typed out, and periodically check at the door so that the friends and media people you've invited aren't stranded outside trying to get in.

Live Performance Roles

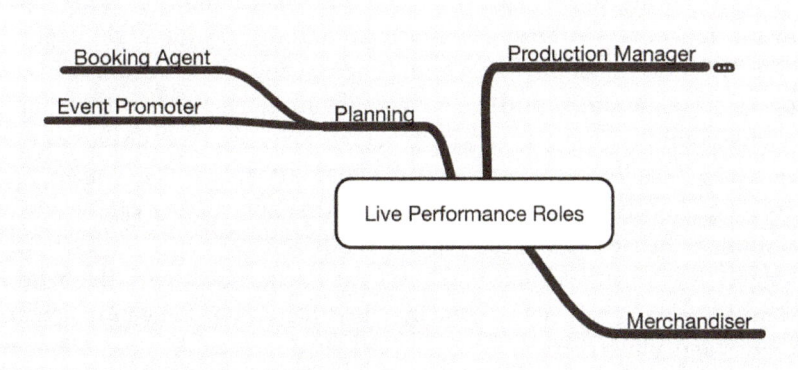

Main branches of support for live performance.

In Chapter 2, we discussed the roles of the booking agent and tour manager. Here are some other jobs that need to be filled for a large national tour with support from a major label. The same functions need to be covered for regional tours on a smaller scale by DIY musicians.

An Event Promoter is an independent operator that puts together concerts, club dates, and other events. They create a budget, put together money to promote the event, advertise, sell tickets, hire a crew, and coordinate all the details with a venue. Some, like Josh Algler of the Bluebird in Indianapolis, do it in order to bring good music to an audience: "If one song that one band plays at one show changes one person's life, then I've done my job." A promoter gets experience by starting to plan small events and working their way up to larger ones. It is important to be a good multitasker in order to handle all the details.

The crew is under the direction of the Production Manager, who oversees all of the technical aspects of a performance, including the sound and light systems, the backline technicians, and power requirements. It is important that this person is detail-oriented as the stakes can be high.

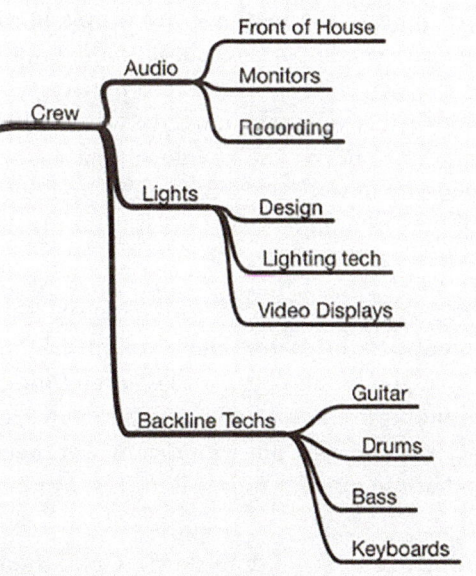

The crew is a combination of traveling and local technicians.

The members of the road crew travel with the band. They work with local technicians to do anything necessary for a show other than perform, including driving, unloading and loading equipment, rigging, security, catering, and selling merchandise. Those involved with the sound system work in two main capacities. The "Front of House" (FOH) Engineer sets up the mix and amplification that the audience hears. Speakers are suspended or "flown" along with the lighting system from the stage scaffolding and the FOH engineer adjusts balancing the volume and the tone of the various instruments on stage to suit the acoustics of the space. The Monitor Engineer takes care of the stage monitors for the benefit of the musicians so that they can hear themselves and each other. Issues are addressed during the soundcheck before the show. A recording of the show can be made during the performance. The Backline Tech Crew sets up, maintains, and tears down the equipment used by the guitarist, drummer, bass, and keyboard players, and the amplifiers and speaker cabinets that their sound comes out of that are placed on stage in the back.

The Lighting Designer is in charge of the shows' visuals. They consult with the band before the tour and design a system that reinforces the music. Local crew members help setup the band's lights, integrate them into what the venue has to offer, and adjust them to focus on the desired areas of the stage. Video panels are an increasingly important part of presentations which make an unlimited variety of effects possible. The settings for the video and lights can be changed over the course of the performance to create variety and suit the flow of the show.

A store to sell merchandise can be set up each day by a crew member or local agent. The Merchandiser works with the band to design products, check inventory, order product when necessary, set prices, hire a sales team, meet fans, and keep track of the money that comes in. They should have good people skills and be knowledgeable about the band, since they have the most contact on a personal level with fans.

If you can't afford a Publicist, you should at least check that the venue you are set to perform in spells your name correctly and links to your website. Send a press release to local media, and if there's someone who will do an interview or review your show, send them a CD and put them on the guest list. It's important to build up a collection of clippings and quotes from reviews for marketing purposes.

Collected Wisdom

1. Don't go on tour unless you are all in. One test of this is whether you are willing to do a great show even if you're not feeling well and only five people show up. Be grateful, and celebrate with those who are there. It should be about the people, not the money. The show must go on. Have fun!

2. Make "win-win" deals. Foster positive relationships with people so that they will want to work with you again in the future. It's nice to be important, but it's more important to be nice—to *everyone*, including the soundman, bartender, and waitresses. Take note of people's names and use them, and remember to say "please" and "thank you." The music business is a small world, people have long memories, and you meet the same ones on the way down that you passed on the way up. You want to have the reputation for being easy to work with. Be humble and honest. Obey the house rules. Never cancel a gig on short notice, and help find a substitute if you can't make it. Be responsible and pay for anything you break.

3. Be cool. Expect change. Be prepared for those around you to act out and go crazy.

4. Go see other bands. Check out their live shows and social media. Subscribe to their email lists. Steal like an artist—if you like what you see and hear, reach out and introduce yourself. Give them a copy of your CD. The music business can be cut throat, but it can also have aspects of a big family. Many of your biggest fans and advocates may be other musicians. Let them and venues know that your band is available to sub if someone cancels. You're all in this together, and a rising ocean floats all boats.

5. Be patient. Build a base and develop relationships slowly. Good things come to those who wait. Rome wasn't built in a day. If at first you don't succeed, try, try, try, try, try again. Don't get discouraged if

no one pays attention to you or seems to love your music as much as you do. Don't be surprised by rejection. You'll need thick skin to survive in this business.

6. Pay attention to the details. Learn from your mistakes. Listen to the opinions of people who have more experience and heed their advice—club owners, people who work in record stores, bartenders, and promoters.

7. Life is a struggle. Make the best of the situation. Remember, this, too, will pass, and in 10,000 years all this will seem much less important. Stop complaining and look for solutions. Be flexible. Improvise.

8. Don't apologize or make excuses to the audience. Most civilians won't notice when something goes wrong. There's no need to draw attention to problems. They are there to have a good time.

9. Add value to whatever situation you're in. Develop your entrepreneurial skills—find out what you're good at, and what you can do with it.

10. Don't leave home without some cash reserves and a credit card. Be prepared for emergencies.

11. Reducing expenses can add as much to your bottom line as increasing your income. Maintain a realistic touring schedule, but avoid planning days off. Play every day. Take breaks when shows are cancelled. Limit the number of members in the group.

12. Get inspired by Amanda Palmer's TED talk. Ask for help. Accept the hospitality of family, friends, and fans. Sleep on couches.

13. Maintain your physical and mental health. Have a plan, and watch your diet, sleep, exercise, and wear earplugs. Don't buy your food where you buy your gas. Stock a cooler with healthy snacks. Stay hydrated. Don't drink alcohol or do drugs—if that's your motivation to play music, stay home where there's a better support system.

14. Be on time. Have a proper map. Compare the directions you get from someone who knows the area with what a GPS tells you. You'll be glad you know where you are and where you're headed if there's a glitch, and you'll save time you would have wasted being fooled and led astray by an electronic device. Get a Rand McNally Dist-O-Map to quickly see the distances that are involved.

15. Maintain the condition and appearance of your car. Be polite with police. If you're stopped at night, turn on an interior light. Keep your hands in sight. Have a designated person who can explain clearly where you are going and what you're up to. Know the laws of the state that you're in.

16. Buddhists and Shakespeare agree: expectation is the cause of suffering. Do your best and don't be too attached to the outcome. Remember why you got into this business to begin with. Music can make the world a better place. Be a force for good.

Booking

Minimize crisscrossing and looping back when you plan your routing. Start your routing three or more months in advance. Contact multiple venues in the same area to see who will give you a gig. See the indieonthemove.com venue database for help with finding suitable places to perform, and their preferences for how whether they want to be contacted by email or phone. Do your homework to make sure you are a good fit in terms of draw and style. Don't shoot too high until you have the stature to back it up. Playing at smaller venues and on off-nights is less risky because expectations are lower, and getting experience at them will help you learn the language and business practices necessary to negotiate bigger shows.

Club managers will appreciate it if you don't waste their time. Call during off-hours and don't leave more than one phone message, and speak your name and phone number clearly so that they can write it down the first time you say it. If you don't get a call back, wait a week or two, and then send them an email. Have your materials well-organized on your website, Facebook page, YouTube channel, SoundCloud, and Spotify sites. Make it easy for managers to find out what bands your members have played in and which ones you've shared a date with. Clearly describe your fan base. How old are they? How do they behave? What is it that they love about your music? How energetic are you on stage? How loud are you? What other artists do you sound like? Who are your influences?

Interviews help artists reach a wider audience and establish their credibility.

Media

Touring bands often take the opportunity to visit with local media when they are in a new city. Research the websites and print publications that deal with your genre of music, and look for opportunities to do interviews on independent local or college radio, television, or in newspapers. Remember to thank anyone that helps you. Review your mission statement and brand statement. Figure out the impression that you want to make. Have your talking points in order, and rehearse the story you are going to tell. Know who their audience is, and figure out what about you and your music is newsworthy and what will be interesting to them.

Never make people wait for more than 10 minutes. Make it easy for the person on the other end of the conversation to do their job. Write out a list of questions and answers for less-experienced journalists to get ideas from, and give them a set list and anything else that would be easy for them to misunderstand or mix up the spelling for. Give reviewers a copy of your CD. Make sure the first track on it is your best song.

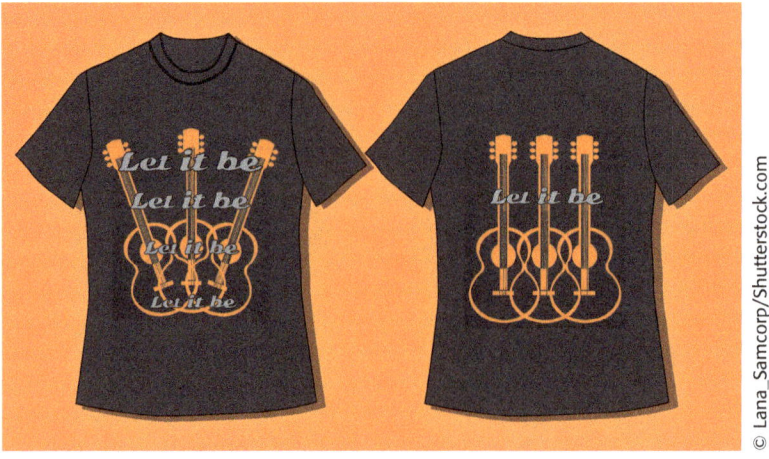

Selling merchandise is one way bands cover their expenses.

Merchandise

In Chapter 1, we looked at some classical music composers from the past and noted how they earned money working for the church or royalty, and found out that Beethoven was one of the first to live off the income from his publications. One wonders how he would have adjusted to today's model of giving away music for free so people will come to shows, and then playing shows so people will buy merchandise.

If you're in a band it's a good idea to maintain contact with people who buy your wares, since it's easier to get them to do it again than to find someone new. You're not going to make much money from performing when you're starting out. Selling merchandise can make the difference between coming home with an empty tank or a few dollars in your wallet. Many fans like to take home souvenirs, especially in smaller markets where they don't get as many acts coming through. Even after paying the club a percentage of what you sell, it can still be your main revenue center.

T-shirts don't have to be fancy or expensive, but it's important to match your design to the market. It's better to get a good design for your logo and style, be consistent, and stay with it for a while to develop your brand. You might consider having some hook lines from your songs on the shirts. If you don't have a lot of money to invest in product when you're starting out you can use just-in-time manufacturing services like Spreadshirt, Zazzle, Cafepress, or PrintFection which make them one at a time when a fan orders online. The advantage here is that there are no up-front costs, you don't have to maintain your stock, and the company fulfills orders. You can try an unlimited number of designs, colors, and sizes, link them from your website and social media, and see which ones sell the best. Make a few for the band and the people at the merch table. After you get an idea which ones are most popular, you can think about investing in a bulk supply, which when you sell yourselves will return a much higher profit. Have two designs in a range of sizes, including M–2XL.

Predicting the tastes of your fans can be a hard thing for bands to do. Study your audience and their buying behavior and income streams in order to get the most benefit from merch sales. For example, many people have more money to spend in the middle of the month than they do at the end. If you're a new band you're not going to make much money anyway, so consider playing for free at the end of the month when the audience is running low on funds.

It's important to have something for sale that's in every fan's budget, from $5 to $70 dollars. Price items so that you won't have to bother making change since the goal is to sell as many things as you can in the shortest amount of time. Limit the number of items for sale, like two types of shirts and two CDs. This will make it easier for people to decide on which one to buy. The more choices there are, the harder it will be for them to make up their minds and the less satisfied they will be afterward. Stickers have the highest profit margin. They're so cheap that you can give them away, or include as a thank you for buying a shirt or CD.

Giving away free stuff will increase your sales. Pass out coupons for merch. Throwing something in for free with a purchase and discounted bundles can stimulate sales. Make your merch table a reason for going to the show, stocked with items that can't be bought anywhere else. Include some special item like a limited edition shirt, remix CD or EP from upcoming album, or autographed poster that is only available at the show. This can create a sense of urgency and promote impulse shopping in fans who feel that if they don't buy then that they won't have another chance.

Bring your own folding table in case the venue doesn't have one for you. Have a system for taking credit cards, and bring receipt paper, a 20-foot extension cord, pens, and a 75–100 watt light with extra bulbs. Set up your booth close to the entrance close to where people walk by. Pay the person who works at the table 10% of what they sell and make them responsible for the inventory. Tape things down to reduce theft. Have a sign that can be read from a distance that clearly lists sizes and prices.

A mailing list is priceless. Come up with some incentives to get people to sign up. Collect email addresses and organize them by city and zip code so that you can target your campaigns to people who live close to the event you are promoting.

When it comes to selling music, there are several options for formats. When you're an independent band, your goal is not to have a major label sell zillions of copies of your CD, but rather for you to sell thousands of them to individuals one at a time. The most profitable and highest quality CDs are "replicated", meaning that they are pressed from a glass master. These are ordered in increments of 500 or 1000. This product has the greatest up front cost, but it has the lowest per-CD cost, and is the most durable. If you want smaller numbers, you should consider "duplicated" CD-Rs. They cost two to three times as much, but you can burn them yourself, or set up an account at kunaki.com for them to take orders from fans online. The company burns them on demand, and ships them to customers for about $6 a disk including shipping. Other options are music download cards and USB thumb drives, which can hold complete albums, artwork, lyrics, photos, and videos, and be reused by fans for other purposes.

Let your fans know that you'll be waiting to meet them at the merch table after the show. If you have the right equipment, you can offer a CD or DVD of the show 30 minutes after you finish. Have a member of the band there to sign autographs and chat up the people. Fans who are visiting with you may end up buying something else while they wait.

You may also wish to give away your music. Your problem at this stage of your career is not that people are getting it for free, but that you are unknown. Your music is your best marketing tool. One of the factors that contributed to the Grateful Dead becoming one of the most lucrative touring bands was that they helped fans make bootleg recordings by providing multiple sets of output wires from the mixing board that they could plug into their own tape recorders during the show. A whole community grew around the exchange of well-recorded live shows. Today you can easily live stream your shows using YouTube or Facebook. Fans appreciate being able to review a show they have attended, or were unable to get to in another city. This helps people become familiar with your music so that when you come through town the next time they will want to come see you play live.

Collecting data is the first step to improving a product or service.

Record Keeping

Humans are not designed to notice trends over time. For example, the sun moves across the sky so slowly that we don't notice it. The years pass, and if you're lucky, you'll get to the point where you find yourself to be a senior citizen. If you want to improve over time, it is important to keep records so that you can analyze data. History is not everything that happened; it's what you have a record of. Without evidence, there is no history. If you want to manage your time better, keep a time log and write down what you do every 15 minutes for a week. If you want to manage your money, keep a list of time you spend. If you want to change your eating habits, write down what you eat. The same thing goes for a band. Keep a record of your shows, noting the day of the week, time of day, weather, number of people who came, which songs you played, which got the best response, how much you were paid, how many people the venue can hold, what publicity you and the venue put out, who else was on the bill, whether you were the headliner, how many T-shirts of each size and color you sold, how many people bought CDs, how many signed up for the mailing list, and so on. Report your CD sales to SoundScan. Record labels, stores, distributors, and other bands will be looking at your numbers as one measure of your status. Analyzing the data can reveal a variety of things and help you make better plans for the future, adjust your set, and order the right merchandise. You can also use it to show a track record to managers to get booked for shows, and even land a record deal.

Review and Preview

Big name acts can make millions touring and are supported by a big staff. Small and mid-sized acts may aspire to growing to the point where they can be signed to a major label and cash in on that action. In the meantime, they need to cover the jobs themselves that a large crew would handle.

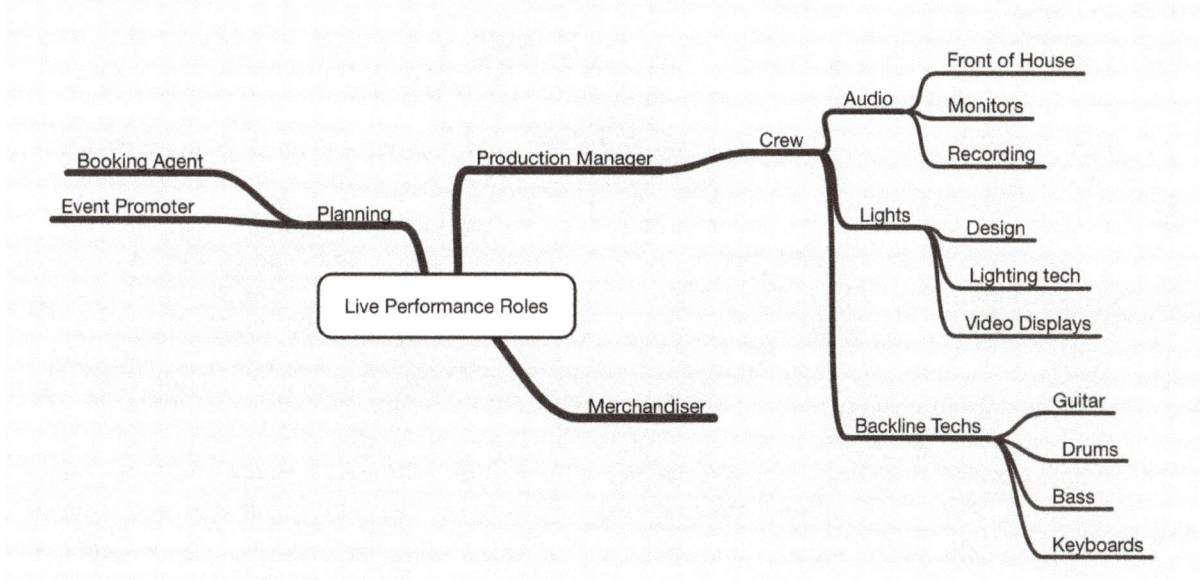

An overview of roles involved with live performance.

Most amateur and semi-professional musicians play because they love it and get an intrinsic satisfaction from performing.

Bands need to develop their craft and fan base at home before they start to tour. It's possible to make a profit if you develop an excellent product and cultivate an audience, and play often enough so that fans remember you, but not so often that they get bored and take you for granted. It's important to be smart about when and where you play, and to minimize expenses.

Bands who want to make money should spend as much time thinking about selling merchandise as they do about creating their music and developing their presentation. Keeping records returns data that can be used to analyze how they are doing over a period of months, so that they can tinker with their approach and make their business be more successful.

Fortunately, there have never been so many powerful and free tools to connect with an audience and develop fans. In the next chapter, we will look at the effect of the new economy, Internet services, and developing an entrepreneurial mindset.

For Further Investigation

1. Visit local venues. Talk to the people who work there and observe the bands who perform.

2. Look at technical riders and stage plots that bands use to specify their equipment and hospitality needs.

3. Research where the opportunities are for musicians to perform in your city and along the routes to the next closest centers. Why have some cities turned into cultural hubs?

4. Find regional bands that you're not aware of on Facebook and YouTube. Create a YouTube playlist with your favorites. Make and share a new Spotify playlist of remarkable music.

5. Make a list of all the shows and artists you've ever met and seen.

6. Many of the suggestions in this chapter for things to do came from my experiences playing in bands and reading books, particularly *Tour Smart* from Martin Atkins. Read that, and talk to working musicians to understand more about live performance and touring.

Do It Yourself

1. Ask your audience what they like most about your work. Focus your efforts on work that leverages your core competencies.

2. Start a blog where you report on what you experience from your regional music & entertainment scene.

3. If you're not satisfied with your reception, think of three ways that you could improve your repertoire or delivery. Start writing a press release for an event to prepare for an opportunity to try out the changes. Find a gig and fill in the details.

4. Keep track of how you spend your time for a week categorized by type of activity, including sleep, taking care of your body, commuting, work, socializing, relaxing, work, etc. Add up the totals for each one. How did you spend your 168 hours? How much time are you working on your music? Can you double that and/or make the use of that time more efficiently? Now, spend an equal amount of time working on your delivery to the audience. Next, spend the same or more time developing a simple line of merchandise and a way to display it. Finally, get a gig and try out your new product.

5. Choose an online delivery system for merchandise. Create a variety of products and link to them from your website.

6. Keep track of everything you spend money on for 2 weeks organized by type. Add up all the expenses in each the categories and see where you are spending the most money. Finding ways to reduce or cut out the less-important items can have the same effect as doubling your salary.

7. Form a co-op with other bands that fit well with each other. You may be able to get some dates by presenting a package to a venue. Take turns opening for each other. Share marketing and crew expenses.

8. Learn about the house concert scene in your area. These are small shows that people host in their homes

9. Plan one lobe of a Figure 8 or Petal Pattern tour.

10. Watch Derek Sivers TED talk on how to start a movement, then recruit a couple of superfans to see if they can light a fire under your audience.

Vocabulary Review

Advance—the process of someone in the band (i.e., the tour manager) confirming the details of a gig with the venue's personnel during the weeks before each show.

Backline Tech—technicians that handle the drums, guitars, bass, and keyboards, and the amplifiers they are played through that are set up on stage.

Demo—a demonstration recording made by a band to show a club owner or record label how they sound.

Front of House—the P.A. system set up to amplify the music for the audience. The FOH engineer is usually positioned between the middle to the back of the hall in order to give them an idea of what is being fed into the room.

Gig—a performance or other job. It may be a single or series of events.

House Nut—the amount of money a venue estimates that they have to bring in per night to meet their bills. It is computed by taking their total costs and dividing by the number of shows.

Merch—a band's merchandise for sale online or at their shows.

Monitors—speakers or in-ear monitors on stage that allow the musicians to hear themselves and each other.

Off night—A Sunday through Wednesday night at a club, when audiences are usually smaller.

P.A. (public address) **system**—amplifiers and loudspeakers used to make the music loud enough for the audience.

Press Kit—an organized collection of information a band can use to efficiently communicate the style of music they play and their value. Many groups use Sonicbids to produce an EPK (electronic version).

Rider—the part of a contract that lists a band's requirements for equipment and hospitality (food, drinks, dressing rooms, etc.).

Roadie—sometimes carries the connotation of being a person who does more physical labor than technical work, but it can also mean someone who works on the road and who may fulfill functions at a higher level.

Stage plot—a diagram that a band supplies to a venue to show graphically how their equipment is arranged and connected.

Win-win agreement—an arrangement that is good for both parties. If only one side benefits from a deal, the other will be less likely to want to work together again in the future. For more information, see Stephen Covey's book *Seven Habits for Highly Effective People*.

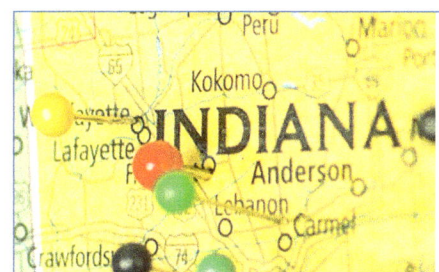

CHAPTER 9

The Music Business Today

Topics

The Perfect Storm
Local, Regional, National, International
The Importance of Being Remarkable
The Experience Economy
Being an Entrepreneur

Main Ideas

- Technological changes at the end of the 20th century set the stage for the new information economy. The digitization of content, increases in processing power and data storage, the growth of the Internet, and proliferation of smartphones transformed the way the music industry works.

- The music industry is divided into levels, and musicians face increasing odds as they try to widen the scope of their business, beginning at a local level and working up through regional to national and international stages.

- In order to be successful, you have to have a remarkable product. Being average won't get you a middle-class lifestyle anymore.

- We're moving from a consumer product economy to one based on experiences.

- There are more ways to being entrepreneurial than running a company.

See the book's companion website for supplemental information, updates, and links: http://willshare.com/mmb

Introduction

In Chapter 1, we covered an overview of the music business and changes in technology around the turn of the century that led up to deep changes in the music. We start this chapter by going back to pick up where we left off with the last three developments—digitization, the Internet, and the Apple iPhone, this time exploring their implications on the way music is consumed and monetized.

The Perfect Storm

Digitization greatly reduces the cost of storage and distribution of data. LP records have to be shipped and stored on shelves, an expense that is partly recouped due to their collectable form, and the space their packaging offers for artwork and liner notes. No matter how big the store, however, there was always a limit to the number of titles that could be stocked, and customers had to travel there to make their purchase. Vinyl discs have mostly been replaced by CDs, and books and films have likewise been converted to binary form, and they, too, can be downloaded or streamed directly to a customer's mobile device. Today, because of the storage capacity of servers and increased access to high-speed network connections, consumers have access to nearly unlimited virtual shelf space, and when the supply went up, prices came down. There is no more scarcity of product in the digital world due to the advances in processor power, transmission speed, and data storage.

The ability to digitize and deliver music over networks changed the music business.

The transistor was invented to replace vacuum tubes. Whereas American companies focused on its applications for the military, Sony developed a process of mass-producing them for portable radios, which as we saw in

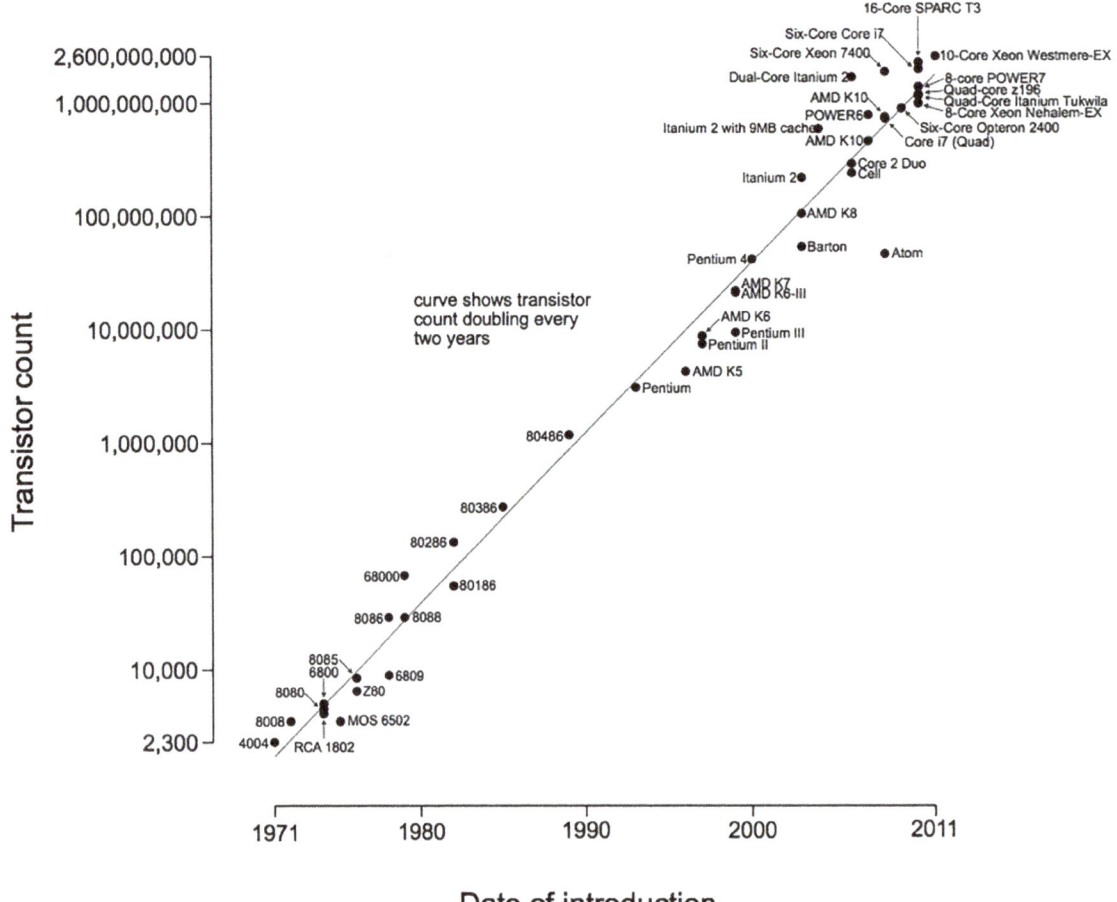

Moore's Law identified the trend that the complexity of integrated circuits doubles about every 2 years. Notice how fast the numbers on the y-axis are increasing.

Chapter 1 became the first personal music listening product. In 1961, a single transistor cost $10. At the time of this writing, the two billion transistors in Intel's latest computer chip sell for $300, or just 0.000015 cents per transistor. Moore's Law expresses the trend in the growing number of transistors that can be produced per unit area, a technological advance that has caused their cost to drop by half approximately every 2 years. Note that the vertical axis in the previous graph was exponential, meaning that it is a much faster growth than might be appreciated from a first glance at the graph:

The increase in memory capacity for hard drives has been equally astonishing, the result of which has been a drop in prices for memory storage similar to what has been seen for computer processors. A gigabyte of data that would have sold for nearly a million dollars in the 1960s costs less than 10 cents today, and you can have gigabytes of it for free online from companies like Gmail and Dropbox.

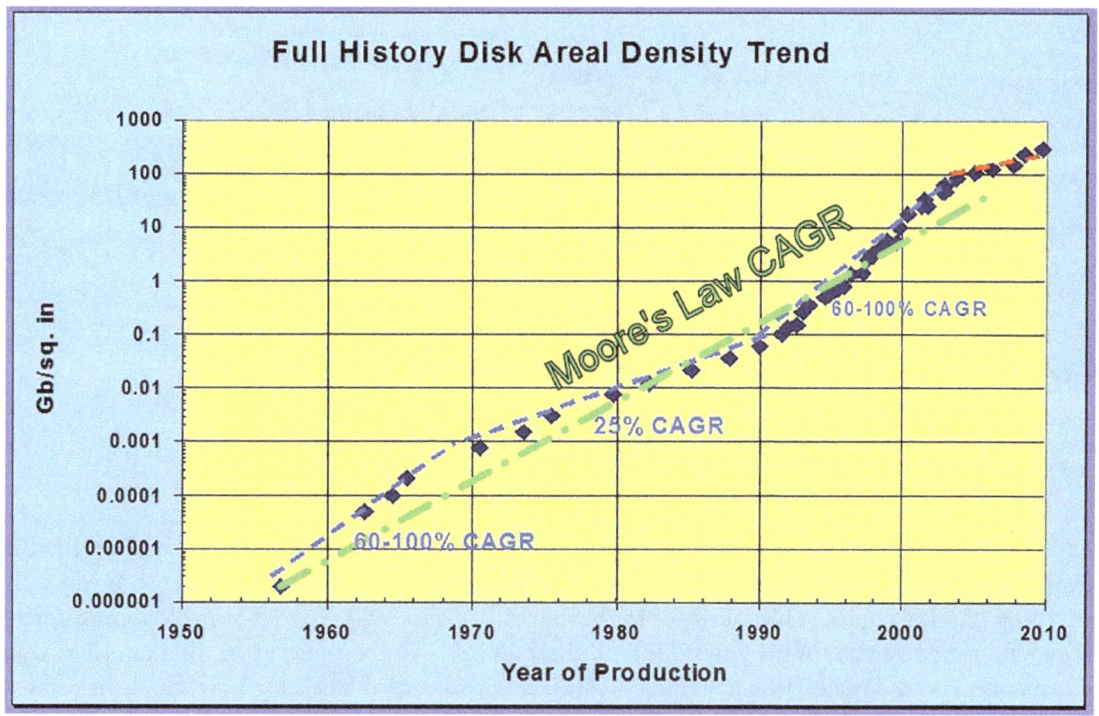

The increase in the capacity of hard drives (shown in blue) roughly follows Moore's Law (in green) as well.

You can buy a Raspberry Pi computer for $35, and it won't be long before computers will be free, too. Having such a valuable resource as a computer becoming free will have profound effects on society.

The rapid and continuing drop in prices for computer power and storage space is one of the forces driving the information age. In the 1970s, I suffered an ethical crisis and decided to retire from playing in bars in order to escape the implications of Willey's Law of Music & Entertainment ("music + alcohol = money"). I enrolled in graduate school to study computer music at the University of California, San Diego after reading the predictions by my future professor of the trend represented in Moore's Law on music. I read an article by Richard Moore (not Gordon Moore, for whom Moore's Law is named) and was convinced by his argument that there would come a time when making music with computer-based systems would become cheaper than with acoustic instruments, since while the price of digital technology was plummeting, the expenses of material and labor for making acoustic instruments was gradually increasing. The two lines probably crossed around 1983 with the introduction of MIDI and personal Digital Audio Workstations. In 1980, U.C.S.D. was one of a handful of places in the world where you could study computer music. One needed to go there or to Stanford or M.I.T., since the computer systems that ran the software cost half a million dollars. Today, the system in your smartphone is more powerful.

The Internet has provided instant access anytime to information stored anywhere in the world, first through the Netscape browser, and later with Google running on a variety of systems. The wealth of information indexed by search engines combined with YouTube's videos on just about any subject have accelerated the rate of change and learning, and when we look back in 50 years, the launch of the Internet on an international scale will undoubtedly be remembered as a pivotal change in human history, and as having a big part to play in ushering civilization into the digital age. File-sharing platforms like Napster and others made it easy to circumvent copyright, but at the same time, offered independent musicians a vehicle to connect with fans through websites and social media without needing the support of a record label:

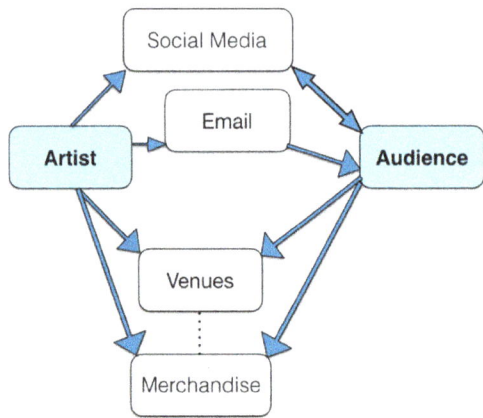

The Internet and social media have brought
artists much closer to audiences today.

In 2017, Chance the Rapper became the first to have a streaming album reach number 8 on the Billboard charts, with 57 million listeners during the first week. He was also the first independent artist to win a Grammy without selling physical copies of his music, or for having much sales at all. The 23-year-old built his reputation by giving away free downloads of his songs. He won three awards—for best new artist, best rap album, and best rap performance, and did it all without signing a contract with a record label. He now stands to make a lot of money, as future income will be all his, instead of giving 90% to a label.

The Internet has also affected international markets. In his book *The World Is Flat*, Thomas Friedman divides globalization into three phases. During Globalization 1.0 (1492–1800), European industrial powers mounted expensive expeditions to colonize the new world and set up trade for raw materials. During Globalization 2.0 (1800–2000), multinational corporations took the place of nations in the new economy. Advances in sea and rail transportation and modern communications made it possible for companies like Nestlé and Proctor & Gamble to act as parent companies with groups of subsidiaries dealing in consumer goods, media, banks, and energy. The opening of Internet traffic for commercial purposes in 1995, and the rise of automation and large connected populations in India and China have, according to Friedman, marked our entrance into Globalization 3.0. When he writes that "the world is flat" what he means is that in a globally-connected society everyone now has more of the same opportunities and is in competition for the same jobs. The Midwest has one advantage over the west and east coasts in terms of its lower cost of living. Here in Muncie where houses are inexpensive, we ask "Why send jobs to India when you can have them done in Indiana?"

The pressure on American workers is now on to refine their skills and become expert in a job that can't be moved offshore or performed by a computer. There is a joke that goes "In the future factories will only need two positions filled: a man or woman to sweep the floor, and a dog to keep them from messing with the robots." It is not clear, however, how much longer even service occupations such as janitors, cosmetologists, plumbers, surgeons, specialized lawyers, or performing musicians will be protected, as artificial intelligence and new technologies become more capable.

The last piece of the puzzle fell into place with the release of the iPhone in 2007. Having the Internet and its services within arm's reach at all times turned out to have more of an impact on sending text messages, access to information, taking photographs, and consuming media than it did on making phone calls, which quickly became the least used of its capabilities. The record industry was teetering on the edge of destruction due to the drop in album sales, but is now coming back thanks to streaming services. Listening to music has moved to cell phones as well, and become a personal experience. In most cases, the audio quality has suffered, since it is heard through budget earphones or built-in speakers rather than a full-range system—just one more example of convenience trumping quality. Music is now everywhere and more often something playing in the background. As supply increases, it turns music from an art form into a commodity.

The expense of copying digitized music and distributing it over networks is insignificant, and we now effectively have an unlimited supply of product. According to the economic principle of pricing a product based on its supply and demand, when supply goes up and demand stays steady, price goes down. After a generation of this many fans have come to expect music to be free. In his book *Free: The Future of a Radical Price*, Chris Anderson argues that businesses can profit more from giving some things away than they can by charging for them. Radiohead experimented with this approach in 2007 with the release of the *In Rainbows* album. They allowed fans to download and pay whatever they wished for it, and over two million copies were exchanged on file-sharing sites by the end of its first month.

The good news for musicians in the "Economy of Free" model is that the more you give away your infinite supply, the bigger your market size becomes of people who are aware of your music, which creates a demand for things of which there is a limited supply. After Radiohead gave away their album for free, they released an $80 deluxe box set, followed by a CD and digital album. The pay-what-you-want experiment generated a lot of publicity for them, and in the end awareness grew as fans had multiple avenues to get the music. The band eventually sold 1.75 million copies, resulting in $3 million dollars of sales worldwide.

Another example of creating demand for scarce items was Trent Reznor and Nine Inch Nails' *Ghosts I-IV* project, which they released as a limited deluxe edition with two hardcover books of high-resolution photos, Blu-ray high-resolution and high-quality audio .mp3 files, a 40-page PDF book, a data DVD with multitrack recording sessions that fans can remix, computer screen wallpapers, icons, and other graphics.

The Wu-Tang Clan is another group that has taken creative approaches to their marketing. For one album they released only 1,000 sequentially-numbered copies, which provided the true fans who bought them a feeling of exclusivity. They partnered with Boombotix to make 3,000 wearable speakers loaded with nine songs from their upcoming album *A Better Tomorrow*. Probably their most creative campaign to date was for *Once Upon A Time in Shaolin*, a double album that they worked on in secret over a 2-year period. When they were finished, they made a single copy of the record, and deposited it in a vault in a Moroccan hotel. It was then auctioned off to the highest bidder, who was rumored to have paid $5 million dollars. The only other way to hear the music was to catch up with it on its tour of select museums and universities, where for $30–$50 you could listen for two hours on headphones.

Local, Regional, National, International

The music industry works on a number of different levels. Some of the forces are the same for everyone but happen on such a different scale that they feel different to those who are involved. For example, everyone from the most successful artist to the musician playing their first gig thinks about social media, but the star has a marketing team to help them with publicity, while the beginner has to do it all themselves. An artist may continue to perform some of the same songs as they move up through the different levels represented in the following diagram, but the music industry that they are in once they reach the national stage as a signed artist is quite different from when they played locally.

The path diagrammed by the flowchart below starts in the lower left corner with songs. It's important that you like your own songs. You are their first audience. Writing and polishing songs at this stage has intrinsic value, and can satisfy one's curiosity and innate drive for discovery and self-expression. Musicians who don't write their own songs focus on their repertoire and performance. In either case, the musician at home keeps returning to

A simplified flowchart of a musician's rise to international stardom.

the same question (represented in a diamond) of whether they are happy with their songs or not. If the answer is yes, they move up a level, otherwise they continue to work on their material some more. They may not be interested in performing at all and just do it because they have a taste or love for it—the literal meaning of the word "amateur". They may be doing it as a hobby—a regular activity they do in their spare or leisure time for pleasure and relaxation. Once they leave their home and try to earn money by performing, they may lose some of those pure feelings about music.

Performing locally gives the musician a chance to be heard. Once they are paid, they become members of the unofficial federation of semi-pro musicians, who perform for money but not as a full-time occupation. Most people at this stage have a "day job" to pay their bills and perform at night after work and on weekends. Getting commercial radio play at this level is not possible, but they may get some exposure on a local college or public station. Podcasters are often looking for free music and can get your music heard in places near and far. A music aggregator like CD Baby will put your tracks on Spotify, allowing you to reach more of your fans where they already are. You may want to stream your shows using Facebook Live so that people who can't come out can catch your act, or watch it at a later time. Some artists like Justin Bieber and Jacob Collier were discovered on YouTube.

After a musician has developed their act and established a local following, they may try to approach in indie label to get a record made, or save up the money to do it themselves. Whichever way they get the record done, the next level, as was outlined in Chapter 8, is reached by having radio-ready songs and growing a following and a track record of successful regional gigs and CD sales. The more a band can do themselves, the more interest an indie or major label will have in them. For bands who want to go on, everything they've done so far has been leading up to a shot at getting signed with a major label.

Most civilians wouldn't recognize musicians as being part of the music business until they are on national tours with the support of management and a label. The three major labels are the only ones with the organization, financial resources, and connections to get a song played on commercial radio, and media exposure for their artists. It's only at this point that the group has entered the major leagues. All their development work in their home town and surround region was farm club and minor league action in comparison. The label gives the band a limited amount of time to have the public catch on. If the album's single doesn't become a hit, the band will be dropped and sent home. If they are a hit on the national stage, they may be sent abroad to see if they connect with fans in other countries. However high a band goes, their career will probably be fairly short lived, as the public's tastes are constantly changing, and there is always a steady stream of new acts waiting in the wings to take their place.

© Barbara Willey. Reprinted by permission.

The glamorous music industry.

Music is a glamour industry, meaning that many people are attracted to it by the fantasy of its exciting image. Because they have the dream of hitting the big time someday, many are willing to play for free, or even to pay to play in order to get into the pipeline. Many are mistakenly operating on some level with a case of association fallacy. This happens because the musician overestimates their abilities and has made mistakes in reasoning. The transitive law "If A is equal to B, and B is equal to C, then A is equal to C" holds true in some, but not all cases, and can result in an overestimation of the odds of becoming famous. For example, for many years I myself suffered from a case of delusional honor by association expressed in this faulty logic:

1. I can dance as well as Michael Jackson (A = B)
2. Michael Jackson is a star (B = C)
3. I will be a star (A = C)

While it *may* be true that in my prime I could dance as well as Michael Jackson (in hindsight, I'm not so sure anymore), and Michael Jackson *was* the King of Pop, it was a logical error to conclude that I would therefore become as famous as him just because we had a level of skill in common. There are so many other factors besides raw talent, such as drive and work ethic, one's community, connections, and luck, not to mention which of the infinite parallel universes your particular instance happens to be in. I worry about this often when I meet young producers who create beats with tools like FL Studio hoping that they are going to win Grammys, have multiple homes, cars, and a beautiful entourage. The beats usually sound OK, as they should since they are based on well-recorded pre-fab ingredients. The problem is that just because your beats sound like those on records ($B = C$) doesn't mean that you are going to have hit records, in the same way you're never going to see me on a Pepsi ad or playing at the half time show at the Superbowl ($A \neq C$). There are a lot of people with the same dream, and only a miniscule number are ever going to get through the eye of the needle and end up making serious money. I suspect that you have a better chance of going from success on your middle school basketball team to being drafted by the NBA. It's hard to predict success in music since there aren't the obvious characteristics of height and speed to use as indicators. It's a little easier to judge instrumentalists than producers since they create each note one-by-one themselves instead of using sampled sounds and loops.

There are many reasons to perform. Some people have something they want to communicate, and choose the songs that resonate, and focus on crafting and delivering their message. Some want to be entertainers and help people have a good time, and concentrate on reading a crowd, going with the flow, and leading them on a journey. Other people are in it to get attention or their egos stroked. Some are looking for dates, or to party. What interested me most about it was being in the middle of the sound, the opportunity to interact with the other musicians, and the challenge of figuring out of how my part fit with theirs. At some point, every musician has to decide which way they want to go:

> "There are three kinds of artists. The first kind are the ones who hurt to do what they do. It hurts to write. There's pain involved. There's experience and there's blood. The second kind of artist imitates the ones in pain. The third kind just does what someone tells them to do: 'Learn this step. Wear this wig. Shake your ass. Watch yourself.' The first kind of artist is more popular than the amount of money that they receive. The second kind are usually the rich ones. The third kind gets dropped from the label 'cause there's millions of them walking around."—Erykah Badu, in *Before the Music Dies*

It's said that music makes the world go round. That is true in a poetic sense, but in reality, it's a luxury and is not required for survival. To my knowledge, no one has ever pounded on a composer's door in the middle of the night, pleading to them to help their child who was badly stuck on finishing the composition of their latest song, unable to find the right chord to lead off the bridge with. The difference between music and medicine, which is reflected in the relative salaries between the professions, is that most parents would go to any expense to hire a doctor if their child had been injured and needed surgery. On the other hand, making music is a noble calling, since once the doctor has stitched you back up and sent you home there isn't much that they can do to make life beautiful and worth living.

The Importance of Being Remarkable

Seth Godin is a marketing expert, and in one of his talks he described the "TV/Industrial Complex"—an informal partnership that found success from the 1960s up until recent times through placing ads put on TV to advertise a product, which predictably would then cause an increase in sales, the profits from which could be

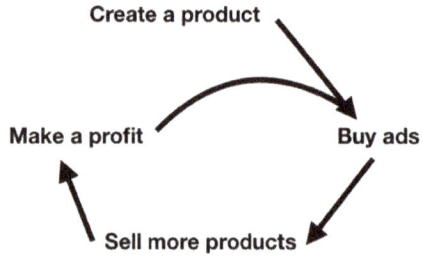

The advertising cycle of the TV/Industrial Complex

used to buy more ads and grow the business further. For many years, network TV was supported by ads that developed brand loyalty.

In his best-seller *Purple Cow*, Godin argues that it is no longer possible to sell mediocre products just by piling on the advertising. Tom Friedman says the same kind of thing about globalization—that you can't get by anymore by making average products for average people. Audiences are jaded and don't pay attention to the ads that they are inundated with. Godin says that if you were traveling through the country and passed some beautiful cows freshly showered, sanitized, backlit, and arranged in a lovely setting of rolling hills and freshly painted barns, you might point them out to your companion as you passed the first group, but after a few hours of seeing the same quality of animals in herds on both sides of the road you would no longer pay any attention. Should you at some point see a *purple* cow, however, you would surely sit up and take notice, and would probably even stop to snap a selfie with her to post on Instagram or a video clip for Vine. You've got to make remarkable products, something that people will literally feel an irresistible urge to remark to others about.

Godin says that the average person is too busy and uninterested to pay attention to advertising. The only people that you have a hope of reaching even with a remarkable product are the early adopters. They are alert and curious, and always on the lookout for the new thing that will give them an edge in their business or cool status among their friends. If they like it, they will tell the majority about it— people who may pay attention to them as they are identifiable as trendsetters.

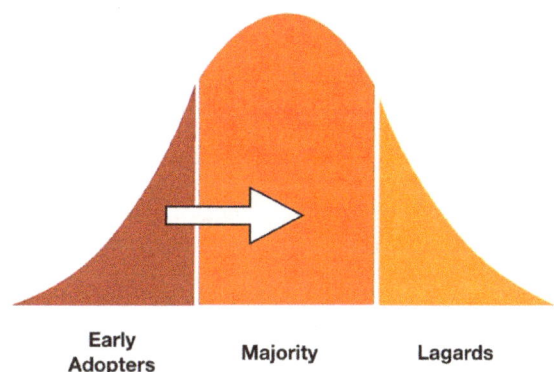

Early Adopters   Majority   Lagards

The early adopters are the best people to target in marketing campaigns. If they like your product or service they will spread the word to the majority, who listens to them more than they do to you, like they listen to a friend's recommendation to see a film more than to a professional reviewer.

Godin also says not to wait until a product is finished to start marketing it. In order to make a remarkable product he recommends starting on the marketing from the beginning. If you wait to try to find out what is unique and worth advertising until after it is finished, there may not be anything of interest there. Don't miss the opportunity to bake greatness into something from the beginning of the design. Write the outline of a press release for it as part of the initial planning process, and don't commit to moving forward until you have something solid that people will take notice of.

The Experience Economy

In his book *Future Shock* (1971), Alvin Toffler predicted a future with an experiential economy in which people would be willing to spend a big percentage of their income on in order to have to have amazing experiences. The term "experience economy" was first used in an article by Joseph Pine and James Gilmore in 1998 to describe an

Musicians can orchestrate memorable events for their customers.

approaching wave of economic change, and pointed to current examples in industry like Disneyland that aim to be the happiest place on earth. The authors categorized economic offerings into five categories:

1. A commodity business with undifferentiated products. Muzak is an example of this in the music field. Every song has the same mundane arrangement. The closer cover bands come to playing the hits as they were played by the artists who made them famous, the more nonmusical things they must feature in their show in order to be remembered.

2. A goods business with distinctive things. The challenge for musicians is to be unique, but even when they achieve that, consumers still want their recordings to be free.

3. A service business charges for activities they perform. Consumers and businesses are willing to pay someone else to do things more efficiently and effectively, and with better quality. Musicians are hired to teach someone to play an instrument or to provide entertainment when employers don't have the time or necessary skills. DJs sometimes get work over bands because they can reproduce the exact sound of records and at a lower cost.

4. An experience business. In 2010, Cornell psychology professors Gravis Carter and Thomas Gilovich demonstrated that people become happier from buying experiences than goods, and that *doing* something makes you happier than *having* it. Whereas possessions can be broken, lost, or stolen, the sensations of experiences take place within the buyer, and their value lingers in memory. The value of the memory becomes the product. Pine and Gilmore recommend one way of customizing products is to differentiate one from another, which is especially effective if it can be done in front of the customer, or better yet, with their participation. An example of this could be an autographed poster or CD in which the musician adds the customer's name and allows them to be photographed together during the signing. Some musicians offer to compose a song for a client. Individualized products such as these are more easily remembered. The communication skills of merch sales people at shows and their knowledge of the band and music influences the customer's experience, and any exchange provides an opportunity to get to know the customer better and to learn what is important to them.

     Watching sports can be a powerful experience. The audience can project themselves on the athletes, and feel happy when they win. Watching performers is another activity with a visual element, and even if you can't relate to what a virtuoso is doing, it can still be interesting to watch the performance unfold over time. Some restaurants have exposed parts of their kitchen to diners in order to let them see what's going on. Bartenders and sushi chefs have the closest contact with customers as they are in such close proximity and can carry on a conversation with the customers.

Carter and Gilmore caution that advertising an experience is risky, as it can create a suspicious atmosphere. The experience must be authentic, and needs to be so engaging that potential customers cannot resist giving their attention to it, after which they may become buyers. Having a TV monitor outside showing a good time going on inside can serve to increase the number of people who decide to come in. The value of attending a show is the experience of the music and being surrounded by other people. Charging a cover charge or selling a ticket to a concert is the most common way to monetize it.

A company should try to understand all the aspects of the customer's experience and make sure that each is completely satisfied in order to maximize long-term success. One way to develop brand loyalty is by having a series of positive experiences, which leads to word-of-mouth advertising. For this reason, movie studios take lower risks when they produce sequels of popular movies.

5. The highest category in the new economy is a transformation business, which may collect money from "guests" rather than "customers" who receive benefit from spending time at the location, like a spa. V.I.P. packages are an intense form of experience and could be transformational. Universities refer to their customers as "students" and focus on the "college experience" in their marketing materials. Many students pick a college based on their expectations for campus life more than the reputation of the faculty.

Bands can tap into the experience economy by orchestrating memorable events for their audience. Merch is an important profit center, but its real value may be as memorabilia functioning as a memory aid. Bands like the Grateful Dead and festivals like SXSW and Lollapalooza created brands that have to do as much with the experience of being there as the music that is presented.

Some artists offer V.I.P. concert packages for superfans, such as this offering from Britney Spears:

- Early entry to the venue if desired
- A personal escort using a dedicated entrance to bypass the line for the general public
- Backstage access
- A meet & greet with Britney including a photo op
- A chance to appear onstage with Britney
- A seat in the first row of reserved seating
- An autographed special edition poster
- A souvenir goodie bag

If you're a superfan (or super parent) you might consider paying hundreds, if not thousands of dollars for the once-in-a-lifetime experience of interacting with an idol—a greatly loved and admired hero or heroine.

Being an Entrepreneur

There's a lot of interest in entrepreneurialism these days. As big companies shuffle their divisions or shut down, and with the acceleration in change in society and the economy, it's unlikely that people are going to learn everything they need in school and run off that knowledge for 30 years at the same company, get honored at a party, and retire to enjoy their pension. If you go to college, it's been predicted that 5 years after you graduate half of what you learned will no longer be true or will be obsolete.

"Entrepreneurial learning" sounds great to politicians who are eager to find shortcuts to economic growth, but it isn't necessarily about developing entrepreneurs—though people who intend to start their own business would certainly benefit from it. Instead, it is about developing a portfolio of skills and applying them in order to build a life. Figure out what you're good at, and then what you can do with it. The goal of entrepreneurial learning is for the student to become a creative problem-solver and to develop transferable skills. It helps if you can hone your communication, leadership, and persuasion skills and become a good collaborator.

Students are asked to take a risk, jump in, and figure out how to do things along the way. It can be uncomfortable after years in public school, where you were taught that failure was the worst possible outcome and something that should be avoided at all costs. After years of taking standardized tests and filling out worksheets, students adapt to being passive, and just try to figure out what the teacher wants of them and what the minimum effort is needed to pass the class. Jeff Bezos, the founder and CEO of Amazon says that failure and invention are "inseparable twins" and that "those who fail the most often win", and then pivot and try something new, taking advantage of what they learned.

An entrepreneur is a self-directed person who is willing to take a risk and show initiative, instead of being passive and waiting to be told what to do. One of the key activities of an entrepreneur is opportunity recognition. Develop your critical thinking skills and become a problem solver. You can do this at any level in an organization, whether you are an unpaid intern or the owner of the company.

There are two conditions of life that conflict with each other every day:

1. People resist change. It is more comfortable to go along with the way things are (status quo). It takes effort, and for some people worst of all—thinking—to adapt.

2. The world is constantly changing. It has changed more than you realize from the last time you looked at it.

It's natural to look for and capitalize on opportunities.

An entrepreneur relishes change, since it creates new opportunities where they can insert themselves, like a seed that takes root in a crack in the cement and over time grows into a bush or tree. One way to maintain the right mindset, make the day more interesting, and keep you on your toes is to start off the morning reminding yourself that it's likely that there will be unexpected changes that day, and to be ready to use them as opportunities to develop your ability to improvise and adapt. Be flexible and act quickly to respond to new information, obstacles, and setbacks.

I wish I had a nickel for every time I've heard the advice to "follow your passion." I used to say that, too, until I read Cal Newport's book called *So Good They Can't Ignore You: Why Skills Trump Passion in the Quest for Work You Love*. He says that following your passion is a bad idea, that too many people become disillusioned when they don't love their first assignment, take that as proof that they aren't cut out for that line of work, and then switch to something new that they think better fits with their desires. Newport recommends buckling down instead and developing the skills and experience necessary to be given more autonomy on the job. That leads to success, and ultimately makes people more satisfied with their work.

We are asked from an early age what job we would like to do when we grow up and are shown pictures of some of the best-known options, such as fireman, doctor, baker, soldier, Hey, now that I think of it, how come there's rarely a picture of a guitar player or singer in there?

Kids, which job is for you?

Those sorts of images have a way of sticking in your mind, and many people gravitate towards a career on some level based on the costume they think they would look good in, and the surroundings they would wear it in. The star musicians that you see in photos are usually dressed nicely and in pleasant surrounds with smiling cohorts. It looks pretty good, but what are they actually *doing* and what skills are they using all day when the cameras are turned off?

Another approach to searching for one's life work is to find your calling. It may not be the profession you always imagined that you were destined for:

"Your calling is the thing that you can't not do. Everybody has a calling. You don't plan it. You can prepare for it and do the most to respond when the opportunities present themselves. Your calling is not just one thing, it's many things. It's your body of work and the accumulation of all the things you do, it's a portfolio. You've got skills, you've got gifts, you've got things you can do, and you've got burdens. You need to do something with it. Your portfolio is your curating those things you're good at, your passions, your skills, the things you can use to help other people. It doesn't have to be one thing, some big epiphany. You can take intentional actions that move you closer to your purpose, that thing that you do that adds value to the world and makes you come alive…It's not who you know, it's who you help that defines your trajectory to greatness." – Jeff Goins, (Episode #463 of "The Art of Charm" podcast)

One of the pressures when considering being an entrepreneur is worrying how you will support yourself, and your family if you have one, especially when you know that most businesses fail. A good option can be to start out as a 10% entrepreneur, investing part of your time and resources in your own side project, while holding down a day job that pays the bills. Ideally what you do during the daytime can also be rewarding, while your side project adds to your experience and increases your value to your employer. If you become successful as an entrepreneur, you can later expand your operation, or even quit your day job to dedicate yourself to it fulltime.

Grit, self-control, and communication skills are vital for success for everyone, and particularly so for entrepreneurs. Another word for grit is perseverance—not giving up on what's important despite the difficulties and delays that may arise. Self-control is the ability to monitor yourself and keep your emotions from interfering. It helps to avoid distractions, like constantly checking social media, so that you can get the work done that is needed to achieve your goals.

It is important to be aware of your thoughts, feelings, and behavior in order to recognize where your weaknesses are, and where you need to develop. Read Clara Dweck's book *Mindset* if you want to find out how people can change more than they might think. She says that you shouldn't conclude that you're not good at something just because it doesn't come easily.

Musicians, like most other people in the 21st century, are going to benefit from being entrepreneurial. People are increasingly going to be working for themselves and deciding each day where their time and effort will best be spent.

Today is the first day for the rest of your life. Bon voyage!

Review and Preview

In this chapter, we traced some of the key technological developments that have changed modern life, including the music and entertainment industry.

As profits declined from record sales, the competition for record deals increased along with the pressure to have instant hits. Only a tiny fraction of artists ever achieve stardom, but the glamour of the business attracts many musicians who are willing to put up with difficult conditions and uncertain futures in order to have a chance at someday becoming famous. There are, however, many opportunities to develop your art and participate in the culture if you are realistic, practical, and understand how the business works. The faster you rise, the faster you may fall. People who want to have long and steady careers may find more satisfaction running their business themselves, as semi-pros playing on a local and regional level with a day job to pay the bills.

Whatever level you are on, it's important to offer your customers remarkable products, services, and experiences.

For Further Investigation

1. Make a list of the shows you have seen, and then add to it details about what made each one memorable. What sticks in your memory more—visuals, sounds, smells, emotions? Which of the things you remember were under the performers' control, like their costumes, backdrop, lights, and use of video, and which happened randomly in the environment and the audience members? The events you have forgotten most likely lacked something special. How much did it have to do with the people that you attended the show with? Did you bring back any souvenirs?

2. We are all becoming addicted to being addicted, to the little burst of dopamine that drips when we check our devices and get a little lift from the control we exert and electronic feedback. Try leaving your phone off for a day. What did you notice? How did you deal with the urge to check your messages? If you could spend some time alone with your thoughts, what did you come up with? Try journaling with the time you save. In what way was your day better and worse? If you want to learn more, set aside a "digital Sabbath" one day each week where you leave your electronics off and connect with physical objects, other activities, and human beings. When you return to your phone, notice how you are serving it rather than the other way around.

3. Do some research about global opportunities related to your profession. Is there an opportunity to connect with people in another city, state, or country?

4. Read Jeff Goins *Purple Cow*. It's short, and may give you some ideas for something you could do to be remarkable.

5. Read Sally Hogshead, *Fascinate: How to Make Your Brand Impossible to Resist.* Take her free online quiz to learn what about how other people perceive you, and what they find fascinating.

Do It Yourself

1. Find a way to send more fans home with a souvenir that can stimulate their memory of your show. Make each performance a special event, and in the planning, make a plan for something that will make it a memorable experience.

2. Make a video of your next show. Play it back and look for elements that you think could have made the experience more memorable for the audience. Did the audience react more at some point? What could you do the next time to make it unforgettable?

3. Make your next project be something remarkable. What could you do that would be so interesting that people who find out about it will feel an irresistible urge to tell others about it on your behalf? Sounds difficult? Get used to it, and welcome to the new economy! We are done making average products for average people. Get on board, or resign yourself to staying home and watching daytime TV.

4. Do some brainstorming about opportunities that you could exploit using your portfolio of skills. Pick two or three that seem most promising to mull over, then select the most auspicious one and tackle it.

5. Do you feel like you don't have enough time to do everything you need to get done? One of the biggest sucks on your time is probably your cell phone. Set a limit for the amount of time you're going to let it use you per day. Set aside some blocks of time in which you get rid of all distractions, focus, and get the most important business done. One system is called the Pomodoro Technique, where you do nothing but one task for blocks of 25 minutes, with short breaks in between. The most important resource you have is time. Get a grip on how you are spending your 168 hours per week. You can use the time that you reclaim to start and maintain a new 10% entrepreneurial venture, which could change your life.

6. Throughout the day be on your toes to see where your skills and talents can be used to make things better. Keep your shoelaces tight and the weight balanced between your feet so that you can leap in any direction when a need arises. Keep a record for a week of how you have added value to situations. Reviewing it to see if you notice a pattern can help you start to identify your calling. Over time and with repetition, this practice will also create actual new physical pathways in your brain that get faster and stronger in looking for and capitalizing on opportunities. It's said that you can't tell Einstein's brain from a barbarian's by examining them physically, but you can tell the difference between a musician's brain and a civilian's because of the extra connections between the hemispheres that grow due to the communication between the various parts of the brain involved with time, listening, memory, movement, monitoring, emotions, etc. that are activated while playing an instrument. If you put in the time and effort, the structure of your brain will actually change physically and become more complex and powerful.

7. Read Gabrielle Oettingen's book *Rethinking Positive Thinking*. Her research shows that imagining the benefits of achieving your goals actually lowers the chances of achieving them. She says that it's not until you go on to make plans for getting around the obstacles that may arise in your environment and in yourself that your odds actually improve. Try out her free app for the WOOP technique (W-ish, O-utcome, O-bstacle, P-lan) for one of your goals and see if you notice any benefit.

8. Ask an entrepreneur if you can shadow them for a day. Offer to keep track of what they do and to deliver a detailed report of how they spent their time and which communication channels they used. People who might be interested in having this information but don't want to take the time to keep the records themselves might see your visit as offering some value to trade off the inconvenience of having you around.

9. What is your calling? Who can you help? Go help them!

Vocabulary Review

Auspicious—something that shows signs of pointing to success and/or a happy outcome.
Day job—employment that musicians maintain while they play music on the side on nights and weekends.
Digitization—converting analog materials like audio recordings, books, and films into a binary form (i.e., strings of 0s and 1s) that can then be easily and accurately stored in memory, copied, and transmitted over the Internet.

Entrepreneur—someone who is willing to take a risk and initiate action; or to plan, organize, and exploit an opportunity which may result in an innovation or improvement of a product or service.

Experience Economy—an economic model in which the consumer pays for an experience rather than a product or service.

Globalization—an integration of markets, information, and communication systems that is shrinking the world, and enabling each person to reach around it faster, farther, deeper, and more cheaply than ever before.

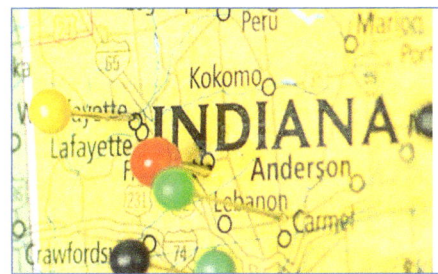

Music and Entertainment in the Midwest

Topics

Main Ideas

- Some Midwest musicians play in an "Americana" style.
- Musicians in the Midwest have seen firsthand the collapse of manufacturing in the United States, and may be a step ahead of their cousins on the East and West coasts in preparing for a DIY future.
- The Midwest is good place for a band to develop its act. There are more cities in close proximity to each other, and the cost of living is lower.
- Opportunities in Indiana include careers in live sound, manufacturing, and music product sales.

See the book's companion website for supplemental information, updates, and links: http://willshare.com/mmb

Introduction

The "Midwest" in this book is defined as the states of Minnesota, Iowa, Missouri, Wisconsin, Illinois, Michigan, Indiana, Ohio, and Ontario. The reason for this idiosyncratic grouping is that the author lives in Indiana, and these are the states that we can reach more reasonably in a day. Another way to look at the grouping is as a Great Lakes and Mississippi River collection. I included Toronto because of its status as the world's most diverse city, in an effort to balance Indiana's homogeneity.

One of the defining features of the Midwest is that it is distant from the oceans. I grew up in the San Francisco bay area and went to graduate school in San Diego. I later worked in Argentina, Brazil, upstate New York, and Southwest Louisiana. I love the West Coast but couldn't afford to return there due to the high cost of living. The challenge for us music producers in central Indiana is that we're off the beaten track for professional bands that want to record an album.

In this chapter, we will look at some distinctive characteristics of the music industry in the Midwest, and the special opportunities for musicians who want to have careers here instead of moving to a major market.

Americana and the Heartland

In 1995, San Francisco DJ Rob Bleetstein coined the term "Americana" to describe a new radio format to suit listeners who did not fit in straight country or folk genres. The playlists he developed for this category were broader than most, and included such artists as Alison Krauss, The Band, Bonnie Raitt, Bruce Hornsby, Bruce Springsteen, Calexico, Danny O'Keefe, David Lindley, Doc Watson, Grateful Dead, John Fogerty, John Mellencamp, Leon Russell, Levon Helm, Linda Ronstadt, Loretta Lynn, Lucinda Williams, Lyle Lovett, Mary Chapin Carpenter, Mavis Staples, Mumford & Sons, Neil Young, Pete Seeger, Porter Wagoner, Robert Plant, Rosanne Cash, Ry Cooder, Tom Petty and the Heartbreakers, The Weavers, and Willie Nelson. The American Music Association adopted the new genre, describing it as "contemporary music that incorporates elements of various American roots music styles, including country, roots-rock, folk, bluegrass, R&B and blues, resulting in a distinctive roots-oriented sound that lives a world apart from the pure forms of the genres upon which it may draw. While acoustic instruments are often present and vital, Americana also often uses a full electric band."

Similar to the Midwest, America's "heartland" is described as not reaching the coasts, and is based on cultural ideas such as the value of hard work, simplicity, and honesty. It is associated with small towns, a rural heritage, and family-owned farms. At a Live Aid concert Bob Dylan (from Minnesota) mentioned that he wished that some of the money raised there could be used to help American farmers who were in danger of going bankrupt due to mortgage debt. In 1982, John Mellencamp (from Indiana), Willie Nelson (from Texas), and Neil Young (Toronto, Ontario), decided to take up that challenge and launched the Farm Aid festival in Champaign, Illinois. They then brought family farmers to testify before Congress, which led to the Agricultural Credit Act of 1987 intended to save farms from foreclosure.

Some Midwest artists such as Pokey LaFarge are continuing to produce and perform music in this genre, which resonates with a wide spectrum of listeners, who find it refreshing in an age of slick, over-produced pop music.

The Canary in the Rusted Cage

There are signs for hope as long as musicians keep playing music.

In the 20th century, miners began to use canaries as early-warning systems for toxic gases. Today it is artists who serve as indicators of the health of a cultural economy. The "Rust Belt" is the region of the United States from the Great Lakes region to the Upper Midwest, roughly the area that *Midwest Music Business* focuses on. The term refers to the decline of population and urban decay caused by the de-industrialization of an area that was once a powerful manufacturing center. Ball State University is in Muncie, Indiana. The Ball brothers who contributed financially to the school's development grew their wealth from manufacturing glass jars and lids. They had been attracted to the area in the 1880s for its supply of natural gas, which began to be depleted around 1910. In the 1960s, an exodus began as iron and steel mills, automobile manufacturing, and auto parts operations closed or moved elsewhere. From 2001 to 2011, Muncie lost thousands of jobs as it transitioned from a blue collar workforce to a white-collar service economy involved with health care, education, and retail. The retail sector will be the next to be squeezed as companies such as Walmart and Amazon draw customers away from smaller stores and malls. Many of the hospital and university employees who work in town choose to live in the more up-to-date suburbs of Indianapolis that offer more amenities and opportunities for entertainment.

People living on the West, South, and East coasts do not see as many daily reminders of closed factories and abandoned houses as we do in the Midwest, and have not yet had to deal as much with the early warning signs of changes in the economy as we enter a postindustrial era. Because of this, it is possible that the DIY musician scene has a head start in the region as Midwest artists adjust to 21st century music scene, with lower record sales and fewer record contracts, in an industry that is increasingly dominated by a small number of artists promoted by the three major record labels. As we saw in the last chapter, we are moving from a commodity (farming) and services (performing) economy to one based on experiences, and finally to transformations. T.J Müller says in his interview (found on the book's companion website) that engaging an audience with live music that connects with a city's history is more important to him than stardom, and that teaching and coaching amateurs is the way to nurture the community that will, in the long run, sustain the culture.

As we move into a postindustrial society, the purpose of music may be more about education, participation, and transformation than writing hit songs to soothe the masses and selling diversions and drinks at the neighborhood bar. The Midwest has a strong folk music tradition, and the repertoire drawing on its cultural reserves is accessible on a variety of levels to anyone who wants to join in. Like Pete Seegar said, "Participation—that's what's gonna save the human race."

The Midwest Music Scene

The Midwest offers musicians and audiences some unique opportunities. We're generally nice people, helpful, and not so jaded as some fans in other states. The cost of living is lower—in Muncie they'll *give* you a house if you'll fix it up, and the lot next door if you'll maintain it. As Ariel Hyatt says (see her interview on the book's website) that it's a lot more affordable for bands to live in the Midwest than in major markets such as Los Angeles and New York City.

Gas prices are lower, making it more affordable for both musicians and fans to drive from one show to another. The young people that you want to bring to your shows are more likely to go to smaller venues with less expensive tickets. One of the common bits of advice for touring bands is to avoid taking days off, as income stops while expenses go on. As T.J. Müller says, it's a lot cheaper to travel to surrounding mid-sized markets in the Midwest due to closer proximity of cities as compared with the those in the South and west of the Mississippi river. The shorter driving distance between gigs doesn't just limit the number of gallons of gas you have to buy, it also reduces wear and tear on vehicles and the musicians they transport, and reduces the risk of falling asleep at the wheel while driving at night.

Frank Sinatra extolled the virtues of New York City as a proving ground in the song "New York, New York" when he sang "If I can make it here I'll make it anywhere." That sets the bar very high, due to the competition and the cost of food and lodging in The Big Apple. There is less financial pressure in the Midwest, and a band has more time to hone their craft. Because audiences in the Midwest are in some ways "average" they are representative of typical music-lovers and provide a laboratory where bands can test themselves in a different and more affordable manner: "If you can make it here you'll make it everywhere."

What follows are some sketches of the music scene in Midwest cities that each represent a different type of market:

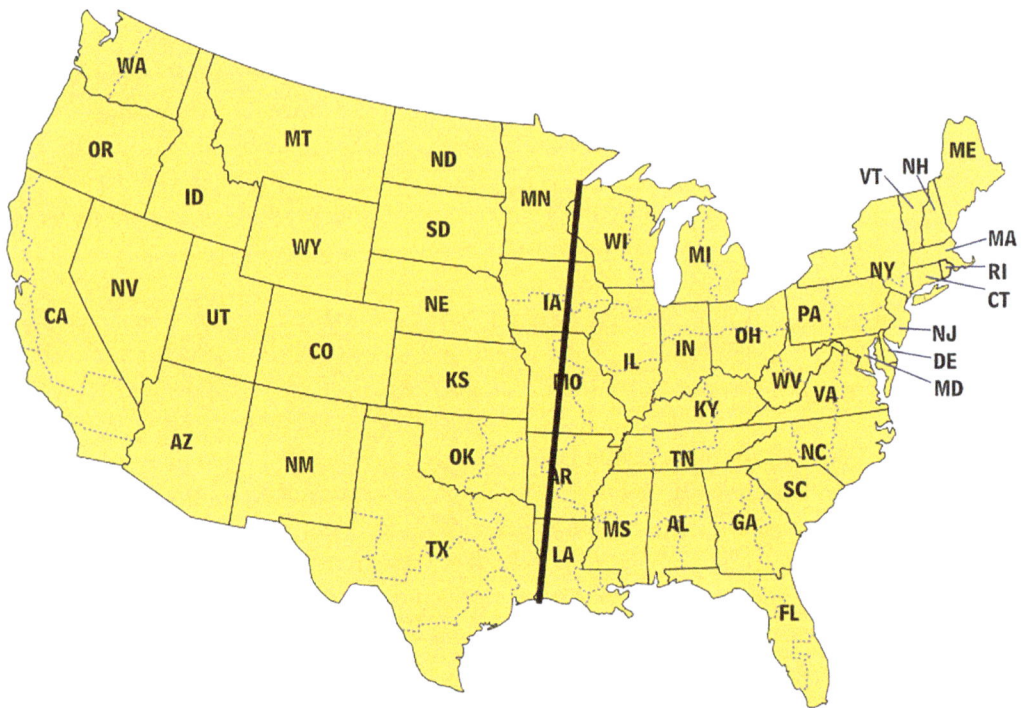

Most big cities in the United States are to the right of the line on this map.

Chicago, IL—3rd largest city in the United States, the Midwest's regional megopolis

The Jay Pritzker Pavilion serves as the centerpiece for Chicago's Millennium Park. Rather than having a large sound system in front of the audience which has to be turned up to dangerous volume levels to reach those seated in the back, the Pavilion's sound system is the first of its kind—distributing sound via an overhead trellis with 52 loudspeakers that envelop the audience and produce a clear sound at comfortable listening levels for all.

In 1915, poor black workers began moving to Northern cities in order to find work. They brought the blues and jazz with them in what became known as the "Great Migration". By 1960, five million migrants had headed to the large industrial centers of Detroit, Pittsburgh, New York, and especially to Chicago.

As a result, distinct versions of the blues, Dixieland, boogie-woogie, and jazz developed in Chicago. Blues and jazz are still very much alive in venues, and the process of evolution has continued in other genres such as soul, rock, house music, and hip-hop. As Timothy Hays points out (see his interview on the book's website) Chicago also has a top-level classical music scene centered around the world-renowned Chicago Symphony Orchestra and Lyric Opera.

There are hundreds of venues to choose from in the city. Here are a few examples:

Cobra Lounge—A little bar attached to a brewery. Regional underground and emerging music.

Green Mill Cocktail Lounge—The city's oldest continuously-running jazz club, still connected to the left-over tunnels Al Capone used for illicit alcohol deliveries during Prohibition.

The Hideout—Surrounded by factories. Punk rock, alt-country, indie rock.

Honky Tonk BBQ—variations on country and Americana: Western Swing, Honky Tonk, Rockabilly, Bluegrass, Blues, Old Time, Soul, and occasionally new age indie and rock.

House of Blues—Part of the national chain. Blues, R&B, gospel, jazz, roots rock & roll seven nights a week.

Jazz Showcase—A favorite jazz spot.

Martyrs'—A musical oasis dedicated to the musicians who give their life to their art.

Schubas Tavern—A historic landmark, elegant, renovated saloon, with all styles of music. See the book's companion website for a link to contact info for all the different members of their production staff.

Subterranean—Two floors, all styles, live entertainment and DJs, open mic night.

Chicago resident artists have included Muddy Waters, Junior Well, Howlin' Wolf, Nat King Cole, Benny Goodman, Elmore James, Paul Butterfield, and James Cotton, King Oliver, Jelly Roll Morton, Louis Armstrong, Lou Rawls.

Bands like Styx, REO Speedwagon, Cheap Trick, Chicago Transit Authority, Smashing Pumpkins.

Born there: Sam Cooke, Lou Rawls, Curtis Mayfield, Alice Cooper, Chaka Khan, Jennifer Hudson, and Chance the Rapper.

Fort Wayne, Indiana—Home of music retail giant Sweetwater Sound, Inc.

The pavilion at Sweetwater Sound, Inc. can be used for community presentations, or for gatherings of its growing number of employees.

Fort Wayne is not a big tourist center like Chicago, but it is nevertheless developing in interesting ways. Indianapolis has Indiana's bigger live music scene, but Fort Wayne has the second highest concentration of studios outside of Nashville, in large part because of Sweetwater's employees, who make good money and can afford to buy their own homes and trick out their own project studios. They are also music lovers and practitioners, and have significantly increased the gene pool for live sound and performance in the area.

Sweetwater is the Google of music stores, with a circular slide to get from the second story to the ground floor. They are the third-largest music store in the United States and are growing at a rate of 20% a year. Most sales are done over the phone. The "Sweetwater Difference" of doing the right thing, satisfying customers, and following up with after-sale support is the key to their success. Each June they present Gear Fest, the largest music trade show in the United States open to the public.

Fort Wayne has many restaurants and a growing jazz, jazz-rock, and blues scene, which can be heard in venues such as:

Auer Center for Arts and Culture—includes music as part of the arts and culture.

The Brass Rail—A dive bar with a lot of character. Encompasses the entire spectrum and premier shows on the weekend for a 20s–30s crowd.

Calhoun Soups Salads and Spirits (CS3)—Live concert and comedy venue, restaurant and bar.

Club Soda—food and drink with jazz, soul, and blues acts.

The Clyde Theatre—brings the world's top touring talent to a beautifully renovated space, powered by Sweetwater (read Rick Kinney's interview on the book's companion website).

Embassy Theater—A converted movie and vaudeville theater listed in the National Register of Historic Places. Broadway touring shows, all types of concerts, educational programming.

Foellinger Theatre—A concert venue with big-name acts.

The Hub Entertainment Center—Located in a strip mall. Comedy, music concerts, dance.

Nick's Martini & Wine Bar—food and drinks, live music most weekends.

The Phoenix—A smaller venue with a chill atmosphere. Jazz and food.

Piere's Entertainment—Draws a younger clientele. Five rooms, including one for dancing.

Skeletunes Lounge—Posters and pictures everywhere along the walls and ceilings. Punk and heavy rock.

Allen County War Memorial Coliseum—Arena with big shows.

Madison, Wisconsin—The upper Midwest's progressive cultural hub

Powerman 5000 performing at the Taste of Madison festival.

With a population of 246,000, Madison is college boom town with the feel of the old country of rural Wisconsin now fueled by 21st century hipsters. The city has a reputation for diversity and being liberal and open-minded.

The music scene has a small-town feel but still offers an eclectic array of styles and national talent. Many of the musicians, especially those from the punk/rock community, connect their music with political causes.

Madison's vibrant musical life has ranked second in polls behind Austin, TX in the ratio of rock shows-to-residents. Audiences enjoy the relatively-affordable ticket prices. Livibility.com rates the city 8th in their list of best music scenes outside of Nashville, New York City, and Los Angeles.

In addition to venues, there are a lot of record labels, distributors, recording studios, and music publishers for the size of the city, following behind Nashville, Los Angeles, New York City, and the Oxnard/Thousand Oaks area of Southern California. Madison's dynamic music scene is reflected in the number of record stores the city supports: Strictly Discs, B-Side Records, Ear Wax Records, MadCity Music Exchange, Strictly Discs, The Exclusive Company, Resale Records, Jiggy Jamz Records and CDs, and Sugar Shack Records. Venues include:

> The Frequency—Unpretentious, tiny music oasis with local, regional, national, and international acts seven nights a week.
>
> High Noon Saloon—Rock, alternative, metal, indie, alt-country, pop, punk, bluegrass, folk, jam, hip hop, world music, etc., seven nights a week.
>
> Liquid Nightclub—Electronic dance music.
>
> The Majestic Theatre—Wisconsin's oldest theatre, with a mission to make Madison a more expressive and fulfilled cultural center. Comedy, music, 80s and 90s theme parties, movies, burlesque.
>
> Native musicians: Clyde Stubblefield, Butch Vig.

Detroit, MI—Post-apocalyptic car town, home of Motown and Techno

Detroit was founded in 1701 by Antoine de la Mothe Cadillac. The region grew initially due to its proximity to the Great Lakes and its associated fur trade with Native Americans. Following World War II the auto industry

The original home of Motown Records founded by Barry Gordy.

grew to become one of the largest in the United States, but jobs began to be lost to the suburbs after 1950 due to changes in advances in technology and automation, and the construction of a highway system that made it easier for workers to commute. Global competition in automobile manufacturing caused a collapse in the industry, and the city went bankrupt in 2013. By 2015, over 60% of the population had moved away. Local crime rates are among the highest in the United States and large areas of the city are in a state of severe urban decay.

The Motor City's styles of blues, gospel, jazz, soul, classic rock, electronica, and hip-hop changed American music. Detroit has also been cited as the birthplace of techno music. One of the highlights of the city's musical history was the growth of Motown Records in the 1960s and 1970s. Auto worker Berry Gordy built an empire with records by some of the world's most popular acts, including Marvin Gaye, Aretha Franklin, Smokey Robinson, The Temptations, Anita Baker, Stevie Wonder, Diana Ross & The Supremes, The Four Tops, and The Spinners.

Detroit's music scene declined along with its economy, but it has at least stabilized and is showing some signs of coming back. Some of the most interesting new music can be heard in house shows. Here are some of the top clubs:

The Raven Lounge—The oldest blues bar and social club in the city.

Cliff Bell's—Upscale, jazz and dancing.

The Fillmore Detroit—A renovated movie house that seats 3,000, whose beautiful grand lobby and three floors of seating have earned it a place in the National Register of Historic Places. Concerts and EDM dance shows.

Harpos Concert Theater—Heavy metal, rock, punk, and alternative acts.

The Magic Stick—A converted bowling alley, now with 10 pool tables and a dance floor. The basement motif serves as a backdrop for Detroit's growing garage, alt rock, and electronic scene.

PJ's Lager House—The bar was hidden behind a furniture store façade in the days of Prohibition. Since the punk revolution in the 1990s, it has become a hangout for rock bands.

Saint Andrews Hall—a legendary and iconic music venue and concert hall, which has hosted groups such as Eminem, Iggy Pop, Bob Dylan, Paul Simon, Tool, Nirvana, R.E.M., and the Red Hot Chili Peppers.

Home away from home: Detroit has provided residences to many famous jazz and pop musicians, including Duke Ellington, Elvin Jones, Yusef Lateef, Kenny Burrell, Ron Carter, Donald Byrd, Betty Carter. Madonna was born 35 miles outside of the city and attended the University of Michigan on a dance scholarship. Aretha Franklin was born in Memphis, Tennessee, but her family later moved to Detroit. Bands such as Ted Nugent, Alice Cooper, and Grand Funk Railroad got their start in the city.

Natives: Jack White, Eminem.

Minneapolis/St. Paul, MN—The Twin Cities' eclectic music scene

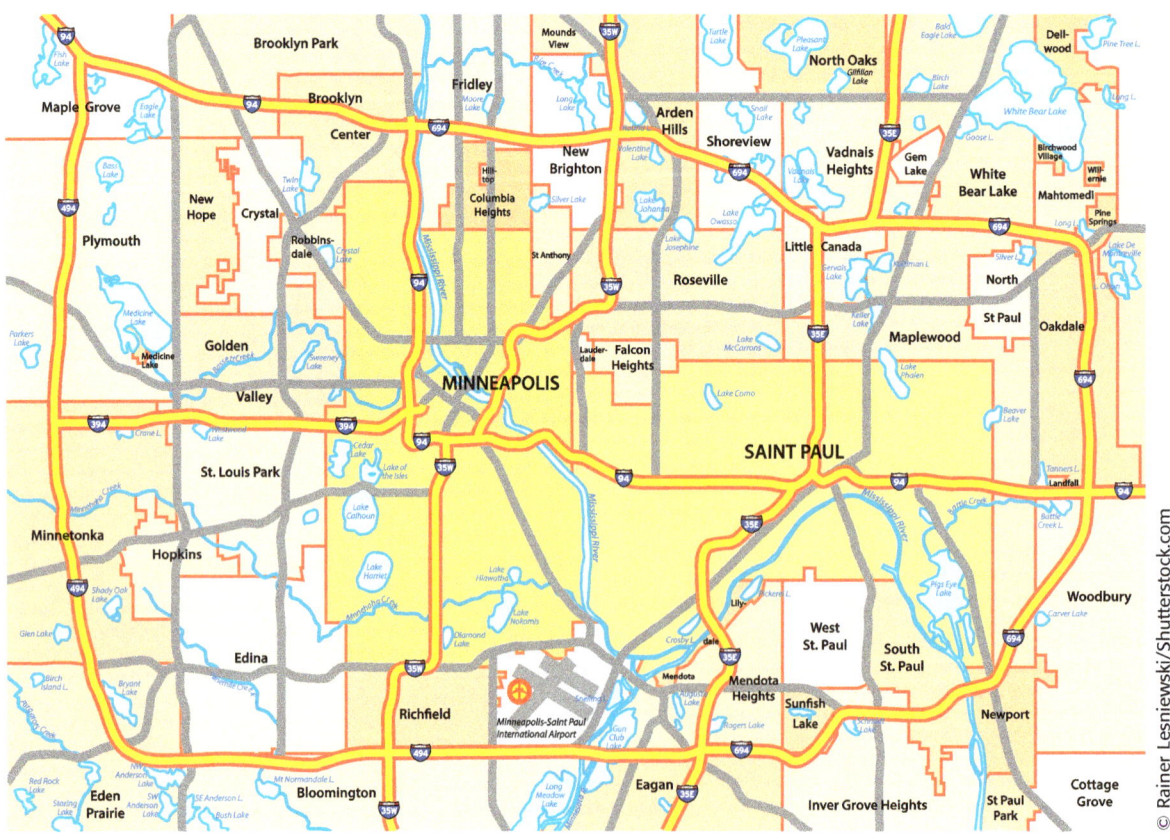

The Twin Cities of Minneapolis and St. Paul, Minnesota

The Twin Cities of Minneapolis and St. Paul have a musical culture that is as unique as their geography. Its heritage includes the original indigenous peoples including Dakota folk songs, and French, Slavic, Scandinavian, Irish, English, Polish, and Czech traditions, and continues to be seen in the continuing influence of old-time music. Livibility.com has chosen Minneapolis as having the second-best music scene outside of Nashville, New York City, and Los Angeles.

Bob Zimmerman (aka Bob Dylan) arrived in 1959 and enrolled for a short time at the University of Minnesota. He later recorded *Blood on the Tracks* at Studio80, a Minneapolis recording facility that has produced records for other famous groups such as Dave Brubeck, Leo Kottke, Cat Stevens, and Yanni.

The Minneapolis music scene's subsequent claim to fame was the sound created by Prince, who built a recording studio called Paisley Park for his own projects and others by Madonna, Boy George, the Fine Young Cannibals, and his protégé Paula Abdul. Today Minneapolis/St. Paul is a major hub for hip-hop and indie rock acts that play in the Target Center and Horthrop Auditorium.

Minnesota values its educational system and offers music in the schools. Youth music venues operate as youth centers during the day and provide listening and performing opportunities in the evening for young people. The community supports the St. Paul Chamber Orchestra, the only professional full-time chamber orchestra in the country. Here are some of the clubs in town:

Amsterdam—Bar and music hall, versatile facility with moving wall dividers. Variety of music and other events seven nights.

Cabooze—Intimate live rock bar. Bands from all over the world perform in a variety of styles, including rock, alternative, metal, indie, country, pop, punk, bluegrass, folk, blues, and hip-hop.

7th Street Entry and First Avenue—One of the longest running independently owned and operated clubs in the US. They have two separate performance spaces: 7th Street Entry is a 1550-person live music venue with over 200 concerts per year. First Avenue is a 250-person rock venue with a tiny side bar that presents 300 concerts annually. In 1984, it served as the backdrop for Prince's movie *Purple Rain*.

Icehouse—Vibrant location with lots of restaurants nearby. Jazz club and restaurant, eclectic and adventuresome music.

Orpheum Theatre—Historically and beautifully restored. Broadway musicals, concerts, and other events.

Triple Rock Social Club—Edgy punk rock with live music most nights, jukebox on the rest.

Varsity Theater—Standing only, theater, dance, live music, modern dance, Shakespeare, trade shows, weddings, you name it!

Vieux Carre Bar & Jazz Lounge—A New Orleans-style club in a historic space. An open mix of jazz, blues, and roots rock.

Minnesota Music Café—Local jazz, R&B, blues, rock seven nights a week.

Target Center—Multi-use arena (first to have a green roof). Don't try to book it if you're a baby band, as it seats 20,000.

Got their start here: Janet Jackson, Courtney Love, Yanni, New Edition, Boyz II Men, Patti LaBelle.

Interesting trivia facts: (1) Tiny Tim died of a heart attack while performing at the Minneapolis Women's Club in 1996 and is buried in the Lakewood Cemetery; (2) After the Beatles performance in 1975, the police complained about the Fab Four's behavior, and nearly arrested Paul McCartney for luring a girl to his room, who turned out to be a 21-year-old from Cleveland.

Local Musicians: The Andrews Sisters, Prince, Jimmy Jam and Terry Lewis, and radio personality Dr. Demento—the DJ who discovered "Weird Al" Jankovic.

St. Louis, MO—From Traditional Americana to Hip-hop

The Mississippi River and city of St. Louis's skyline at twilight. The Gateway Arch was built in 1965 as a monument to westward expansion.

St. Louis stands at the crossroads of America. Due to its location in the center of river and rail transportation, it served as a cradle of ragtime blues, and jazz. It is home to both the National Blues Museum and the Scott Joplin Residence, where the composer lived from 1901 to 1903 while composing his first opera (lost) and some of his better-known compositions (The Entertainer, Elite Syncopations, March Majestic, and Ragtime Dance). W.C. Handy is said to have been inspired to write the classic "St. Louis Blues" after a chance meeting with a woman on the street who was upset over her husband's absence.

Whereas New Orleans's traditional jazz scene caters to tourists, its counterpart in St. Louis is enjoyed by locals who are participating in its renaissance, thanks to young players like Pokey LaFarge and T.J. Müller (see his interview on the book's website). The city has scores of venues where music is performed. Here is a sampling:

BB's Jazz, Blues and Soups—Southern food, live blues and jazz every night.

Beale on Broadway—Atmospheric, intimate bar, music seven nights a week including blues, soul, rockabilly, soul, and R&B.

The Firebird—A small concert hall with standing room, hosting national and local rock acts.

The Fox Theatre—Great architecture, Broadway shows, comedy, national music pop and rock acts.

The Gramophone—A small listening room with different kinds music every night of the week.

Jazz at the Bistro—An elegant place to dine, big enough to be lively and fun, small enough to feel intimate. The home of St. Louis jazz.

Kirkwood Station Brewing Company—In the suburbs, music on the weekends, rock, R&B, swing dance.

Off Broadway—An old brick garage converted into a bar. From local punk to national alt-country.

Old Rock House—Cabaret-style dining area and bar. Hip-hop to indie rock and jam bands.

The Pageant—St. Louis's premier mid-sized venue.

Schlafly Bottleworks and Tap Room—micro-brewery, eclectic music mix, lighter traditional and acoustic offerings in the Bottleworks, Americana and rock acts in the Tap Room.

Local Musicians: Chuck Berry was born in St. Louis. Ike and Tina Turner launched their careers there. Nelly was born in Austin, TX, moved to St. Louis as a teenager. Pokey LaFarge was born in Bloomington, Indiana, and lives in St. Louis when he is not on tour.

Cleveland, OH—Rock and Roll Hall of Fame, home of American Punk and Techno

The Rock and Roll Hall of Fame is located in a glass pyramid on the shores of Lake Erie.

Cleveland's international influence on music began with its radio stations. In 1951, DJ Alan Freed's "Moondog" show exposed a massive audience to R&B on WJW for which he coined the term "rock and roll". Tapes of his program began to air in the New York City area over station WNJR in Newark, New Jersey, and his popularity caught the attention of record industry executives who began to think of Cleveland as a breakout city where national trends began. Soon after, they began sending bands to perform in shows in the city, and sent representatives to try to get their music played on the air. Freed's career ended in the early 1960s after he was convicted and fined for taking money ("payola") from record labels to play their songs on his show. There were other conflict of interest issues as well, such as taking co-writing credits for songs such as Chuck Berry's "Maybellene" in return for putting them into heavy rotation. Despite that scandal, Cleveland continued to be a tastemaker. It's WMMS radio became one of the most influential rock station, and *Rolling Stone* magazine named it "Radio Station of the Year" every year from 1979 to 1987.

The Rock and Roll Hall of Fame moved from New York City to Cleveland in 1983. It celebrates the best-known artists, producers, engineers, and others who have contributed to the evolution of the genre. Displays include historic artifacts from the Beatles, Jimi Hendrix, Michael Jackson, Elvis Presley, John Mellencamp, Johnny Cash, the Rolling Stones, Blondie, the Doors, U2, David Bowie, the Who, and the Supremes.

Cleveland also has bragging rights to being the birthplace of techno, and one of the most important scenes for punk rock in the United States. Here are some of the venues operating today:

Agora Theatre and Ballroom—Three bars, big names.

Beachland Ballroom and Tavern—Has two venues with a vintage feel and a run-down esthetic: the 500-seat Ballroom, and an intimate 150-person Tavern. A top favorite for music with a wide variety of styles.

The Brothers Lounge—Three room: a restaurant, wine bar with acoustic music, and roomy music hall with local rock, blues, jazz, and reggae bands.

Grog Shop—Hot indie, punk, and pop bands.

Happy Dog—Gourmet hot dog emporium and neighborhood bar with local, regional, and national acts.

House of Blues—Another franchise in the chain.

Pete's Tavern—Jazz, blues, rock, and acoustic fare.

State Theatre—National acts.

Quicken Loans Arena—Big concerts in between basketball games.

Fans at an outdoor concert. I suspect this picture was posed—"it's hard to believe anyone would look this fresh after dancing in the sun for six hours!"

Festivals

Another opportunity for bands and fans to get together are at the many outdoor festivals that happen in the summer months. Here is a sampling organized chronologically:

June/July:

- Milwaukee, WI: Summerfest. Two weeks with hundreds of bands on 11 stages. The Top 40 bands headline at night, regional musicians cover almost every possible genre during the day.

Early June:

- Detroit, MI: Detroit Music Weekend.

Early July:

- Detroit, MI: Movement Music Festival—electronic music and yoga.

Mid-July:

- Walker, MN: Moondance Jam—rock and classic rock

Early August:

- Chicago, IL: Lollapalooza—the three-day festival has moved around the United States and now takes place here. 8 stages, 170+ bands playing alternative rock, heavy metal, punk, hop-hop, and EDM, as well as dance, comedy, visual arts, crafts, and politics.
- Detroit Lakes, MN: WE Fest, country music stars to karaoke contests
- Madison, WI: Sugar Maple Traditional Music Festival

Mid August:

- Eau Claire, WI: Eaux Claires, Indie-rock, balance of local and national acts.

Early September:

- Chicago, IL: Chicago Jazz Festival
- Champaign-Urbana, IL: Pygmalion

Late September:

- Bloomington, IN: Lotus World Music & Arts Festival, one of the oldest world music festivals in the United States Inspiring encounters with the new and unfamiliar.

Opportunities in Indiana

Depending on how you look at it, Indiana University has the best music program in the United States, and is among the top 5 in the world. It is located in Bloomington and has 1,600 music majors, 13 choirs, 7 symphonic orchestras, 8 wind bands, and the 600 concerts they present each year include 6 operas.

Like most states, there are more opportunities for young engineers to work in live sound situations than recording studios. Live sound in churches is the fastest growing segment of the live sound industry, and some of our students find work doing technical work at larger churches. Other recent grads have found employment as recording engineers, performers, tour managers, radio staff, web designers, and multimedia developers. Some have gone on to graduate school to study theory and composition and have been hired for university teaching positions.

Map of Indiana.

Indiana's music industry opportunities are concentrated in manufacturing and sales. Here is a variety of types of operations:

- Auralex Acoustics (acoustic treatment material)—Indianapolis
- Conn-Selmer (band instruments)—Elkhart
- Gator Cases (instrument cases)—Grabill
- Goulding & Wood (pipe organs)—Indianapolis
- Jamey Aebersold Jazz (educational materials)—New Albany
- Harman International (audio equipment)—Elkhart
- Klipsch (loudspeakers and headphones)—Indianapolis
- Joyful Noise (record label)—Indianapolis
- Smith's Bell and Clock Service, Inc. (carillon maintenance)—Camby
- Wampler Pedals (guitar effects)—Martinsville

As was mentioned in the description of Fort Wayne above, Sweetwater is a growing company with positions in sales, technical support, and customer service. They are always looking to hire Sales Engineers who are smart, good communicators, and love gear. You have to like running fast, but if you have a music technology degree and want to be part of a winning team you should go for a tour, or visit them during Gear Fest. See our free online course materials on the book's companion website to help prepare for their challenging and comprehensive products examination.

Review and Preview

Cultural and economic factors have shaped the music and entertainment industry in the Midwest. While the region has common features due to its shared geography, culture, and economy, each state has something unique to offer. The region in general can be a good place for musicians to develop since the cost of living is lower, and there are so many secondary markets within close proximity to each other.

The book's companion website includes a series of interviews that tie together many of the topics presented throughout the book.

For Further Investigation

1. Listen to some original Americana artists such as Alison Krauss, The Band, Bonnie Raitt, Bruce Hornsby, Bruce Springsteen, Calexico, Danny O'Keefe, David Lindley, Doc Watson, Grateful Dead, John Fogerty, John Mellencamp, Leon Russell, Levon Helm, Linda Ronstadt, Loretta Lynn, Lucinda Williams, Lyle Lovett, Mary Chapin Carpenter, Mavis Staples, Mumford & Sons, Neil Young, Pete Seeger, Pokey LaFarge, Porter Wagoner, Robert Plant, Rosanne Cash, Ry Cooder, Tom Petty and the Heartbreakers, The Weavers, Willie Nelson, and the Zac Brown Band. What are some characteristics that you notice that they have in common? Find some new artists that seem to have the same qualities.

2. Visit a company involved with music and entertainment. Observe their operation and what they offer their customers. Where would you say they are on the commodities-products-services-experience-transformation spectrum? What do you think they would have to do to more toward the transformation end of the new economy?

3. Visit one or more of the venues described in this chapter, and others listed in indieonthemove .com website. What did you like most about the experience? What would you change if you were in charge? What would you change if you were at the level of one of the employees that you observed?

4. Interview people working in the music and entertainment field. Arrange a phone call or visit, and before you get together, research what they have done and the environment in which they orbit. Prepare a list of questions and organize by category. Highlight the questions that you are most interested in getting answers to, listen intently, and be ready to follow where the conversation leads. Offer to transcribe and edit the interview and send it to them to use for any purpose they wish. Do some follow-up research on your own about one of the topics that came up that you are most interested in.

Do It Yourself

1. Analyze some Americana music. Make a list of the top five features that you identify as being in common. Pick two that you are most drawn to and create a song that incorporates them.

2. Visit Gear Fest at Sweetwater in June in Fort Wayne. Prepare a list of questions for product reps and presenters. What part of the country do they mostly live in? Pay attention to how the event is run, making note of as many little details that you can. Talk to Sweetwater employees about the Sweetwater Difference.

3. Listen to college radio stations in the region and Middletown Radio. Create some music that you think would be appropriate for them to play and get it on the air.

Vocabulary Review

Dive bar—a slang term for a bar that is either a neighborhood bar where locals go to drink and talk, or one that is somewhat disreputable or unrefined.

Heavy rotation—playing a song frequently throughout the day.

Payola—"pay to play" money collected from record companies by disk jockeys to play their records on the public airwaves without revealing the relationship.

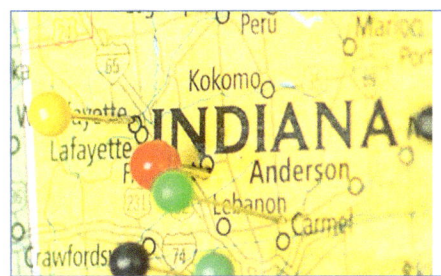

About the Author

Robert Willey was born in Menlo Park, California, and grew up in Palo Alto playing classical, pop, and Dixieland piano, and harpsichord with the Palo Alto Chamber Orchestra.

After receiving his Bachelor of Arts in Music from the University of North Texas, he played keyboards in San Francisco peninsula bands and performed with Stanford University's new music ensemble under the direction of visiting composer Pauline Oliveros. This led to graduate studies at the University of California, San Diego where he studied with F. Richard Moore, Joji Yuasa, Gareth Loy, Robert Erickson, John Silber, Ed Harkins, Cecil Lytle, Jimmy Cheatham, Mark Dolson, and Gerald Balzano.

While working as a Research Associate at the Center for Music Experiment, he developed interactive computer music performance systems supported by Yamaha Corporation of America using their FM synthesizers, Disklavier, and MIDI grand. He worked with Conlon Nancarrow on the arrangement of his player piano *Studies* for synthesizers, and collaborated with János Négyesy on a series of electronic violin intermedia performances in California, Finland, and Argentina. He assisted a computer music exchange program for a number of years between UCSD's Computer Audio Research Laboratory, Stanford University, and the LIPM studio in Buenos Aires supported by the Rockefeller Foundation, and received a Masters in Computer Music and a PhD in Theoretical Studies. Willey owned a project studio in San Diego and had clients in multimedia publishing, jingles, audio production, and cell phone ring tones, while performing in a variety of bands.

He has taught music business, computer music, computer programming, pop music theory, rock and jazz combo, audio recording, video production, music technology, synthesis, songwriting, and senior projects at the University of California San Diego, San Diego State University, University of San Diego, University of California Santa Barbara, the State University of New York Oneonta, and the University of Louisiana at Lafayette. He lived in Argentina and Brazil for 2 years as a Fulbright Scholar and Visiting Research Professor teaching computer music composition and performance, arranging, piano, and improvisation at the Laboratory for Information and Musical Production, the Federal University of Minas Gerais, the Carlos Gomes Conservatory, the State College of Pará, and the Federal University of Pára.

He has also written books and produced DVDs on Louisiana Creole Fiddle (Mel Bay), Zydeco music (Center for Louisiana Studies), and *Getting Started With Music Production* and *Brazilian Piano* (Hal Leonard).

Since 2013, he has been teaching music business, songwriting, senior projects, and computer music in the Music Media Production and Industry program at Ball State.

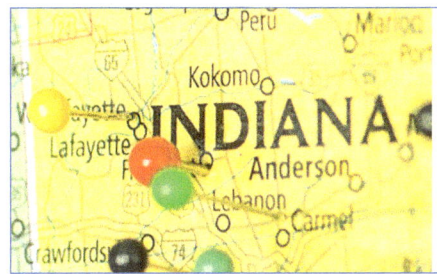

Bibliography

Music Business

Martin Atkins, *Tour Smart.*

Randy Chertkow and Jason Feehan *The Indie Band Survival Guide.*

Randy Chertkow and Jason Feehan, *Making Money with Music: Generate Over 100 Revenue Streams, Grow Your Fan Base, and Thrive in Today's Music Environment.*

Mark Halloran, *The Musician's Business and Legal Guide.*

Ariel Hyatt, *Music Success in 9 Weeks: A Step-by-step Guide to Super Charge Your Social Media & PR, Build Your Fan Base, and Earn More Money.*

Bobby Owsinski, *Music 4.1.*

Donald Passman, *All You Need to Know About the Music Business.*

Derek Thompson, *Hit Makers.*

Sales and Marketing

Chris Anderson, *Free: The Future of a Radical Price.*

Bob Baker, *Guerrilla Music Marketing Guide.*

Nir Eyal, *Hooked: How to Build Habit-Forming Products.*

Seth Godin, *Purple Cow: Transform Your Business By Being Remarkable.*

Seth Goodman and Barry Nalebuff, *Mission in a Bottle: The Story of Honest Tea.*

Sally Hogshead, *Fascinate: How to Make Your Brand Impossible to Resist.*

Daniel Pink, *To Sell Is Human: The Suprising Truth About Moving Others.*

Songwriting and Creativity

Julia Cameron, *The Artist's Way: A Spiritual Path to Higher Creativity.*

Mihaly Csikszentmihalyi, *Flow and the Psychology of Discovery and Invention.*

Sheila Davis, *The Craft of Lyric Writing.*

Austin Kleon, *Steal Like an Artist: 10 Things Nobody Told You About Being Creative.*

Cathy Lynn, Dave Austin, and Jim Peterik, *Songwriting for Dummies.*

Pat Pattison, *Writing Better Lyrics.*

John Seabrook, *The Song Machine.*

Andrea Stolpe, *Popular Lyric Writing: 10 Steps to Effective Storytelling.*

Biz Stone, *Things a Little Bird Told Me: Confessions of the Creative Mind.*

Personal Growth

You become the people you hang out with and the books you read. Here are some good influences:

Jenny Blake, *Pivot: The Only Move That Matters Is Your Next One.*

Susan Cain, *Quiet: The Power of Introverts in a World That Can't Stop Talking.*

Stephen Covey: *Seven Habits of Highly Effective People.*

Angela Duckworth, *Grit: The Power of Passion and Perseverance.*

Carolyn Dweck, *Mindset: The New Psychology of Success.*

Jeff Goins *The Art of Work: A Proven Path to Discovering What You Were Meant to Do.*

Bob Nelson: *Please Don't Just Do What I Tell You, Do What Needs to Be Done: Every Employee's Guide to Making Work More Rewarding.*

Cal Newport, *So Good They Can't Ignore You: Why Skills Trump Passion in the Quest for Work You Love.*

Gabriele Oettingen, *Rethinking Positive Thinking: Inside the New Science of Motivation.*

Randy Pausch, *The Last Lecture.*

Their Stories

You may think that your heroes were just naturally good at things as it came easily to them. No—they may have been naturally talented, but they also worked harder than everyone else.

Miles Davis with Quincy Troupe, *Miles: The Autobiography.*

Walter Isaacson, *Steve Jobs.*

Richard Kostelanetz, *Conversing with Cage.*

Mark Lewisohn, *Tune In: The Beatles: All These Years*, v. 1.

Brad Stone, *The Everything Store: Jeff Bezos and the Age of Amazon.*

Ashlee Vance, *Elon Musk: Tesla, SpaceX, and the Quest for a Fantastic Future.*

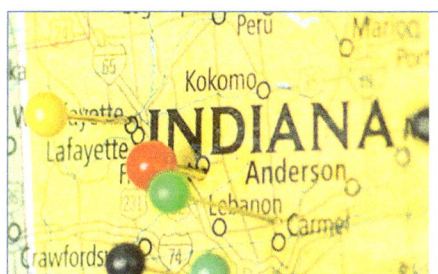

Companion Website

Be sure to visit the book's companion website at http://willshare.com/mmb. It follows the organization of the book and provides updates and links for each chapter.

More from Robert Willey:

http://rkwilley.com

http://robertwilley.com

http://purplecalves.com

http://lovelythinking.com

http://scottjoplinarchive.org

http://brazilianpiano.com

http://willshare.com/creolefiddle

http://willshare.com/zydeco

http://conlonnancarrow.org

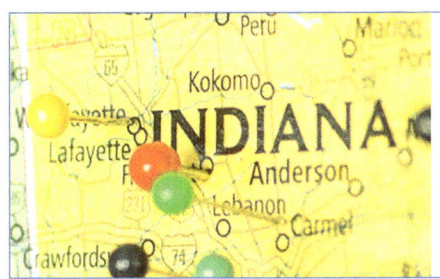

Index

CPSIA information can be obtained
at www.ICGtesting.com
Printed in the USA
LVHW060949080119
603097LV00002B/3/P